FRANKLIN HORTON

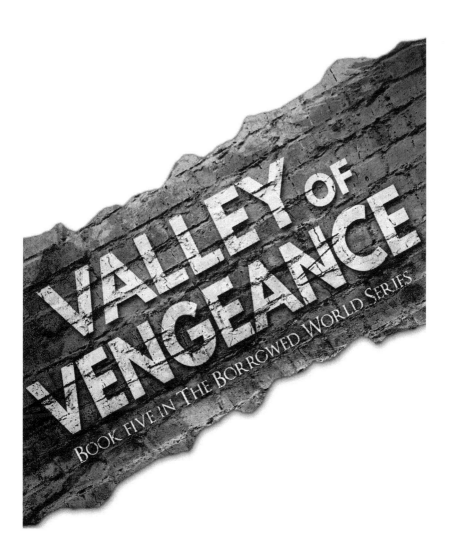

VALLEY OF VENGEANCE

BOOK FIVE IN THE BORROWED WORLD SERIES

ALSO BY FRANKLIN HORTON

The Borrowed World Series

The Borrowed World

Ashes of the Unspeakable

Legion of Despair

No Time For Mourning

Valley of Vengeance

Switched On

The Ungovernable

The Locker Nine Series

Locker Nine

Grace Under Fire

Compound Fracture

Blood Bought

The Mad Mick Series

The Mad Mick

Masters of Mayhem

Stand-Alone Novels

Random Acts

ABOUT THE AUTHOR

Franklin Horton lives and writes in the mountains of Southwestern Virginia. He is the author of several bestselling post-apocalyptic series. You can follow him on his website at franklinhorton.com.

While you're there please sign up for his mailing list for updates, event schedule, book recommendations, and discounts.

VALLEY OF VENGEANCE

PREFACE

In the nearly twenty-five years she'd spent with her employer, Alice had made the trip to Richmond, Virginia hundreds of times. Despite it being several hundred miles round trip, it had become as routine as a trip of that length could become. She could practically drive it blindfolded. She knew where the good restaurants and the clean bathrooms were. She even knew where the speed traps were. The last trip had been anything but routine. It had become a gnarled and convoluted nightmare that she hoped would soon be nothing but a memory. If she could just reach her family she could start putting it all behind her.

The ill-fated trip had started going downhill when the nation was hit with a series of devastating terror attacks in the early morning hours after their arrival. She and her travelling companions had woken to no power, no water, and little information as to the extent of the damage. Despite some debate and disagreement among the group of six, they made the decision to leave Richmond and head back home before things got worse.

They were soon to learn that one target of the terror attacks had been some of the nation's larger fuel refineries. With the refineries offline and the ability to produce gasoline severely diminished, the president of the United States issued an executive order freezing the fuel supply. It would be available only to those taking part in the offi-cial disaster response. The group learned of this executive order while stopped at a travel plaza not far outside of Richmond. News of the fuel seizure inflamed scared and angry travelers, leading to a riot. Gunfire broke out and one of their party was killed in the chaos. It became clear very quickly that the rules had changed.

Forced to abandon their vehicle when it ran out of fuel, the group made their way to an overcrowded interstate exit where they paid an exorbitant price for a room in a hotel with no electricity. There they had a disagreement over the best course of action. Some in their party wanted to wait for the official Federal response and take charter buses to the nearest FEMA assistance center. Others in the group, whom Alice did not agree with, wanted no part of that and split from the group, foolishly choosing to walk home. It would be a while before Alice accepted that this had not been such a foolish decision after all.

She and her friend Rebecca had gone the route of trusting FEMA to deliver them home. After spending some time in a FEMA camp it became clear to Alice that the intention of the camp was not to get stranded travelers home as they'd been told, but instead to just get them centralized so they wouldn't bother the small communities along the highways. Not only was there no plan to get them home, but striking out on their own was strongly discouraged.

When she finally realized the futility of the FEMA camp situation, she escaped in the luggage compartment of a charter bus, but again, things didn't go well for her. Out of loyalty, she chose to include her coworker Rebecca in her plans since she was the only person in the FEMA camp Alice knew. Rebecca suffered from a streak of narcissism that required constant feeding, however. In the camp, it was fed by a man she met named Boyd.

To Alice's horror, Rebecca shared their escape plans with Boyd and they had no choice but to include him when he showed up at their rendezvous point. Rebecca and Boyd quickly paired off, ignoring Alice for much of the trip. Clearly the third wheel, she struggled with whether to split off on her own and travel solo. She didn't decide in time. One morning, Alice found her coworker brutally murdered by the volatile Boyd. Had Alice not slipped off and slept away from the pair that night it was likely she would have been murdered too.

Her trip continued to get worse. Desperate, she drank untreated water from a ditch. It soon made her nauseous and eventually wracked her bowels. She became delirious from dehydration and fever, but was buoyed by having reached territory that was familiar to her. This excitement was short-lived. She crossed paths with Boyd again and ended up chained in his basement. There she found Boyd to be a mentally ill young man with intentions of marrying her and making her his wife. When she did not respond appropriately, there was a ferocious struggle. She killed Boyd with his own knife.

The experience with Boyd changed her. She didn't know if it came from having to take his life so violently or if it came from the experience of being totally at his mercy in the dark prison of his basement.

She salvaged enough gear and clothing from Boyd's house to eventually make it back to her office. There, by sheer luck, she reconnected with Gary, one of her original group of travelling companions. His offer to treat her with antibiotics and help her get home led her to stay with his family for several days. While the stay was supposed to help her recover and gain strength, it was not a respite from the escalating violence of their collapsing society. There were attacks on Gary's innocent family by a marauding group of neighbors and she was forced to kill again. It had been easier for her the second time. The things that happened to her at Boyd's made her harder inside.

Gary lost his son-in-law in that attack. That led Gary to the difficult conclusion that he had to leave his home. He would pack his family into vehicles and bug out to the rural valley where Jim, another of their original group, lived. Alice helped them pack and travelled with them to the valley. True to his word, Gary gave her a fueled vehicle after they reached Jim's valley. Before she left, Jim told her that she was welcome to come back with her family if she needed to. There would be strength in numbers.

She appreciated his offer but the truth was that they'd never gotten along that well. They were always clashing over something at work. Those things seemed silly now. She'd changed and he'd changed. The world, too, had changed around them.

Staying in that valley was not her plan. Her plan was to get home to her family, perhaps head out to her mom's farm and build a life of her own until things returned to normal. She had healing to do, both mentally and physically. She needed to put this whole experience far behind her. She needed to become a mother again, and a wife. She needed to be shed of the bloodstained knife she carried on her belt. She needed to be free of the blackness she wore like a gown of ice cold water.

CHAPTER ONE

Alice

Alice drove quickly but cautiously from the isolated valley in Russell County, Virginia. Her two-day trip to Richmond, Virginia had run into several weeks now and she was ready to get home, though she knew she had to maintain caution. Her home was on the other side of town and she wanted to get there alive and in one piece. It would be easy to lose focus here on the home stretch and do something stupid.

From the condition of the roads it was clear that this was not the same world she'd left. They were covered in debris that would usually have been cleaned up by the local highway department. There were tree branches, roadkill, and trash that forced her to drive slowly and stay vigilant. There were abandoned vehicles on the shoulders and partially blocking lanes, stopped where she assumed they ran out of fuel. They would have presented an obstacle to vehicle traffic if there had been any traffic other than her.

She passed some folks on bicycles and a few walkers. She saw a few folks working in gardens or in fields, though most didn't have any fuel and were having to do the work by hand. When she'd left for her trip, people in this rural community would have thrown a hand up in greeting to anyone they met on the road. Now everyone was greeted with suspicion. She'd already lost that reflexive wave of greeting and these folks apparently had as well.

Around a turn she hit a straight stretch of road with no debris in sight. Either it had been cleared or simply spared the abuse that the rest of this country road was suffering. With no obstacles to dodge, she pressed the gas pedal and picked up the pace, anxious to get home. She was doing nearly fifty miles per hour when a dog leapt out in front of her. She was afraid to swerve around it for fear it might jump in front of her. She slammed on the brakes and lurched to a stop. It wasn't that she was a dog lover, it was simply reflex.

The dog was so close to the front of the vehicle that she couldn't see it over the hood. She lowered the driver's side window and leaned out. She could see then that the dog was pulling against something. A glint of light hit what must have been fishing line tied to the dog's collar. The animal had been pulled into the road on purpose.

It was a trap.

Alice caught movement from the corner of her eye. A man with a baseball bat, dressed in camo, sprang from the ditch. Alice yanked her head back in and began rolling up her window. It was not a logical reaction but an instinctive one. Then he was at the door and the bat was drawn back. The bat would shatter the half-raised window, then it would shatter her skull.

She felt for the revolver that lay against her thigh. She raised it and pointed it at the man. He saw it but didn't even pause. Did he not think she'd do it? Did he think it was unloaded?

She pulled the trigger and there was an enormous boom. The sound was deafening inside the car and she flinched. The round punched through the glass and hit the man just below the sternum. He doubled over, then fell backward, screaming.

Alice was rattled by the attack, stunned by the sound of the gunfire in the confined space of the car. Paralyzed, she watched the man writhing in the ditch, clearly about to die.

Then her passenger window shattered, spraying her with glass. She spun toward a man clutching a short piece of rebar, using it to rake glass from the opening. She raised her gun toward him, ready to pull the trigger as soon as she had it centered on him, but he grabbed it through the window. She tried to aim it toward him but he was pushing against her and throwing her aim off. Then she tried to pull the trigger, hoping the round would either hit him or scare him. She pulled and pulled but it wouldn't go back. She noticed he'd slid a finger in behind the trigger so that she couldn't pull it.

Shit!

Alice tried to wrench the gun from him. She put both hands on it, screaming and pulling violently. Far from being deterred, the man actually grinned at her reaction. He continued to maneuver his body through the shattered window, eventually getting a second hand on the gun.

Then he was yelling too. Not at her, but for help. She stole a glance at her rearview mirror and saw movement. There were more of them. This was bad.

She had no choice. She had to get out of there or die. She stomped the gas, hoping the dog was able to get out of the way. There was yelling behind her. She took one hand from the gun and used it to steer.

The man still had both his hands on the gun to her one hand. He would win this battle if she didn't come up with something fast. She began weaving the car from side-to-side, trying to sling the man from her vehicle. He didn't fall but he did take one hand from the gun and grab at her hair. He pulled at it, trying to use it to pull himself inside the vehicle.

He jerked her head repeatedly, trying to make her wreck. It wrenched her neck painfully to the side. She screamed, both from pain and fear, and tried to pull the trigger again. His finger was still wedged behind it. The gun was useless unless she could get his finger out of there. She didn't know what to do. She was afraid to stop and fight him hand-to-hand. He was stronger and would overpower her. Then his reinforcements would catch up with them and her journey would be over. She would *not* die this close to home.

He tried to push her head into the steering wheel. She spun to bite his hand, but was unable to get purchase on it. The man cursed at her, letting go of her head and drawing back to punch her. She swerved hard, forcing him to grab onto the rearview mirror to keep from being slung out. A tire dropped off the shoulder into a ditch and she yanked the wheel, overcorrecting and almost sending the car off the opposite side of the road. She had to pay attention.

With a solid handhold on the mirror, the man tried again to pull himself completely into the vehicle. There was still glass in the opening, grating and sawing against the pale flesh of his belly as he dragged himself over it. Blood ran down the interior door panel. She could see the look on his face, hear it in his curses. If he got through that window, he would make her pay for his pain.

Alice swerved again and the rearview mirror snapped free of the windshield. Rather than dislodging him from the vehicle, he now had a weapon. He smashed it against her head, shattering the mirror and opening a cut on her scalp. He hit her again. She tried to swerve and make him drop the mirror but he was in the window opening up to his waist now. She was losing this fight. At this point, even letting go of the gun would not help. He would just turn it on her. She had to do something.

Ahead and to her left, she noticed a cornfield with men stacking fodder shocks. The gate leading to the field was open. As the man drew back to hit her with the mirror again, she whipped the wheel to the left and shot through the tight opening between the gateposts. The man's extended legs hit one of the posts at thigh level and jerked him violently out the window before he could even scream.

The men in the field stared in shock as Alice turned the wheel hard. She'd done enough doughnuts in parking lots to know how to make a car spin the way she wanted it. She mashed the gas pedal, keeping the car's momentum up, and spun until she was facing back toward the gate. She could see the crumpled man writhing between the posts.

The car fishtailed as it regained traction, picking up speed. She shot for the opening again, hearing a sickening thud as she drove over the man. The car jumped and jolted, then was back on the road. She looked in her side mirror and saw men from the field running to aid the man she'd run over. He had to be dead. She hoped he was.

CHAPTER TWO

Alice

Alice was hypervigilant for the rest of her drive. She took the four-lane bypass around town and found a few abandoned cars on the road but no people. When she got off the bypass, it was three more miles of careful driving to reach her neighborhood. There she found another roadblock, but this was one manned by people from her neighborhood. They were familiar faces, people who knew and recognized her. Still, that did not reduce her anxiety level. She found herself psychologically preparing for another fight.

This should have been a moment of exhilaration, but she found herself unable to show very much excitement. Everything inside her felt muted anymore. Well, not completely everything. Rage, hate, and violent impulses did not appear to be muted at all, although all of the emotions she would normally associate as being *good* felt as if a damp towel had been laid over them.

In her career, she had often forced herself to be friendly when she didn't feel it. As a trainer, she frequently had to go into rooms full of people who didn't want to be there and try to make them listen to her.

She had to deliver lots of bad news, she had to fire people or tell them that they were not hirable due to a criminal offense in their past. She could put on her game face and perform with the best of them. That facet of her personality had been eroded by the experiences of this trip. She did not think she could make herself ever be friendly again.

One of her neighbors, Adam, pulled an improvised gate aside and let her enter when he recognized her. She stopped the car beside him. She knew him, knew his wife, she'd been to cookouts at their house, and their kids played together. However, she didn't like him. She thought he was creepy. Whenever she was outside gardening he always seemed to find an excuse to come outside. Sometimes he tried to make conversation. Sometimes he just stared at her with an odd smile on his face. She'd also seen him watching from the windows of his house, his featureless dark shape recognizable in profile.

"Haven't seen you since this whole mess started," Adam said. "Where you been?" He crouched down beside her door, putting a hand on the forearm that she rested in her open window and patting it.

She stared at his hand, then moved her arm from beneath it before answering him. She could not focus enough to engage in conversation while he was touching her. "I was out of town," she said. "Just getting back."

"You haven't been home at all?" he asked. "I didn't think I'd seen you for a while."

She met his eye, trying to convey to him that she knew he would have been watching for her, also trying to convey just how unpleasant she found the notion. "No, I've been on the road. I was in Richmond when this all happened."

"Richmond?" Adam said. "That must have been a shit storm. How did you get home?"

"I walked."

Adam burst out laughing until he saw that she was not joking. "You *walked?*"

She nodded.

"I saw your family moving around," he said. "I just assumed you were with them."

She shook her head. "No. It's taken weeks to get here."

He leaned closer, folding his forearms and resting them in the open window. It wasn't intended as a threatening gesture, but Alice found all intrusion into her personal space to be a threatening gesture anymore. It was made worse because it was him. He made her skin crawl. She could feel the reassuring warmth of the pistol hidden beneath her thigh. It was there. It was close. She could get to it if she needed. She could kill him if she had to.

"Your husband and son aren't home," he told her, speaking with exaggerated compassion, as if he were a friend breaking bad news.

Her heart lurched but she forced herself to maintain composure. "Do you know where they went?"

"They said they were going to your mother's house to check on her. That was right after this whole mess happened and they've not been back that I've seen. We've only had this gate up for a few days though, so he could have been back and forth before that and I just didn't notice it."

"So he's been gone a while?"

Adam nodded. "Yep. Right after the power went out. I'll be honest with you, it caught a lot of us unprepared. Water ran out pretty quickly. Food too. A lot of people have left their homes. Those of us who have stayed are having to carry water from the stream down the road. Food is wherever we can find it."

"I'm going up to my house," Alice said.

Adam nodded. "Be careful," he warned. "There's been some break-ins. People stealing food and guns mostly. We don't know if it's neighbors doing it or strangers. Hell, it could be anyone. Just be careful."

"I'll be fine," she said.

"I'll come check on you later," he said. "Make sure things are okay."

"That won't be necessary," she said. "I'm pretty fucking sure things won't be okay. Things may never be okay again."

She drove off. It had been on the tip of Adam's tongue to ask her if there was something wrong but it was clearly a stupid thing to ask. Everything about her was wrong. He tried to imagine what she'd been through, but he couldn't. Despite her assurance, he would try to catch up with her later and make sure she didn't need anything. It would be the neighborly thing to do.

Alice drove down the block and eased into her driveway. She killed the engine and sat there looking at the house. Had this been a normal summer afternoon, there would have been the sounds of children playing, of lawn mowers, and of cars. Now it was unnaturally silent. The grass in her yard was taller than they'd ever allowed it to get, but the grass was tall in all of the yards. Her son's car was in the driveway but the house *felt* empty. She did not sense her family inside, did not feel the warmth of their love radiating through the walls, and into the cold void inside her.

She'd imagined a wholly different homecoming than this. She'd imagined her husband and son stepping out the door and smiling at her from the porch, her husband's arm resting on her son's shoulder like a classic father and son portrait. They would walk down the drive toward her and she would meet them halfway. They would wrap her in a tight embrace that would reboot her systems and start her life over again. While keeping that fantasy alive in her head may have helped her get home, it would do nothing for her now except slow her down and cloud her thinking. Emotions did nothing but muddy the waters and obscure the facts. There would have to be a new plan: accept the circumstances and move on.

She looked around at her neighbors' houses. No one was even outside. Their lawns were as sad as her own. No one would waste precious fuel on mowing. To the left of her house was a brick ranch. It was one of the older houses in the neighborhood, built in the early seventies. Her family had never gotten along with the people that lived there, a man and his nephew. Neither of them worked but somehow they managed to get by.

They always had loud cars that disturbed the peace of the otherwise quiet neighborhood. They would buy one, wreck, it, then buy another, as predictable as the seasons. They always had drinking money, however. They always had money for renting the largest televisions from the rent-to-own store in town. They played music and video games so loud that you could hear them down the street. They also had a constant stream of visitors.

Alice was not naïve. From her job, she knew this racket. Both the uncle and the nephew claimed to have chronic pain and doctor-hopped to get as many prescriptions as they could for pain pills. Some of the pills they used for themselves, some they sold to their steady supply of customers. Alice knew this, just as all the other neighbors did, but they could never prove it to the police.

That neighbor's yard was even worse than the rest in the neighborhood. They'd taken to throwing their garbage in the yard. It wasn't even piled up neatly. It was just tossed out the door and lay where it landed. The first good wind to come up would blow half of it into Alice's yard. She sighed, but accepted that this was an *old world* problem, not a *new world* one. In the current scheme of things, what did blowing trash mean anyway?

As she stared at the neighbor's house and their disgusting yard, she noticed a curtain in their living room part and then drop back into place. Someone was home and watching her. The hair on the back of her neck stood up.

She threw open her door and got out, holding the revolver down against her leg, concealing it against the silhouette of her body. She walked to her front steps, climbed them, and then tried the door.

Locked.

Around her neck, she carried the keys she'd retrieved from her Honda at the office. The car had four flat tires and a punctured gas tank when she finally reached it, but the sparse contents had not led anyone to break into it. She'd lost her car keys along the way home and had been forced to throw a landscaping paver through the window to get the set of house keys hidden in the console.

She opened her front door and pushed it in, raising the revolver against whatever threats might be inside. A powerful smell smacked her in the face, the musty smell of a closed house and the underlying tang of garbage. It reminded her of opening the car trunk on a hot day when a bag of garbage had fermented in there all day. She thought of the contents of the refrigerator and freezer, wondering if her husband had thought to clean those out before he left. Maybe they hadn't intended to stay gone.

She checked all directions but couldn't see much from where she was. The entry foyer didn't present any long-range views. She stepped over the threshold and advanced into the house.

She started to call her husband's name, just as she would months ago if she couldn't find him in the house, but bit her tongue. After her experiences on the road she was more wary. If there were bad people inside her home, yelling out would just tip them off to her presence. The living room was ahead on her right. She pointed her weapon in that direction, advancing. She kept the pistol close to her body. If someone materialized, she didn't want them to be able to reach out and snatch it from her grasp.

When she cleared the doorway and could see further into the house, the state of her living room made her gasp. The room had been ransacked. Books were raked off shelves. Furniture was overturned and the cushions slashed. A potted ficus tree had been uprooted and the dirt shaken out onto the carpet.

For a moment, emotion welled up in Alice and she felt as if she might cry. This was her *home,* the safest place in the world to her. This was the sanctuary she'd walked across an entire state to reach. Why would someone do this? Then that moment of vulnerability was pushed aside by cold rage.

She backed out of the room and continued to the kitchen. It was in a worse state. Drawers were emptied, her flour canister had been dumped out onto the countertops and the canister itself shattered against the floor. The cabinets appeared to have fewer things in them than when she'd left and she couldn't tell if it was because the contents had been stolen or if her family had taken them when they left. Again, she didn't have enough information to know if they left to go stay with her mom long-term or if they just intended to go check on her and got delayed.

She moved through the rest of the house and found it to be in much the same state. Every drawer was pulled and dumped, the contents of closets pulled out onto the floor, mirrors shattered. Every flat surface had been raked clean of the items that once sat there. Everything had been violated. Many of the things sacred to her had been trashed or were missing.

"They're only things," she whispered to herself. "They don't matter." It was a mantra she would have to repeat to herself several times.

She stepped into the master bedroom and tried to separate herself from the personal pain of what she found. The closet doors were open and her husband's gun safe stood there battered and scratched. Whoever tried to get in it had not succeeded. She went to the window and looked out into the backyard. They had an outbuilding there with their camping gear, fishing equipment, and yard tools in it. The doors hung open, one of them canted awkwardly from a broken hinge. Through the now overgrown backyard, she could see a clear path of beaten down grass leading from her back door to that of the next door neighbor.

They had been here often enough to leave a path. She now knew who had violated her home. As if she'd ever had any doubt.

CHAPTER THREE

Alice

Alice could not let herself dwell on the condition of her home. There were bigger concerns. She went to her son's room and found one of the large gym bags that he used for his soccer gear. She took it to her room and began throwing clothes in it, with an emphasis on durability and comfort. She wouldn't be needing the professional wardrobe she wore nearly every day at the office. She stopped packing long enough to change, putting on clothing of her very own for the first time in over a week. Although a small thing, it boosted her morale. It made her feel more like herself.

With a bag of clothing packed, she grabbed a raincoat and a fleece jacket, not knowing how long it would be before she returned to the house. It was hard for her to tell if her husband and son had packed any of their clothing or not. Certainly there were items missing from their closets, but she didn't know if that was from theft or from her family taking them. She packed more of their clothing too, just to prevent it from being stolen once she left.

Making a final sweep of her bedroom for anything she might need in the immediate future, she noticed the gun safe again. She dropped her gear and tried to move the safe, wanting to see if anything rattled inside but she was unable to budge it. The door and lock were battered but it didn't look as if anyone had been able to get inside. It had a rotary lock instead of a digital lock and the dial still turned. She input the combination and turned the handle.

The handle turned freely enough but she was unable to open the door due to the mangled metal around the edges. The door was binding on a lip of metal that had been bent from the attempts to pry it open. She went to the garage and retrieved the biggest screwdriver she could find. Using that, she was able to pry the now unlocked door open. Inside she found most of her husband's guns. She noticed a few missing, which further led to her to believe that her husband had planned on a short stay at her mom's farm.

There had to be a reason why they hadn't returned. Had something happened? Had he been injured? Killed? She couldn't let herself go down that hole. She had to take things one step at a time.

She removed the long guns from the safe, placed them on the bed, and rolled them up in the comforter. She knew her husband would cringe at his guns getting scratched against each other but she didn't have the time to baby them. She didn't want to leave them and she didn't know how else to transport them. She removed the few pistols, placing them in a wheeled piece of carry-on luggage from the closet, along with all the boxes of ammunition. She found a box of spare ammo for the .38 revolver she'd been carrying and she placed that in the bag with her own clothing.

She took the roll of guns, the bag of clothing, and the suitcase of handguns, leaving them just inside the locked front door. She decided that she'd load everything into the car at the same time. Her mind racing, she tried to think of all of the things that she should take but she wanted to believe she'd be back there again.

She needed to keep that hope alive. She wasn't ready to give up on her house and her belongings. She was certain that the garage, the outbuilding, and the basement still had items she needed, however, she didn't have the room to carry everything in this trip, nor did she feel like she had the time to invest in looking for them.

She stood in the entry foyer, trying to think of any things that she'd missed that they might need. Her mind was spinning and she gave up. She'd plan on coming back with her husband in his truck. They'd load it, along with his utility trailer, and maybe they'd just move everything to her mother's house. Right now the most important thing was finding her family; they could deal with the rest later. When she came to this conclusion, she leaned over to pick up her bags. Before her hand closed on a handle, she heard a rattle from the front door.

Someone was trying to get in.

She stared at the handle and listened. It rattled again. It could have been her husband but wouldn't he have just used his key, or at least called out to keep from startling her? The old Alice would have retreated to the bedroom and called 9-1-1. This Alice strode to the door, pulling her revolver from her back pocket. In a single motion, she unlocked the door and whipped it open, holding her gun at the ready.

The young man from next door was clearly not expecting this and threw his arms up, stumbling back a step. "Don't shoot!" He was greasy looking and his shaggy hair stuck out in all directions. She could smell him from where she stood.

"What the fuck do you want?" Alice hissed.

He didn't answer. His eyes were flicking back and forth, searching for an answer. For a *lie*.

"What do you *want*?"

"I d-didn't recognize the c-car," he stuttered. "I was making sure someone wasn't breaking in."

"The hell you were," she replied. "After all this time you suddenly decide to be a good neighbor? You were probably just concerned that someone was in here stealing shit *you* planned on stealing yourself."

He didn't answer.

"Everything okay, Jake?" came a voice from beyond her line of sight. She recognized it as the kid's uncle.

The fact there were two of them didn't faze Alice. She was still comfortable with the odds. If the uncle tried anything, she'd drop this one, and then drop him too.

"Jake?" the man repeated.

"You better back off my fucking porch right now," Alice said. "I don't ever want to see you on my property again. Matter of fact, I don't ever want to see *you* again, *period*."

He started backing up, slightly emboldened both by his suspicion that she wasn't going to kill him and by the presence of his uncle. "Crazy bitch! Think you're all bad with that gun, don't you?"

Alice raised the gun slightly and put a round in the porch light above the punk's head. Glass fragments rained down on him. He flinched and cried out. Funny how a punk's attitude changed when he understood your willingness to pull the trigger.

"Get out of here *now*!" she spat.

He stumbled off the porch, brushing glass from his hair.

The uncle ran into view, concerned by the sound of the shot. He looked from his nephew to Alice. "What the fuck?"

"Take this piece of shit with you," she told the uncle. "Keep him off my property. I find either of you in my yard again I'll kill you."

The uncle bowed up, his chest puffing out, his arms stiffening. "I don't like being threatened."

"And I don't like being robbed," Alice replied. "The men at the road warned me about homes being broken into. I could kill you right now and pull your bodies up into my house. No one would know any better. I'd tell them that I found you robbing my house and you threatened me. They would believe every word of it because I'm a respectable fucking citizen, and you would just be another dead scumbag."

"You don't have the guts," the uncle challenged.

Alice turned her mouth up into a chilling smile. "You don't think so? Try me. *Please...try...me.*"

The uncle could see then that she wanted him to try. She wasn't only ready to kill him, she *wanted* to. She was practically begging him for the opportunity. He grabbed his nephew by the arm and they backed away. Alice kept the gun trained on them the entire time. When they were back in their house, she went back in hers. She had more things to get before she was ready to leave.

CHAPTER FOUR

Alice

Alice was making a pass through the kitchen, packing food and cooking gear into plastic shopping bags, when the front door burst open. She drew her pistol and dropped behind the kitchen island.

"Alice!"

She recognized Adam's voice and stood up cautiously. "In here!" she yelled. "The kitchen."

Adam came into kitchen, followed by the men from the checkpoint, all of them waving their guns around without regard for where their muzzles were pointing.

"Are you okay? We heard a shot!"

"Watch where you're pointing those," she said. "Everything's fine."

"Did you fire that shot?" he asked. "We were afraid you might have caught someone in the act of robbing your house."

Alice tucked her pistol into her back pocket. "No, but I did have a little run-in with the neighbors. They've been breaking into my house on a regular basis. They must have seen the car and thought someone was trying to sneak into their territory. I caught one them trying to get in the front door."

"You think they did this?" Adam asked, taking in the ransacked kitchen.

"Judge for yourself," Alice said. "There's a trail worn in the grass from my house to theirs. They've apparently been making a lot of trips."

"We ought to run those assholes out of the neighborhood," said another of the men. "They're probably the ones been breaking in on everyone else."

"We just can't go accusing people of things like that," Adam said.

"Why not?" Alice asked.

"Yeah, why not?" asked the man who'd suggested running them out of the neighborhood.

"There's such a thing as due process," Adam said. "You got to do these things by the book."

"There is no more due process and there's no more book," Alice spat. "I could have killed him right then and there wouldn't have been anything anyone could have done about it."

Adam frowned. "You can't just go around killing people."

Alice felt her adrenaline rising. She didn't like his lecturing, condescending tone. "I don't know where the hell you've been," she said. "He wouldn't be the first person I've killed recently. He wouldn't even be the first I've killed today."

All the men looked at her then. She could tell from their expressions that they were looking at her differently than they'd ever looked at her before. That seemed to happen when you admitted killing people.

Adam gulped. "You killed someone *today?*"

"On the way out here," Alice said. "I ran into a trap on the road. Some men tried to carjack me. I lived. They didn't."

"They?"

"Let me clarify," Alice said. "I *killed* one man and I *mortally wounded* another. I'm guessing that he's probably dead by now too, what with the lack of available medical care. So if I killed one more person today, I'm just not sure it would be all that big a deal."

Adam approached Alice and put a hand on her shoulder. There was something disingenuous about the gesture, as if he thought it was what he was supposed to do. She turned her head and stared at his hand. He left it there until her eyes began to burn a hole in it, then he moved it.

"Look, I'm sure you saw a lot out there on the road," he said. "We don't live that way here. We're still a civilized community. Things haven't gotten that bad here yet."

"Then either you haven't been out of this neighborhood or you have your head up your ass," Alice retorted. "Things are that bad right up the road from here. Did you not hear me use the words *trap* and *carjack?* That wasn't in Richmond, it was *here.*"

Adam sighed. "I hope it stays up the road. We don't want it coming here."

"It will," Alice warned. "And these boys next door will die anyway. Eventually they'll rob the wrong person or accidentally kill someone. Then you'll be forced to deal with them or they'll kill one of you."

"I don't remember you being like this," Adam said, frowning and shaking his head. "You always struck me as being a bit more polished and professional."

"I don't remember giving a shit what you think about me," Alice said, looking Adam in the eye.

Adam was taken aback. He sighed heavily, as if disappointed in Alice. He wasn't used to confronting this level of hostility. "We'll just be leaving," he said. "We were concerned about your wellbeing is all."

"I appreciate that," Alice said. "I do. It's probably your own wellbeing you should be concerned about. Sounds like you're still living in that fantasy world where things are going to be okay. The world beat that out of me several weeks back."

Adam could sense the hollowness inside Alice, could almost hear the reverberation of her voice echoing in her vast, empty interior. "I'm sorry to hear that," he said, turning to go. "I'll check back with you later."

"Don't bother," she said.

He turned back and smiled at her. "No bother." Then he left.

There was something about him that seemed to be genuine. He came running when he thought Alice was in danger. He almost seemed concerned about what was going on with her emotionally. At the same time, there was that lingering feeling that it was all an act, like he was a serial killer going through the motions of being human while he was far from human on the inside. It was an insight she'd not had into the man before and perhaps it only came to her now because it was similar to how she felt on the inside, like something heartless and cold acting at being human. Like a meat puppet dancing on the stage of the world.

She put the man out of her head and began shuttling her gear from the house to the car. It took several trips. She could tell she was in better shape from her time on the road. Months ago this would have left her out of breath. While stomach ailments had left her a little weak, she had to admit that she was now in the best shape of her life.

Not knowing what she'd come back to once she left the house unattended, she packed the car as full as she could get it. She knew she was overlooking a million things and only hoped they'd be able to come back. Clothes were critical because it might be hard to find any of their sizes without stores to shop at. Shoes were the same way. After that, it was the guns, hygiene items, and their photo albums. She tried to find all their prescription and over the counter meds but they were gone. She hoped her husband had taken them.

During her trips to the car, she kept the revolver in her back pocket, exposed to all the world. She didn't care. She felt eyes burning holes in her back. She knew it was the neighbors, watching her with hate for confronting them, for coming back and taking things that they planned on stealing. She wanted to turn around and shoot their windows out.

Restraint, she reminded herself. *Show a little restraint.*

When the last bags were loaded, she walked through her house again. She gathered some of the things she didn't have room to take − framed family pictures, legal documents, and sentimental items − and packed them back into the gun safe. She shut the door and spun the latch, hoping that it would stay shut until she returned to retrieve the items.

She wouldn't put it past those two neighbors to burn her house down after she left just out of spite. She hoped they didn't; there were a lot of memories here. This wasn't their first house but her son had grown up here. It was where he learned to ride a bike and catch a baseball. It was where her fondest memories were born.

She flipped her hair out of her face and those thoughts out of her head. She stalked through the house, turning the light switch off out of reflex as she went outside. Using her key, she locked the door behind her, and went to her car. She stood for a moment, taking her house in, then cast a wary eye to the neighbors' house. A curtain slid shut. She swallowed the temptation to give them the finger. She didn't need to make it worse.

She backed the car out of the drive and coasted down the street toward the roadblock. The men pulled the barricade out of her way. Adam tried to flag her down but she didn't stop. She had nothing left to say.

CHAPTER FIVE

Alice

Alice's mother lived on a farm on the western side of the county. Alice had grown up there, her father farming for a living. She'd worked on the farm until she started college and had to hold down a full-time job to pay her tuition. Between work and school, she had little time left to help with the farm chores. She enjoyed the freedom too much to experience any guilt over not being there to help out. She was ready to explore life off the farm. She wanted to know what other young women did with their time. She wanted to hang out, go to parties, and she wanted a social life, all things that she felt she missed out on due to the burdens of farm life.

Because she remained in the general area, Alice still went back to help her parents over the years, but she never moved back to the farm. She lent a hand with processing hogs, canning, or putting up tobacco as her parents needed her. They never had to ask. She understood which chores around the farm took extra sets of hands and showed up when needed.

Recalling this made her wonder how she'd gotten so far from the simple life of her childhood. It had been the only life her parents had ever known. Both had been raised on farms and saw no other avenue in life than to one day get married and have a farm of their own to work. That they would one day be farmers had been as inevitable as the change of seasons.

Even though Alice reached a point as a teenager where she grew tired of the unrelenting workload of the farm, it had already shaped her work ethic. While she still enjoyed hard physical work on those occasions that she got to perform it, she'd never wanted a farm, and she hadn't wanted to marry a farmer.

For her generation and those born around it, farming was akin to poverty. It was not a job that she or most people her age aspired to. She thought she understood something now that her father had never been able to convey to her in words, that farming was also about self-sufficiency. It was about having more control of your life.

In trying to escape what she saw as the trappings of poverty, Alice had given up a lot of things, including a working knowledge of how to farm, how to raise livestock, and how to process the things they raised into food and goods. She hadn't passed this knowledge on to her son. She'd never taught him the things she learned as a child. It was like she had a tool in her toolbox that she'd not only failed to pass on, but had allowed to rust from neglect. It had never occurred to her until this moment how much of a failure that was on her part. She hoped there was still time to do something about it.

Her dad had passed away three years ago, leaving her with the responsibility of helping her mother out. She'd never minded, but she did wish her mom would move off the farm. Although she worried about her living out there all alone, still trying to raise a few animals and more garden than she needed, her mother wouldn't budge. She just couldn't see herself in an apartment in town. She liked the taste of food she raised with her own hands on her own land. She liked seeing the smiles when she shared the bounty of her garden with people who didn't have one.

The road between Alice's house and her mother's farm was heavily travelled in normal times. It was a narrow and shoulder-less road. People drove too fast on it and accidents tended to be fatal head-on collisions. Today there were not many people out on it at all. There were some walkers, a few bikes, and a long, rattling Oliver tractor. She saw a few of the Chinese scooters that would run all day on a cup of gas. There were also a lot of vehicles abandoned along the shoulder and in the ditch. Some had rags hanging from the window like flags of surrender. They must have been placed there early in this mess, when people still thought they'd be coming back for them.

Alice was thankful for her functioning vehicle. She was aware that it made her a target so she maintained vigilance throughout her drive. She looked ahead for roadblocks and traps. She studied the people she passed for weapons or any indication that they may be about to launch some kind of action against her. She scanned the road surface for anything that might slow or disable her car. Her gun lay in its regular place now, beneath her right thigh, ready for when she needed it.

At a major intersection, she saw that an oak tree had been cut down across the road at one point but someone had made the effort to saw it up and roll the logs off onto the shoulder. She slowed as she passed by it, noting that what she thought were cigarette butts littering the surface of the road were actually spent shell casings. There were smears that she took for blood but no bodies visible anywhere. Drag marks indicated the bodies must have been tossed over the hill. There had been a roadblock here at one point and the day had ended badly for someone. The memory of coming upon such a roadblock with Gary when she was helping him get a box truck was still fresh in her mind.

A little further down the road she came across a head-on collision. She could see it from a good distance off, the bright colored vehicles sitting at odd angles. While she felt an initial wave of concern for the victims, she noticed that she did not feel the level of concern she might have felt six months ago when coming upon the same scene. She realized that the feeling of *concern* was programmed into her and could be programmed out just as easily. Of much greater importance to her was whether there was room or not for her to navigate her vehicle around the accident. She was pleased to see there was.

It was a tight squeeze on the narrow, two-lane road. She had to put a tire off the edge of the pavement and creep by slowly to avoid getting her vehicle hung on the wreckage. She noted that all the windows in the entangled vehicles were shattered. As she pulled alongside the driver's door of a 1980s model Thunderbird, she was shocked to see that the bodies had not been removed. She couldn't even tell if the driver was a man or a woman, the face being so bloated and fly-encrusted. The passenger had been partially ejected, travelling through the windshield and ending up crushed between the vehicles. It was a gory sight that fascinated her as much as it repelled her.

It reminded her of war photos she'd seen, with the bodies of enemy soldiers left scattered among debris. It was easy to forget that the dead may have been important to someone. In this world as it was now, with no phone and no news, word may never reach the families of these victims. It was like the world used to be before the advent of the electronic age. If you died away from home, outside of the sphere of where you were known, your fate may never make it to the folks back home.

About twenty minutes later Alice approached her mother's farm on a dirt road that seemed more desolate than at any time in her memory. As a child, the road had seemed alive with other farming families and livestock being moved back and forth. There was always something going on. She was never more than a few minutes' walk from a friend's house. She played outside until well after dark, always feeling safe, and any neighboring family would care for her as well as her own family would.

Now the road seemed surreal, winding through a barren and lifeless facsimile of what had once been her community. She saw no farmers working, no children playing. There was damaged fencing that could have been taken down by falling limbs, persistent cattle, or even thieves. It was the kind of thing that most respectable farmers could not have let lie for even a single day in better times. Fences were a sign of the health of a farm. If the fences were dying, the farms, and the families on them, were likely dead or dying too.

Her family's farm extended down to the road and she drove along hundreds of feet of cattle fencing that her father had installed with his own hands. When she reached the driveway, she found it blocked by a hulking hay baler that had been pulled across the entrance. She stopped there, turning off the car and listening. She could hear nothing other than the ticking of the engine. Had her family put this there as a barricade?

She opened her door and got out, revolver in her hand. She stepped away from the car because the baler was blocking her view of the house. She could see no movement. Her mother's border collie would normally be at her side by now but there was no sign of it. Down the road about a half mile, on the opposite side of the dirt road, was the neighbor's farm, and she could see no movement down there either. The emptiness of it all, the surreal feeling, reminded her of the Stephen King story *Children of the Corn*.

She would like to roll the baler out of the way and drive on through but it was too heavy for her to move alone. Sitting perpendicular to the driveway, there was not even an easy way for her to nudge it with the car and move it to the side. She looked toward the house again. There were no lights, no cooking smells, and no vehicles. There were no chickens in the yard and she saw no movement in the hog pen. Where they even still here or had someone else moved in?

She reached back and shut the car door. It closed louder than she expected and the noise stood out in the absolute silence of the pasture-land. She started to walk away, then worried about leaving the car. She reached back through the window and removed the key, then grabbed her pack from the back. There were other things in the car that were important to her but after what she'd been through the pack was her lifeline. The things in the car were things she could live without. The things in her pack were not.

She pocketed the keys and slung the pack over her shoulders and checked the chamber of the revolver, confirming there was a live round ready to go in each chamber. With another look toward the house, she moved toward the gate, turning sideways to squeeze her body between the gatepost and the baler. The pack hung up on a strand of barbed wire and it took her a moment to unsnag herself. When she did, she continued easing around the baler and started to walk toward the house.

She made it one step before a shot rang out and she dropped to the ground.

CHAPTER SIX

Alice

Alice lay on the ground stunned. The side of her face burned and she put a hand to it. When she drew it back, there were blotches of bright red blood on it. The impact had been to her right. The bullet hadn't hit her, so it had to be fragments from the bullet shattering when it hit a thick steel component of the baler. Before she could get her head together and get back to her feet, the front door slammed. She looked in that direction and saw her son Charlie clambering down the porch steps, a rifle held to his shoulder and aimed in her direction. He still did not recognize her. He appeared to be coming down to finish her off.

"It's me!" she cried, but the voice that came from her mouth did not sound like her own. He seemed not to recognize it, either. Had she made it this far only to die in the yard of the home where she was born and at the hand of her seventeen year old son? The dispassionate cruelty of the world was sometimes unfathomable.

It was perhaps fifty yards to the porch and he continued creeping steadily in her direction, the rifle leveled on her. Alice began to slide one arm free of a pack strap, hoping that without the burden of it she could roll toward the baler and take cover behind it.

At her movement he fired again and a divot of grass flew up to her left.

"Don't you fucking move!" he yelled.

He was trying to sound older and intimidating, but she could hear the boy beneath it. He sounded scared. Perhaps even scared enough to shoot a stranger he didn't recognize. Perhaps even scared enough to kill his own mother in this confusing circumstance. The dam of emotion that she'd held back for so long on this trip weakened and crumbled. She began to sob. She had tried. She had given it everything she had to get back here. She didn't want to die here. She didn't want Charlie to have to live with the burden of having killed his mother.

She was laying there with her face in the dirt, crying uncontrollably when he neared. He paused. Awareness seemed to settle onto him like fog settling onto the land. She could not blame him for taking so long to recognize her. She was in a strange car, carrying a backpack, her disheveled hair pulled back in a way that she never wore it before. She was dirty and her clothes ill-fitting. She was not the mother that left home a few weeks ago.

"M-Mom?" he asked, his voice rife with uncertainty.

She couldn't respond.

"MOM!" he yelled, leaning the rifle against the baler and dropping beside her. He rolled her over and lost it when he saw the blood on her face. "I'm sorry, Mom! I didn't mean to. I didn't know who you were!" He said other things but they were lost in the flurry of his own sobs. With all the blood, he couldn't tell the extent of her injuries. He'd been aiming for her head and assumed his round had found its mark.

Alice reached up, touching his face. Seeing his own tears, feeling again the need to take care of someone, she began to regain control of her own emotions. "It's okay, sweetie. You hit the baler. Something just ricocheted off and hit me. I'm okay. Really I am."

She pushed herself up and hugged him. He still felt like her son. He still smelled like her son. Holding him brought back to life a part of her that she thought may have been gone forever. It was different, but there was still the capacity to care, to love.

The sound of the door opening again made both of them look in the direction of the house. Alice's mom, Pat, was coming outside. To Alice's surprise, she was leading Alice's husband by the arm, as if something were wrong with him.

"What's the matter with your dad?"

Charlie hesitated. "He ran out of his medicine."

Alice's husband had developed a heart condition a few years ago and he took medications for it daily. Although the condition was still present, the medication helped control the symptoms and allow him to function somewhat normally. She hadn't seen him in this state. He looked like an invalid.

"Why hasn't he had his medication?" Alice asked. "He orders a three-month supply at a time. He was getting ready to start an unopened bottle when I left. He should still have about two months' worth."

Alice's husband had to take a seat on the top step, unable to continue any further. Alice's mother hurried down to the yard, bunched her apron in front of her, and began trotting toward them, crying at the very sight of her daughter. She was awash in relief.

"She's okay!" Charlie yelled, his voice still shaky. "I didn't hit her!"

"His medication?" Alice repeated.

"He brought a couple of days' worth with him when we came down here the first time," Charlie said. "It was whatever he had in one of those little pill reminder things you carry in your pocket. We were going to check on Gran, help her with a few chores, and then go back home for a while. We figured the power would come back on any time. If it didn't, we'd pack up some stuff and come down here and stay with Gran. When we got back we found our house got broken into. They stole medications, all the gas we had, and a lot of the food. We barely had enough gas to get back down here. Dad tried rationing the medications but he ran out about two weeks ago and he's been getting worse ever since."

"My baby!" Alice's mom cried as she neared them.

Alice reluctantly disentangled herself from her son and stood. She held her arms open to her mother, who slowed seeing the blood.

"You're hurt," she said, saying the words as if discovering this hurt her too.

Alice wiped at her face with the tail of her shirt, flinching at what must have been a bullet shard still stuck in the wound. "It's not serious."

Pat took her daughter into her arms and Alice felt like she was a child again. Not in years had she felt so comforted. She began to cry again. Over her mother's shoulder, she could see her husband on the porch trying to struggle to his feet, the pain of missing this reunion too much for him. He leaned heavily on the stair rail and carefully took one step at a time.

"I have to go see Terry," Alice said. "Let's go to the house."

"Give me your keys and I'll bring your car up," Charlie said. "It's not safe to leave it out along the road."

Alice dug her key out of her pocket and tossed it to him. She picked her pack up from the ground and slung it over her shoulder, then realized she was missing her revolver. She walked around looking at the ground for a moment.

"This what you're looking for?" Charlie asked, crouching and picking up the handgun.

"Careful," Alice said. "It's loaded."

Charlie carefully handed the pistol over to his mother, the muzzle pointed in a safe direction. "When did you start carrying a gun?"

Alice didn't have an easy answer for that. To tell even a part of the story would open a direct channel to experiences she wasn't ready to relate yet. "It was a long trip home, honey."

Charlie nodded as if understanding exactly what that meant. Maybe he did understand it. Maybe he'd seen things the past weeks too. She had no idea yet what they'd gone through in her absence. Had people tried to kill her child? Had he been forced to kill someone? He certainly hadn't hesitated to fire a shot at her.

She began walking toward the house, holding her mother's hand. Seeing them headed in his direction, Terry sagged awkwardly down on a lower step. Alice could not believe how bad he looked. He'd been weaker in the years since his heart condition developed but the medication had allowed him to live a somewhat normal life. This man in front of her appeared to be dying. When she reached him, seeing the dark rings around his eyes, the bloating in his body, she knew that he *was* dying.

He held his arms out to her but could not stand. Coming outside and down the few steps appeared to have taken all he had in him. She could feel the weakness in his embrace, like she was hugging an elderly man. Despite his obvious relief at having her come home to them, she could feel that there was little strength in his body.

"I'm sorry, baby," he said as she embraced him, holding him tight.

His words made her cry. "Why are you sorry?"

He was crying now too. "I can't do a damn thing anymore," he said. "I'm not a bit of good to anyone."

"It's not your fault," she said. "The medicine was helping."

He released her. "The medicine is gone," he said, shaking his head. "The house got broken into and they took it."

She wiped at her eyes. "Any idea who it was?" she asked, already having an idea of her own as to who it might have been.

"No," he said. "They hit several homes in the neighborhood. It got bad fast and has been getting worse every day."

She nodded at this, well aware of how bad things were.

"We're so glad you're home, baby," Terry said. "We didn't know if you were alive or not."

"We've been so worried," her mother agreed.

"How was the trip?" Terry asked. "How did you get home?"

As memories of her trip assaulted her, remembering the deaths she'd seen, the violence, she was overwhelmed. She took a deep breath and let it out slowly. "It was fine," she said. "All that matters is that I'm home now. We can talk about the rest later."

CHAPTER SEVEN

Alice

The table in Pat's kitchen had been a wedding gift. She'd married Alice's father Walter in 1954 when she was fifteen years old. Every meal she'd ever served as a wife and mother had been at that table. Alice thought about this as her mother cooked. She thought of all the meals she'd eaten there, all the conversations she'd had with her father, and all the things she'd told her mother about that she didn't want her father to know.

The table had not been something Alice thought about as she fought her way home from Richmond. She thought of family, of how much she enjoyed her backyard and the time she spent there with her son and husband. On those occasions that she did think of her mother's house she thought of the farm itself – barns, livestock, and the fields. How this table could be so integral to her memory of family and not have crossed her mind at all surprised her. She ran a finger over the wood surface, touching scratches and dings, reading the braille written there. It was the story of a life, of a family.

Around the table, Terry and Charlie sat watching Alice. They were obviously wanting to hear about her experiences but she wasn't ready to talk yet. They studied her, seeing a difference that they couldn't quite put a finger on. Alice could sense their confusion but almost found it amusing. Under normal circumstances, the two barely noticed if she dyed her hair a different color. How could they ever tell what was happening in her murky depths?

Her mother was fixing biscuits from scratch and frying sausage canned from hogs killed on the farm. She cooked on an antique Monarch wood cook stove that had always been in this kitchen, even before it became Pat's kitchen. When she bought an electric stove and didn't need the old Monarch for cooking anymore, she and Walter kept it for backup heat, so used to the way it warmed the kitchen on cold mornings.

When her mother was done with the sausage, she'd make gravy from fresh raw milk. The smell made Alice so hungry that she physically ached. It wasn't just that it was food, because she'd had food. It was that it was her *mother's* food, eaten with her family, and it would feed more than her belly.

"So where's all the livestock?" Alice asked. "I didn't see any animals when I walked up. You must still have a milk cow, right?"

"Locked in the barn," Charlie said.

"Shouldn't they be out grazing?" Alice asked. "If we can't get feed this winter, we'll need them on grass as long as we can."

"We've already lost about half of them," Terry said, his voice so weak that it was almost unfamiliar to her. "You know there isn't a grocery store for twenty miles. The convenience stores were the only source of food once people couldn't get gas. People were paying five dollars each for Little Debbie cakes. I heard jerky was twenty-five dollars a bag. Even at those prices that food only lasted a couple of days. When it ran out, there was no food in this part of the county at all except for what people had in their homes."

Alice hadn't thought about that. Her mother's community had no grocery stores at all. Before cars became so common, every community had its own country store. Now you were lucky if you even had a grocery store in your county. That made driving to the store a big deal in the best of times. People had to take a cooler for bringing home frozen items or they would already be thawing out by the time they got home. What had once been a mere inconvenience became instantly more serious when things collapsed.

"People started breaking into homes and farms looking for food," Charlie said. "We were afraid to go back home and leave Gran alone. We were afraid someone would break in on her."

Pat bristled. "I can take care of myself," she said. "I have for years."

"I know you can, Mom, but it's different when you don't have the law for backup. You can't hide in the bedroom and call the police. You have to finish things."

Everyone looked at Alice for a moment, understanding what she was saying but curious about what was not being said. Had Alice been forced to "finish what she started" on the road? Had she had to finish *people?*

"They took one of the cows first," Terry said. "Someone cut the fence and led it down the road with a bucket of grain. They'd spilled little bits of it here and there. We tried to track them but I couldn't get very far and I wasn't going to let Charlie go alone."

"I wanted to go," Charlie said. "I wanted to get them."

"I wanted to get them too," Pat said, reaching out and patting Charlie's hand. "But a grandson is worth more to me than a cow."

"Gran, that's the sweetest thing you've ever said to me," Charlie said, smiling.

"What about the dog?" Alice asked. "Didn't it bark? I didn't hear it when I pulled up, either." The farm had always had a couple of dogs, though they were down to a single blue heeler/beagle mix.

"They killed it," Terry said. "It was too friendly with people to be a decent guard dog. They beat it to death with a stick. We found it laying in the ditch just the other side of the fence."

There had been a day Alice would have cried over the death of a sweet dog but not anymore. She was almost surprised to find that she could still love people. She'd been worried that all her softness and compassion had been pushed out by her experiences on the road. Still, there was less room in there now. She could feel it. The people and things she could feel love for would be fewer than they had once been. She also wondered if the only reason she still loved *these* people was that they had already been in her heart before the horrible experiences she went through. Did that mean there might not be room for anyone new?

"We started keeping watch after that," Charlie said. "I stayed up all night but someone still got two of the hogs. I never even heard a thing from in here and Dad wouldn't let me stay out in the barn." He cast an accusing glance at his father.

"I didn't want him out there on his own at night," Terry said. "The boy seems to think he's invincible or something."

"I told Charlie if he ran into the wrong people he'd end up like that dog – beaten to death," Pat said. A practical country woman, Alice's mom never did sugarcoat things.

"A lot of this is my fault," Terry said, looking down at the table and shaking his head. "Since my medicine ran out, I'm not much help at all. I'm too damn weak to stand watch at night and I can't do any of the chores. It's not fair on Charlie and your mom to have to do it all."

"So you're not standing watch anymore?" Alice asked.

"We try to," Pat said. "It's just hard after working all day. We've had all this canning to do, taking care of what animals we have left. We're exhausted."

"Have you considered leaving?" Alice asked.

They all looked at her stunned.

"Honey, we've got water, wood heat, a springhouse for storing milk, and the animals. This is a much better setup than we've got back at our house," Terry said. "It's a better setup than most people have."

"How much longer will it be ours?" she asked. "How much longer before, instead of stealing from you, someone decides to kill you and take the place for their own? Once the weather turns cold, people will start looking for more than food. They'll start looking for homes with chimneys that they can take by force. If you can't keep the animals, how can you hope to keep this house?"

Alice could tell from the look on their faces that they hadn't considered this. She could almost understand, considering that they were so sheltered here from the events taking place in the outside world. "People are doing those things," Alice said, pressing her point. "They're behaving in the worst ways you can imagine. I've seen it. I want to stay here and I hope we can keep it, but it may be harder than you think."

"Maybe we can talk to some of the neighbors and work together?" Pat suggested.

Alice shook her head. "No offense, Mom, but everyone up and down this road is around your age or close to it. Defending homes is probably not one of their strongest skills."

"I don't want to leave," Pat said. "This is the only place I've ever known."

"I'm not saying you have to, Mom. I'm just suggesting that we might need an escape plan in case staying here falls through."

"Escape to where?" Charlie asked. "If the world is *that* dangerous now, where the heck can we go and hope to be safe?"

"I know some people," Alice said. "People I work with. They would welcome people with your skills, Mom. They helped me get home and they offered to let us join them if we needed to."

Pat shook her head and made a sound of disapproval. "I don't have any skills, Alice," Pat said. "I'm just a plain old farm wife. A country girl. It's all I've ever known."

"Those are *priceless* skills right now," Alice said. "Being able to farm, to raise food, and to preserve food, it's nearly a lost art."

"I'm not so sure about giving this place up to throw in with other people," Terry said. "I hate the idea of strangers moving in here and having the run of the place."

"The idea makes me sick," Alice said. "And I'm not saying we have to leave. I'm saying that the people who *plan* are the people who *live,* and we need to plan for everything. I saw it on my way home. There are actually people out there who did plan for things like this and they were ready. I wasn't."

Pat came around the table and put her arm around her daughter. "I love you, Alice. I'm proud of what you've become in life. I just want you to know that you all can leave if you want to. I wouldn't be mad and I wouldn't blame you. If you aren't comfortable having your family here, then you all can go stay with your friends. I've been tending this farm by myself and I can still do it."

Alice's eyes moved between her mother's hands and her face. "We won't leave you, Mom," Alice said. "We'll try to make it work."

Terry reached over and patted Alice on the back. "I think your mom's probably right, honey. We just need to get ourselves organized a little better and we can get through this. It's like one of those crazy ice storms that paralyzes everything. Eventually the power will come back on and people will start acting right again. This will all become a memory."

Alice looked in her husband's eyes. He believed every word he'd said, just as she had when she and Jim parted ways in the dark hotel on the interstate. At that time she believed everything would be fine too. She believed FEMA would get her home. She believed life would return to normal. Now she knew better.

CHAPTER EIGHT

Alice

Near Alice and Terry's home there was a country church by the road-side. The poplar clapboards were stark white and there was a galva-nized metal roof that was beginning to show rust at the seams. At one corner of the roof was a bell tower with an actual brass bell instead of the more modern system of a speaker that played a recording of bells. There was no air conditioning and on warm evenings the minister opened the windows and doors to allow the cooler air in. From her house, Alice could hear the sound of the congregation singing on those nights. It seemed an odd contrast to her, to be sitting on the porch outside her modern home, using a tablet with a Wi-Fi connection while listening to old Baptist hymns sung without piano or organ accompaniment, just as they may have been sung a hundred or even two hundred years ago.

Alice pulled off the two-lane road and into the church parking lot, her headlights not finding another soul. She cut the lights and used the moonlight to park the vehicle behind the church. She turned the engine off and listened. She allowed her ears to adjust to the night the same way her eyes would. She wanted to be as certain as she could that no one was nearby.

She dug into her Go Bag and pulled out a flashlight, tucking it into her pocket. She unfastened her belt, pulled it free of a few loops, and threaded on a Buck hunting knife that she'd gotten from her father's dresser. It had been in the same place where he'd always kept it, her mom treating his things with too much reverence to ever move them, as if they contained a magic that would be broken if she disturbed them. Alice knew the black-handled knife was razor sharp. Her dad skinned deer with it. She knew what it could do in a determined and steady hand.

She opened her car door as carefully as possible, trying to minimize the groaning of the hinges, closing it just as carefully. She wanted to lock the car but it was pointless with so many windows broken out. Knowing that it would be best to have both hands free when walking on unfamiliar terrain in the dark, she tucked the revolver into her waistband and started off.

She knew from her son's explorations of the neighborhood that there was a trail leading from their street to the church. In the summer, with everything leafed-out, you'd never see it. When the leaves fell, the steeple of the church was visible from the master bedroom of her home.

She walked carefully, feeling her way along with her feet. She didn't want to fall. Not because of fear of getting hurt but because she didn't want to make any noise. With the nights warm and no air conditioning available, people would probably have windows open. After a few minutes of determined walking she emerged from the woods, leaving the rich blackness of the forest for the pale silver of the moonlit neighborhood.

According to the car clock, it was nearly 1 a.m. when she parked. With no power and no electronic distractions most people would be asleep unless they were standing guard. In the far distance, at the entrance to their subdivision, Alice could indeed see a bonfire going. She couldn't see anything in detail, but assumed that men still stood guard there just as they had when she came in. They would be a nervous lot, uncertain as to what awaited them out in the world. She would have to avoid drawing their attention as fearful men might be quick to shoot.

From the woods, she cut across the dew-soaked grass, her sneakers growing wetter with each step. When she passed her family's home, she paused and took it in. Without power and without her family inside it seemed lifeless, like a body viewed in a funeral home, merely the husk of what it had once been. She had no desire to go inside and be reminded of how life had been. She moved on, walking through the grass to avoid the sound of scuffing gravel on the asphalt, and stopped in front of her neighbors' house.

The boy and his uncle had broken into her house. She was certain of it. They'd made enough looting trips that they'd worn a trail between the two houses. She didn't like it but she could almost understand it. By taking her husband's medications, they had handed down a death sentence on him and she couldn't accept that. She certainly couldn't prove it was them but who else would have taken it? These were the men who were raiding her house. They were known drug users. This was the place to start.

As she stood there in the dark, Alice accepted there would likely be a time soon when her husband ran out of medications again. Even if she found what had been stolen it would not be an indefinite supply. All she could hope for was to buy him some time. She hoped that if she could keep him alive she might be able to learn more about the pharmacological mechanisms of the medication and see if there were natural alternatives. If she could find someone knowledgeable about herbs and plants then maybe there was something they could try. Even if it didn't have the same level of effectiveness as the prescription medication, if it could just keep him alive. That was her hope.

Besides, there had to be an end to this disaster eventually. While she had to admit it had gotten much worse than she ever expected and people's behavior had been more along the lines of what her pessimistic coworker Jim had predicted, she did honestly believe there would be a point in the future where it took an upturn. Things would get back to normal one day.

Yet she hadn't come all this way to ponder. She was on a mission. She watched the house the two men lived in and saw no lights, no

movement through any of the windows. With no power and the difficulty of getting gas, even the scumbags were beginning to feel the
pinch. There were some things that even thieves and drug dealers had
trouble laying their hands on. She stepped into the tall grass of their
yard, feeling an immediate increase in her level of tension. She was in
new territory, both literally and figuratively.

She raised her feet high as she walked to avoid kicking any trash or
other debris in the yard, of which there was plenty. She paused when
she reached the porch in front of the house and listened again. No
sounds at all. There were two brick steps leading up to a porch of brick
pavers. Even though she couldn't see it, she knew there was a cheap
black welcome mat on the porch. She also knew that there was a door
key beneath it. She'd seen Jake use it many times to get inside the
house when he forgotten his house key. She hoped it was still there.

She lowered herself to her knees, shocked at the loud pops and
creaks they emitted, a reminder of her age. She waved her hands
lightly against the gritty surface of the bricks, feeling for the mat.
When she found it, she carefully rolled back the edge and felt under-
neath it. She moved her hand in a searching pattern, concerned when
she didn't immediately find it.

She paused. She wasn't particularly nervous or scared. She was just
impatient and needed to slow down. She willed herself to take her time
and began feeling for the key again, moving her hand in a circular
pattern this time. She was rewarded with a light clinking sound when
her fingers bumped the key.

Not wanting to lose track of it, she laid her palm flat across it, then
used the other hand to pick it up. She clutched it tightly and stood up,
her knees protesting again. With her other hand, she removed her
revolver and held it pointed toward the ground. It was not the most
tactically proficient stance, but it was how she'd become accustomed
to handling her weapon. She was not a trained shooter. She was a reluc-
tant warrior who was learning as she went.

She stood in front of the door and listened. There was still time to
change her mind if anything seemed wrong, but she knew she couldn't
change her mind. How could she go back empty-handed after being
this close? With her husband's pallor and growing weakness, she

couldn't imagine he'd last the month without his medication. This had to happen tonight.

She took the key and raised it to the lock. With her other hand holding the gun, she felt for the keyhole. That was when she dropped the key, hearing it ring as it bounced off the brick at her feet. She lowered her head and shook it.

Fuck!

She struggled to calm herself. This was not a time to rage and curse. She had to stay on-task. Getting angry would not solve the problem.

She remained still and listened until she was sure no one was alerted. Then she put the gun back in her waistband and knelt down, feeling around with both hands in ever widening circles. She found cigarette butts, the caps from beer bottles, and several sticky clumps of what she thought must be chewed gum. The smell of urine rose strongly from beneath her nose and she realized that the men probably relieved themselves on this porch sometimes. Although this disgusted her, it was too late to worry about that now. She continued to feel around and finally her hand landed on the familiar shape of the key. She sighed with relief.

This time she used both hands to find the keyhole. She carefully inserted it into the lock, advancing it slowly, feeling it slide past each pin in the cylinder. Only then did she retrieve the revolver from her waistband again. She took a deep breath and turned the key ever so slowly.

CHAPTER NINE

Alice

Jake Fisher was sound asleep, dreaming about playing Frisbee and getting high, when he felt himself being choked awake. It was a sensation so sudden, so violent, that he thought he was going to throw up. He felt himself gagging, felt the sickness rising in his throat. A light clicked on directly in his face and he was blinded. He tried to turn his head away from the light but a sharp pain in his forehead stopped him. He tried to call out but realized there was something in his mouth preventing that. He tried to move his arms but someone was sitting on him. He rocked his body, trying to throw the person off. The pressure on his forehead increased, something cutting into his flesh.

"Stop moving," a female voice hissed.

Jake blinked his eyes, struggling to get his bearings and make sense of what was happening. The light turned away from his face, the beam resting on his chest. Though still squinting against the bright light, his eyes adjusted enough that he could see a woman sitting on him, holding a pistol to his forehead. He panicked again, trying to suck in air but his mouth was blocked. Air came through his nose but it wasn't enough. He was hyperventilating. She pressed the gun against him harder.

"Breathe slower," she whispered. "Slow, deep breaths."

He tried to talk again but couldn't form words.

"You can't talk. I shoved a pair of your nasty underwear into your mouth. You should do a better job picking up your room. You should also change your underwear a little more often."

He made another sound but she pressed the gun against his forehead so hard he was sure he could feel it cutting a circle in his flesh. He closed his eyes against the pain. It was like the worst brain freeze he'd ever had multiplied ten times over.

"Do you know who I am?" the woman asked.

Jake tried to focus on her, his brain struggling to make sense of the visual input. Wild, dark hair, angry eyes. He thought he might know her. The neighbor?

She could see the light of recognition come on his brain. "I'm going to ask you one question and you better tell me the fucking truth. Did you steal medications from my house?"

He said nothing, just stared at her wide-eyed, still feeling like he was suffocating. He started to hyperventilate again.

"Did you hear me?" she asked. She was not pleased by his failure to respond. He was not taking her seriously and that was a mistake. She raised the gun about a foot above his head, then clubbed him viciously before placing the barrel back on his forehead. He grimaced and tried to twist his head away but she held him tight. Then she thumbed back the hammer of the revolver, the click of the mechanism unmistakable in the quiet of the room.

When he still failed to respond, she lay the flashlight on the bed beside them. It shined upward onto her face, illuminating her in a ghastly manner that did nothing to decrease his level of fear. Her dark hair, gone wild from a month of inattention, splayed around her face, giving her a Medusa-like quality. Although she'd tried to stay clean, the dirt of the road had settled into the lines of her face, etching and exaggerating them. Perhaps most frightening was that with the light on her face, he could better see the complete absence of fear. He could see in her eyes what he, even as a young, inexperienced man, recognized as a wildness that bordered on insanity. She was a woman over the edge.

Alice unsnapped the black sheath on her belt. There was a faint hiss as the blade slid from the leather. She leaned forward over his face, all her weight resting on the barrel of the gun, which in turn rested on Jake's forehead. She lowered herself and whispered in his ear. "I don't have the patience to make threats. I just want to know where our medication is. I'm going to pull that underwear out of your mouth and you're going to answer me real quietly. Do you understand?"

He nodded, but there was something in his eyes that betrayed an insincerity, a streak of noncompliance, that didn't sit well with her. She didn't like the boy – never had – and she didn't want to waste any more time on coercion. She needed to get out of there.

Without hesitation, she put the razor sharp blade of her dad's knife to the tip of his nose, placing her thumb against the underside, just above his lip. She cut off the tip of his nose as casually as one might snip the tip off a carrot. The domed sliver of flesh stuck to the blade, the way a sliced mushroom might.

His eyes widened in pain, but before he could make a sound, she pressed her hand over his mouth, pushing the underwear in further. His nervous system was overloaded, his body confused by the fear, the waves of pain, the gagging sensation, and the impending suffocation. She continued to hold her hand over his mouth until he looked as if he were losing consciousness. Then she violently jerked the underwear from his mouth in a single tug.

He retched and started to cough. She could feel his hands twitching beneath her legs, trying to fly up to his mouth in reflex. She put the knife against his throat, laying it in the blood running from his nose, around his mouth, and down his neck. His body trembled as he tried to hold in the sounds wanting to fight their way out of his body. His eyes watered and his face grew red.

"You see how easily I did that?" she whispered.

He didn't reply. He could see that she was pleased with herself. Pleased that she had elicited this reaction from him. Pleased that she'd hurt him.

"Did you?" she repeated.

He nodded this time, afraid that any failure to respond might bring more pain.

"I used to be a good woman," she said. "I looked after hundreds of employees at my company. I'll be honest with you. After the shit I've been through – shit you couldn't even imagine – I'm feeling a little unhinged. You do not want to push me." The gun still pressed against his head, she lowered her other hand until the knife blade lay against his groin. She felt a shudder pass through his body. "You know what I'm considering next and you know I'll do it."

He didn't hesitate. He fully understood that she'd do it. He was afraid to even twitch his legs for fear of her reaction, that she'd snip him there as easily as she'd snipped the tip from his nose.

"The backpack," he hissed. "By the door."

Leaving the gun and knife in position, she turned her head slightly and observed that there was indeed a student backpack hanging from a nail on the wall. "You better not be lying," she whispered.

"I'm not," he said. "Just take it and go. Get the fuck off me and get out of here."

His tone was defiant but whiny. She hated whiny people before. Now she couldn't tolerate them at all. She pressed her knife against him harder. He had to be feeling the tip of the blade poking through the denim now. He had to know how close he was to permanent and irreparable mutilation.

"Do *not* take an attitude with me," she warned. "I might not be able to stop myself from giving you what you deserve."

He did not make a sound or move a muscle.

Leaving the gun tight against his forehead, she sheathed her knife and eased off the bed, picking up her flashlight as she went. She backed away from the young man until she was beside the backpack. It was partially unzipped already.

Jake sat up and gingerly pressed the dirty underwear over his bleeding nose, wincing as it made contact with the wound. Alice hit the button on her flashlight and directed the beam inside the pack. The bag was indeed full of pill bottles. She could tell that there were many more than they'd ever had at her house. The little bastard had been robbing a lot of other houses.

She caught a flash of movement from her peripheral vision and looked over in time to see Jake yank a vicious-looking hatchet from beneath the bed. It was a garish black and neon green, like the kind of weapon supposedly designed for killing zombies. It would still be highly lethal.

He whipped it back over his head and launched it at Alice. She lunged to the side, raised the pistol, and fired at him. His throw was rushed and the hatchet clattered harmlessly off the closed bedroom door several feet from Alice. Jake was not so lucky. Alice's aim was true.

Her round caught him in the throat and he threw both hands to his neck, trying to staunch the geyser of blood. His eyes flew wide with surprise. He tried to yell for help but only emitted a gurgling sound from deep in his throat. It was the sound of a man drowning in his own blood.

Alice grabbed the pack and slung it over one shoulder and pulled open the bedroom door, her light breaching the hallway and revealing a wide-eyed man in boxer shorts coming toward her. It was the boy's uncle. He had a baseball bat in his hands and lunged toward her. Her gun was at the ready and she fired twice into the thick mass of his torso, dropping him at her feet. His cries for help followed her as she stepped over him and hurried down the hall.

She knew she only had seconds before the men at the bonfire were up there. She'd probably woken the rest of the neighbors with her gunfire. She bolted down the steps and ran through the unfamiliar house. She turned a corner and collided with a half-open closet door before her brain could tell her to slow down. She was stunned but pulled herself together and staggered out the front door. She could hear voices, see flashlights approaching, their beams cutting through the night air like spotlights.

They would be on her quickly and she didn't want to have to explain herself. She felt like she was justified. She was saving her husband's life, stealing back what had been stolen from her, but would these men see it that way? What if they shot her on sight?

Using the flashlight inside the house had already blown her night vision so she opted to continue using the light to expedite her escape.

She could run faster if she could see. She sprinted across the yard and toward the woods, hoping that uncertainty would keep her sheltered, docile neighbors from firing on her. She reached the trail with at least fifty yards head start over the nearest pursuer.

She hadn't run in years but gave it her all, negotiating the rock-strewn and root-laced path with a nimbleness she hadn't known she possessed. She felt like a quarterback playing one of those games where everything was going just right. When she burst into the church parking lot, she began digging for her keys. With the aid of the light, she quickly found the correct one and was in the car as lights began coming down the trail toward her. She'd hoped everyone would go to the house but they must have split up. They were coming for her.

Voices were rising, getting closer. Lights were beginning to hit objects around her. They must surely be able to see her now. She flinched, knowing that if the lights were hitting her, bullets could also. No sooner had she thought that than a shot rang out. She heard it whistle overhead, clipping leaves and small branches. She threw the pack into the car and dropped into the seat, jamming the key into the ignition. There was another shot.

She was panicking. What if they shot out the tires? What if they hit the radiator? What if they hit her? She said a quick prayer as she turned the key in the ignition. It started. There was no time for relief. She flipped on the headlights and floored the gas pedal, spraying gravel in her wake. She slid onto the paved road, the car fishtailing as it clawed for traction.

"Concentrate," she warned herself. "Do not fucking wreck!"

The tires caught and she shot off down the road. With distance growing between her and her pursuers, she forced herself to pay more attention to the road, trying to remember all of the obstacles she'd encountered earlier. She hadn't come this far to collide with an abandoned vehicle or a downed tree.

She knew it was a dumb move but she reached up and flipped on the overhead light. She had to know if what she'd done was worth it. She reached into the open top of the backpack in the passenger seat and extracted a bottle. She didn't recognize the name and angrily tossed it into the back seat. She dug another out with the same result.

"Don't tell me..." she said, anger and frustration in her voice. "*Please*! Be there!"

Another bottle. This one a name she recognized. A neighbor with prostate problems. She tossed it in the back, becoming more desperate. There were dozens of bottles. She found another. Pre-natal vitamins. Another bottle. She read the name, tears stinging her eyes. Had she risked her life for nothing? Had she shot those men for nothing?

Then the name on a bottle sank into her brain. "Terry Watkins."

Her husband.

CHAPTER TEN

Alice

Alice shook her husband awake a little before 4 a.m. She expected him to wake with a start, as he always had in the years they'd been together. If there was a noise in the night or if Charlie woke with a bad dream, he always sprang from the bed. Now his eyes fluttered open weakly. Her flashlight sat on the nightstand, casting indirect light off the ceiling. In the glow of the LED bulb, he was pale and his skin puffy. She couldn't help but think that he looked like a bloated corpse.

She had used her dad's knife to scrape the label off the pill bottle. She didn't want Terry to ask how she'd gotten his exact bottle of pills back. It was difficult enough to tell him about her experiences on the road. She couldn't just come out and tell him that she'd killed their old neighbors to bring back his meds. He definitely wasn't ready to hear that. Maybe one day they could talk about it and all the rest of the things she'd been through, but this wasn't the day.

She held the bottle up in front of his glassy, half-lidded eyes.

"What is it?" he asked.

"Your medicine."

"How?" he asked, too weak to form the rest of the question.

"There's a nurse. Someone I know from work. She owed me a favor. She helped me get a refill."

Terry raised an eyebrow, sensing there was more to the story. Alice opened the bottle and shook a pill out. She reached for a cup of water she'd set on the nightstand.

"Go ahead and take one right now," she said. "The sooner we get this in your system, the sooner you'll start feeling better."

Terry struggled to sit up in the bed. He couldn't do it. After watching him for a moment, Alice set the water and medication down to help him.

"I'm sorry," he said, embarrassed that he'd been unable to do it on his own.

Alice sat back down beside him, handing him the pill. He swallowed it, then she gave him the cup of water. He settled back, continuing to sip on the water.

"I thought about killing myself," he said. "In this condition, I'm just a burden on everyone. I felt guilty about leaving Charlie with nobody but your mother. If something happened to her, he'd have no one."

Alice shook her head. "You don't have to worry about that now. Once we get this medication back to a therapeutic level you'll start feeling better."

Terry took a sip of water and looked at Alice. He shook his head despondently. "For how long? Until the meds run out and then we're doing this all over again?"

"We deal with the problems one at a time," Alice said, her voice firm.

"I'm not sure I want to live like this," Terry said. "With you back, Charlie would be in good hands if I died. I could die in peace, on my own terms."

"You're not going to die." It was not meant to be reassuring. It sounded more like an order.

"Yeah, I probably am," he said. "I just want to have control over when and where."

"What are you saying?" Alice asked.

"I think I want to end it," Terry said. "I want to kill myself." He looked her in the eye, defeated. He had given up.

Alice's hand lashed out and struck Terry across the face. The glass in his hand flew against the wall and shattered. Terry was frozen in shock. Never in all the years they'd been married had he seen anything like this from her. They didn't disagree often. In fact, they barely ever raised their voices at each other.

"You don't know what I went through," she spat, her finger hovering in front of Terry's face. "I don't know if I'll ever be able to talk about it, but I didn't go through it to come home to shit like this. I expect you to be a fucking man. I expect you to fight with everything you have. That's what I had to do."

Alice rose from the bed and strode toward the bedroom door. When she reached it, she spun toward her stunned husband. "I better never hear you say anything like that again."

She did not wait for a reaction. She left the room and shut the door behind her. When she turned, she found her mother standing at the top of the stairs.

"Is everything okay?" Pat asked.

Alice considered her answer. "Terry dropped a glass."

"Dropped?" Pat asked.

Alice brushed by her mother, stroking her arm lightly as she passed. "I need some fresh air."

CHAPTER ELEVEN

The Valley

"You sure it's safe to abandon my post?" Pete asked.

He was standing with his dad in front of Outpost Pete, his brow furrowed with uncertainty. It was the concealed observation post that Pete had constructed in the early days of the collapse, allowing him to keep an eye on his family home until his dad could reach them. It also allowed him to continue playing a role in the safety of the community even after his dad made it back. He wasn't so sure about giving it up.

"We are decommissioning your base," Jim said.

Pete looked glum.

"It's not a bad thing," Jim said. "With the road blown at each end of the valley, I'm not as concerned about just guarding our house. We need to look at the bigger picture now."

"I hate to give it up," Pete said. "This was my job."

"You'll still have a job," Jim said. "I'm putting you on the list to rotate in and out of the guard posts at each end of the valley with the other men. It's a big responsibility. You'll still be guarding the folks of the valley."

"Really?"

"Really," Jim said. "You'll learn a lot working with the other men."

"Is it dangerous?" Pete asked.

His voice didn't convey fear, but instead a note of excitement that worried Jim a little. He was a boy, though, and boys always wanted adventure. Jim hoped there wouldn't be any, other than the normal daily adventure of trying to stay alive and stay fed.

"We're only hauling out the things you may need in other places," Jim said. "We're not tearing down Outpost Pete. It's always possible we'll need it again. I won't undo all the hard work you put in up here."

Pete seemed satisfied with that, then got a serious look on his face. "If we blew up the road, why are we still having to keep watch on it?"

"People could just walk in cross-country from any side," Jim said. "People are pretty lazy, and the road is the easiest walking for a man or a horse. Those guard posts won't be the only line of defense. We're going to make a run to Pop's house and get his diesel utility vehicle. We're going to use it to patrol the perimeter of the valley."

"Can I go on those patrols?"

"We can put you in the rotation, just like everyone else," Jim said. "Now get in there and start sliding stuff out to me, anything you think we can use at the guard posts."

The entry into the outpost was like an obstacle course but Pete maneuvered through it with an ease that Jim envied. In a moment, Pete crawled back with a milk crate jammed with gear.

"Do you think they'll come back?" Pete asked as he got to his feet.

"The people who left the food and fuel?"

Pete nodded.

"I don't know," Jim said. "Depends on how desperately they need it. Seeing that we killed the men they left here, they may be scared to come back."

"Or they may be mad that we killed their friends and they're busy getting reinforcements."

"The thought crossed my mind," Jim said. "Still, we can't obsess over all the bad possibilities. There are too many of them. You'll go nuts if you dwell on it all the time. You still have to take time to enjoy life, to go fishing, and to be as happy as the current state of the world will let you be. You remember that, okay?"

"I will," Pete said.

Jim took the crate and they walked back toward the house.

"Who's going with you to Pop's house?" Pete asked.

"Me, Pops, and Buddy."

"You take Buddy everywhere you go," Pete said. "Is he your best friend?"

Jim laughed. "No, I think Lloyd is probably my best friend because I've known him so long. I like Buddy because he reminds me of my grandfather."

"How?"

"It's complicated," Jim said. "I'm not sure I could put it in words. It's something about the way he sees the world."

Pete considered this for a moment. "Can I go with you all?"

"Sure," Jim said. "With the road gone, we have to drive out on farm roads and then ford the creek when we get closer to town."

"How are we getting the UTV back?" Pete asked.

"We're driving it."

"Through town?"

Jim nodded. "Yep."

"Cool," Pete said, a smile spreading on his face. "Can I ride with Pops?"

"Sure."

CHAPTER TWELVE

Randi

"I knew you were sweet on me," Lloyd said. "I knew it all the time. You were afraid of losing me, weren't you?"

Randi was examining the cauterized stumps of Lloyd's missing fingers. He'd lost them to the psychopath Valentine who'd been trying to extract information from Lloyd about the residents of the valley. Randi had gone looking for Lloyd and, just as Randi had predicted, he couldn't let it go.

"Don't let it go to your head. I went looking for you because I knew you couldn't take care of yourself," Randi said. "Sure enough you were bumbling through the woods like Winnie the Pooh and nearly got yourself killed."

"I had things under control. I was just getting ready to open a can of whoop ass."

Randi frowned at him. "I think you've spent a lot more time opening jars of moonshine than you have cans of whoop ass."

"He only got the jump on me because I was distracted thinking about you," Lloyd said, winking at her. "If I hadn't been fixating on your beauty and charm he'd have never got the chance."

"You're fixing to lose another finger," Randi warned, taking an intact finger in her hand and pinching it with imaginary clippers.

In truth, she did appear to be softening some. Her daughters encouraged Lloyd, but everyone suspected that they only did so because it kept Lloyd in the crosshairs of Randi's sarcasm and earned them some peace. Randi did visit him daily, stopping by Buddy's house to check his healing wounds.

"I reckon I can spare another finger if that's what it takes. As long as I can still bang out a tune on the banjo I'll be fine," he said.

"It does kind of sound like banging when *you* play it," Randi said.

"I can hold a tune."

"Not as well as you hold a mason jar."

"The two go hand-in-hand. Picking the banjo and holding a jar of liquor are both tools of the musician's trade."

Randi looked at him sideways then went back to focusing on his fingers. "They're healing nicely but they'll be tender for a while. There's no indication of any infection. I'd keep them bandaged to protect them for a while."

Lloyd stared at his damaged hand, then looked seriously at Randi. "How are you doing?" he asked.

She looked at him like he'd just fallen out of the sky. "What do you mean by that? I'm fine. I didn't lose any fingers." She held them and waved them around as proof.

"You know what I mean. You lost more," he said. "You lost your parents and your brothers. I just wondered if you were doing okay."

Although her reflex was to aim her radioactive sarcasm in his direction and watch him curl up like an ant under a magnifying glass on a sunny day, she held back. When she realized she wasn't breathing, she forced herself to blow her air out slowly, then took several more breaths.

"I'm fine," she said.

"You don't look it," he said. "You're wound tighter than a two dollar watch. Looks like you're about to blow your cork."

Randi continued to show restraint, to breathe deeply. She looked toward the road, not meeting his eye. "Look, I appreciate what you're trying to do but I'm not all about sharing feelings and singing campfire songs."

"Good damn thing. Your voice seems a mite gravelly for singing," Lloyd said. "Must be all those cigarettes."

"Asshole."

Lloyd smiled. "All I'm saying is that if you need to talk, I'm here."

She breathed, nodded, and sighed. "Understood. Now let's change the subject."

She hoped he was done trying to be nice. All that talk of feelings made her uncomfortable. She dug in her pocket for a smoke. She'd given them up, then restarted knowing that she'd be forced to quit eventually when the supply dried up. For better or worse, dozens of cartons had turned up in the gear left behind by Valentine's men and now she was a smoker again. She lit up and leaned back against a porch post, her arms crossed in front of her and resting on her raised knees.

She stared at the crumpled mountains. It was late summer closing in on fall. The warm air was thick with haze. There was no breeze and not a single sound to be heard anywhere.

"Got one of those jars handy?" Randi asked.

Lloyd grinned. "Is a frog's ass watertight?"

"Got more of that blackberry?"

Lloyd got up and went into the house, the screen door clacking shut behind him. She heard singing, the clinking of glass, and Lloyd's heavy steps on the hardwood floors. When he returned, he placed two jars and two clear glasses on the porch.

"We ain't drinking out of the jars?" Randi asked. "You think this is a date or something?"

"Nah, honey, I know it ain't a date. If it was a date I'd have worn underwear."

"And I was just wondering why a prize like you hadn't been snatched right up."

Lloyd chuckled and poured Randi's glass half-full of the blackberry moonshine. He filled his own glass half-full of the clear stuff.

Randi took a sip of her drink and stared off. She could see now why Lloyd favored the stuff, though she knew the blackberry was not as strong as the clear. With the formal introduction between the liquor and her taste buds out of the way, Randi drained her glass. She licked her lips and placed the glass back on the porch, noticing that Lloyd was staring at her wide-eyed.

"What?"

"You just moved up a notch in my estimation."

She huffed. "Like I give a damn."

Lloyd sipped his drink while Randi took the liberty of refilling her own glass. The first glass worked its way through her body, soothing her nerves and hammering down the sharp edges. She enjoyed a more relaxed pace with the second, taking measured sips.

"Seeing the way you sucked down that shot of liquor makes me inclined to ask again if you're feeling okay but I've already asked once. If you want to talk, the ball's in your court."

She bit at her lip. "I can't let it go," she finally said, carefully annunciating each word.

Lloyd took a sip and smacked his lips as if the crude gesture so was the only way to explore the intricate bouquet of the homemade liquor. "Can't let *what* go?"

"That the bitch who killed my family is still walking around. She got away with it. I let her get away with it."

"Now wait a minute," Lloyd said, shaking his head as if trying to erase a bitter taste from his mouth. "I thought you chose not to pursue this matter right now. I remember you saying that somebody had to call an end to the war and it was going to be you. You said you needed time to mourn and to heal."

She took a sip of her drink and nodded in agreement. "I did. I said all those things. I meant them too. The person who said those things is the person that I *want* to be, not the person I *am*."

Lloyd nodded in understanding. "You tried to get above your raising."

Randi laughed. "I guess you could say that."

"I do understand. Just because a decision seems like the right thing to do doesn't mean you can live with it."

"That's where I'm at," she said, looking Lloyd in the eye. "I don't know where to go from here. My family needs me to be one thing. I need to be another. What should I do?"

Lloyd narrowed his eyes at her. "You're seriously asking *me*?"

She nodded.

"I say you have to do what gives you peace. What lets you sleep at night," he said.

"That means I have to go kill Lisa Cross."

"Then so be it," Lloyd said, raising his glass to her. "Here's to decisions made."

She raised her glass to him, feeling a burden lifted from her. She smiled to herself, finding surprise in the realization that the decision to kill someone could feel so right.

CHAPTER THIRTEEN

Pop's House

Just before they reached his parents' house, Jim pulled his truck onto the shoulder of the road.

"Why are you stopping?" Pete asked.

"I'm going ahead to make sure no one has moved in." Jim hopped out of the truck and slid an AR pistol from beneath the seat. He'd left his M-4 at home, opting for the smaller and more easily concealed weapon. Jim switched on the Vortex optic and raised the weapon to verify that the optic was functioning. He smacked the magazine to make sure it was seated and checked the chamber, seeing the glint of brass just where he wanted to see it.

"I don't think you'll find anyone up there," Pops said. "We're close to the state police substation and the 911 center. There are cops in and out of here all the time."

"There used to be," Jim said. "We don't know if they're still moving around here or not. We don't even know if they got desperate themselves and decided to take a look in your house since it was sitting empty."

Pops furrowed his brow at that, clearly not liking the thought.

"You want me to go with you?" Buddy asked from the back seat of the crew cab.

"No," Jim said. "When I'm sure it's clear, I'll wave you up. One of you just scoot over and drive the truck up."

Jim slipped on his plate carrier with its pouches of spare mags and trudged off up the hill toward the house. Halfway up the long drive, he slipped off into the weeds, disappearing quickly among the cedars and underbrush. There were trails in the woods around the house he'd used as a kid. Years later, Ariel and Pete used the same trails. They led to various spots along the property, including to the back of the house.

Pops watched Jim disappear onto the trail, his own mind having trouble processing everything. His old life in the home where he'd raised his son, and his new life living in his son's spare room, were clashing.

"I don't know if we'll ever get to live in this house again," Pops said out of the blue. It was spoken without bitterness but with resignation.

Buddy and Pete looked at him, unsure of how to respond.

"Nana and I are both getting older, and who knows how long it will be before this mess gets straightened out. It may not happen in my lifetime. I don't like the idea but I'm trying to be practical."

Buddy and Pete looked at each other, not exactly sure what to say. "I'm sure that's difficult. Is there something we can do?" Buddy asked.

"I'd like to take as much back with us as we can," Pops said. "I'd like Nana to have as many of her things as we can fit in the vehicle. I might make it back here again but I want to pack like this is the last time."

"We can do that," Buddy said. "Right, Pete?"

Pete nodded. "I bet Nana would like some of the stuff out of her flower garden. If we have time, I could even pull up some of her bulbs and take them back."

"I think she'd like that," Pops said.

"You just tell us what to do," Buddy said. "We'll do it."

"I've got an open utility trailer here at the house," Pops said. "We can hook it to this truck. I've also got a smaller trailer that hooks to the UTV."

"He's back!" Pete said, pointing. "There's Dad."

At the bend in the driveway, Jim was visible, his gun lowered. He was waving them up.

"Pete, can you drive us in?" Buddy asked.

Pete had been driving a lot around the farm and was pretty good at it. He climbed eagerly into the driver's seat and started the truck. They eased up the hill. Jim walked ahead of them.

"Good job, Pete," Jim said when he parked.

Pete smiled. "Can I drive back?"

"We'll talk about it," Jim said.

"Does that mean no?" Pete asked.

"Probably," Jim said.

"You can drive the UTV," Pops said. "You've been driving it since you could reach the pedals."

Jim looked at Pops questioningly but Pops shrugged. "I'm going to be riding shotgun," Pops said. "I'll be keeping an eye out for trouble."

Jim nodded, but without conviction. Pops was not always aware of the places danger lurked in the current state of the world but he wasn't going to argue with him. Jim would just have to watch his own back as well as theirs.

"Any signs of damage?" Pops asked. "Has anyone broke in?"

Jim shook his head. "Looks like you were right. The yard needs mowing, the flowers need weeding, but otherwise everything looks fine."

"Pete, how about you and Pops go hook that trailer up to Jim's truck," Buddy suggested.

"What trailer?" Jim asked.

Buddy gave Jim a look and a gesture that told him to hold any questions until the other two were gone. Pops slid into the driver's seat and started off around the house, Pete walking behind him to help guide him as he backed up to the trailer.

"What's up?" Jim asked.

"Coming back here seems to have shaken your dad up a little," Buddy said. "He says he's not sure he'll ever be able to live here again. He wants to hook trailers up to both vehicles and haul some more stuff back. He wants to take things that are important to your mother so she'll be more comfortable there."

Jim nodded as this sank in. "That would be hard. In his shoes, I'd be feeling the same way."

"Glad to hear you're okay with taking the extra time," Buddy said. "I know you're not always real patient about these things."

"I'm working on it," Jim said with a smile. "This will be my act of patience for the day, then it's back to being an asshole."

Buddy laughed.

They heard the roar of the diesel engine and Jim's truck came around the house, the empty trailer bouncing and clanking loudly. Pops parked it in the yard, close to the front door. He got out and looked at Jim. Pops assumed that Buddy had told Jim that he wanted to take things back. He wasn't sure how Jim would react and he tried to read his son.

"Do you have a plan?" Jim asked.

"I'm going to fuel up the UTV with the diesel you brought. I've got a trailer to hook up to it. I'll take care of that. I want you to take this trailer to the outbuildings and look for any tools or building materials that may be of use. Put them in the trailer. I want to save the back of the truck for the things I'm bringing out of the house. Buddy will help me in there. Pete is going to work on getting a few things out of the flower gardens."

"That your idea, Pete?" Jim asked.

Pete nodded proudly.

"That was a good idea," Jim said. "Let's get started then."

CHAPTER FOURTEEN

Pop's House

They worked for about three hours, which was nearly three hours longer than Jim had planned on being there. He found patience, though. For whatever reason, the thought was in his dad's head that this could be his last trip to the home that he'd built to raise his family in. Jim could relate to that and wanted to help his dad do what he needed to get done there. They worked fast and efficiently.

Pops had been in a rush when he left his home the first time and his subsequent visits home had just been to check on the place or pick up a few odd items that he needed. He had always assumed he'd be returning home eventually and for whatever reason he wasn't feeling that now. If the first time had been a bug out, this was more like a move out.

Jim looked through the outbuildings trying to find things that the group might have a need for. He took all the fasteners— nails, screws, and bolts. He grabbed wire, electrical fittings, odd lengths of rope, and all of the plumbing supplies he could find. He looked for hand-powered tools that would have been stored here because they'd been replaced with more efficient gas or electric versions. He found several axes and splitting mauls, even taking the ones with broken handles, knowing they could be fixed. There was a coffee can of hammer heads, placed there after their handles broke. They went in the trailer also.

He pitched in old lengths of water hose, every bucket he could find, and a spare set of posthole diggers. He stacked in every board and sizeable scrap of plywood he saw. He packed everything as neatly as he could, wanting to maximize what could be fit into the trailer. In the weeds around the outbuilding he found partial rolls of various types of fencing, a small pile of metal fence posts, and a complete roll of barbed wire.

At a different outbuilding that was used more for storage than a workshop he found some metal folding chairs, folding plastic tables, and two storage totes of old bedding. He took all of it. There was also an older mattress that he tied onto the roof of his truck. With the camper shell on the back, there was plenty of room up there for hauling gear. Gary and his family were still pretty crowded in their house and an extra mattress might help a little. In the same outbuilding, he found several bicycles that had belonged to different members of the family. He threw those on top of the mattress and tied them down. As much as he enjoyed bikes, he didn't relish a day where they might be the primary transportation. Still, he wanted to have as many as possible and a supply of spare parts if that day came.

When he'd found all he felt he needed for this trip, Jim drove the truck around to the front yard. Plastic totes, boxes, and garbage bags were lined up on the sidewalk. He stopped the truck beside the stacks and started packing things tightly into the covered bed of his truck. Pete came along in a moment, soaked in sweat. He was carrying two buckets of flower bulbs, any remaining stalks snipped off and discarded.

"Go ahead and put those in the trailer," Jim instructed. "You have anything else that needs to go?"

"I thought about taking some of the knick-knacks Nana put in the flower garden," Pete said. "Some of the decorations that Ariel and I made. I'd like to take the garden bench if there's room."

Jim had made the bench himself as a gift. It was probably twenty years old and he was pleased that it was still around. "We'll find room." While Pete and Jim were tilting the white garden bench into the trailer, Pops and Buddy came out, each carrying a garbage bag. Pops paused when he noticed the garden bench being loaded.

"Your mother will like that," he said.

"You guys putting a dent in it?" Jim asked.

"A few more loads," Pops said. "It's mostly sentimental stuff but I think it will mean a lot to her to have it. She needs things of her own around her."

"I understand," Jim said.

Soon both trailers, Jim's truck, and the UTV were full. The men sat on the porch and drank spring water they'd bottled at Jim's farm. When they were ready, Pops went inside and checked all the windows and doors to make sure they'd locked them. He went inside by himself and was gone a long time. Jim wondered if he was saying good-bye to the house or just trying to imprint it into his memory in case something happened.

When Pops came out, he locked the front door behind him, took up his shotgun, and tossed the UTV key to Pete. "You driving?" he asked.

"You bet!" Pete said, springing to his feet.

"You guys go in front," Jim said. "We'll follow. Pete, chamber a round in that handgun."

Pete did as he was told, slipping the weapon back in his holster.

"Let's roll," Jim said.

The house was on the fringe of an office park. His parents had been there long before the office park was built. Businesses came and went. Two of the empty buildings were purchased to house law enforcement agencies. One was a Virginia state police substation. The other became a 911 operations center and provided office space for both county and town law enforcement.

As they left, Jim didn't notice anyone at any of the offices. They noticed him though. Two cops within the operations center watched the heavily-laden vehicles heading out of the office park.

"Somebody has fuel."

Deputy Willard Ford was scrawny and balding, with a thick

mustache that attempted to make up for what wasn't growing on his head. He'd been with the sheriff's department for twelve years and people would describe him as loyal.

"Maybe we should let the sheriff know," said the other man, Bruce Deel, also a deputy, though he'd been with the sheriff's department less than a year. He was fresh out of the law enforcement academy and looked more like a high school student than a police officer.

Deputy Ford nodded.

Deputy Deel removed a radio from his belt and thumbed the transmit button. "Unit Sixty-two calling Unit One. Sixty-two calling Unit One."

Deel waited for a response. When nothing came, he transmitted again.

Still no response.

"Sixty-two, Sixty-two calling Unit One."

"*Unit One,*" the sheriff replied, irritation clear in his voice.

"Sorry to bother you, Sheriff," Deel said.

"*It's okay, Deputy. I was just feeding the stock. Damn goat snatched my radio right off my belt and took off with it.*"

"Sorry about that," Deputy Deel said. "Just wanted to let you know that we had a couple of civilian vehicles moving around out here by the 911 center. They seem to be moving stuff out of one of the houses. Whatever they're doing, they have fuel and I haven't seen any civilians with fuel in about a week now."

"*We're about out too.*"

"That's what I was thinking," the deputy said. "Should we follow them? Maybe they have access to resources that we could use?"

"*Just pull them over and make sure they're not stealing that stuff. That's Mr. Powell's house up there by the office. That's all the excuse you need. Pull them over and make sure they're not stealing stuff.*"

"Roger that, Sixty-two out," Deputy Deel said. He looked at Deputy Ford. "Let's roll."

CHAPTER FIFTEEN

Town

The diesel utility vehicle that Pete was driving could barely manage fifteen miles per hour so they'd only gone two miles when the sheriff's department cruiser fell in behind Jim's truck. Jim couldn't see out the back of the truck with it so full but it was part of his paranoid nature to continually monitor the side mirrors for any approaching concerns. It seemed ridiculous with no other cars on the road but it was a habit ingrained from years of interstate driving. As soon as he saw the cruiser, the hair on the back of his neck went up. Then the flashing lights came on.

"Shit," Jim mumbled, checking his mirror.

"What is it?" Buddy asked, craning his neck to catch a glimpse in his own side mirror.

"Cops."

"You're shitting me."

"I shit you not."

Spotting the approaching vehicle, Buddy shook his head. "I found it a lot easier to respect them when they were driving Plymouth

Furies," he said. "Man in a Ford Escape doesn't have nearly so commanding a presence, regardless of what's painted on the outside."

Jim laughed. "No kidding."

"Of the multitude of laws we're violating, any guess as to which one they're pulling us over for?" Buddy asked. "Maybe they noticed someone cut the *Do Not Remove* tag off the mattress on the roof?"

"No idea, but you know it can't be good. I'm expecting it to be a shakedown of some sort."

At first Jim looked for a wide spot where it would be safe to pull over. Then he realized that was a pointless consideration. There was no other traffic. He slowed and stopped in the middle of the road, honking the horn at Pops and Pete. When they saw what was going on, they stopped too.

Jim rolled down the power window and put both hands on the wheel. In his mirror, he could see one deputy get out and walk toward his window. In the other mirror, he could see a second deputy coming alongside Buddy.

"Keep your hands in sight," Jim said. "Don't give them any reason to get squirrelly."

When the deputy reached his window, Jim looked down to see that the man's hand was resting on his gun but it wasn't drawn. His name badge said Ford. Jim had seen the man but didn't know him. It was a small town; eventually you would lay eyes on everyone. There were only so many grocery stores, gas stations, and places to eat.

"Can I help you, Deputy?" Jim asked.

The deputy was wearing sunglasses that prevented Jim from seeing where he was looking. He didn't answer at first. Jim sensed the man was attempting to intimidate him like he might a young punk pulled over speeding but Jim didn't intimidate easily. He'd been through too much. Jim suspected this man had never even drawn his gun on the job. At this point, Jim had quit counting the men he'd had to kill. There were better things to keep track of and he didn't think he was done killing.

Still, this didn't need to go south. Jim had his son and his dad to be concerned about. There were too many nervous men and nervous guns. Jim forced himself to take a deep breath, to try and push the adrenaline back to where it came from.

The deputy cleared his throat. "I couldn't help but notice the load you were hauling down the road. I'm assuming you have a legal right to all this stuff?"

"It's not stolen if that's what you're asking," Jim replied. "It's my dad's stuff. He's in that UTV so you can ask him yourself if you want. I'm moving him and my mom out to my house so I can keep a better eye on them. They don't get around like they used to."

The deputy nodded. "Where do you live?"

Jim hesitated. "I'm not sure that's completely relevant."

The deputy scratched his chin. "Then I'll need to see your license and registration."

Jim sighed. "Look, I don't have them with me. You can run my tags and see that the truck is legal, and that my license is in order."

"The network is down. I can't look anything up," the deputy replied.

Jim had assumed that. "Then why would you need to see my license? There some reason you need to know where I live?"

The other deputy was losing patience and slammed his palm against the passenger door, startling everyone. "He needs to know where you live because *he fucking asked!*" Deputy Deel shouted. Jim turned to see the man red-faced and glaring at him.

"Relax, Deputy," Buddy said. "No need for everyone to get on edge. It's clear that no one trusts anyone anymore. We respect the law. We're just a little nervous about sharing information. Surely you can understand that. You just tell us what your concerns are and we'll see if we can put them to rest."

Deputy Deel was still red. His mouth was screwed tight, like he was ready to pull the men out and rough them up. Buddy was unperturbed. He'd lost everything in the world. He'd killed men and burned another to death. What could these men do to him that the world had not put him through already? It made no difference to him if he died today, tomorrow, or next year.

"We just want to make sure that this stuff isn't stolen," Deputy Ford said.

Everyone present knew that was not the entire truth. Ford had obviously decided to soften his approach a little. Maybe he didn't want things to get out of hand either.

"Then talk to my dad," Jim said, gesturing at the UTV. "He'll tell you this is his stuff. Then we can be on our way."

Deputy Ford looked at Jim as if to tell him that the decision as to whether that would resolve matters was not Jim's to make, but he didn't voice it. Instead the deputy strolled forward to the UTV and addressed Pops.

Jim could not hear what they were saying but watched intently. There was a lot that could go wrong. They were driving an off-road vehicle on the public roadway while openly carrying guns. Jim was trying to work out in his head if he could shoot Deputy Deel and then manage to get an angle on Deputy Ford beside the UTV if he had to. It would not be easy and he was not comfortable with part of his family caught in the crossfire.

Sensing the growing tension and perhaps even Jim's violent plans, Buddy sought to deescalate things. If nothing else, maybe talking to the deputy would distract him enough to give them an advantage is shooting did break out. "How are your families holding up at the superstore, Deputy...Deel?"

Deputy Deel was moving his eyes back and forth between the cab of the truck and the UTV. He seemed to expect that the inevitable result of all this tension would a boiling over into violence. He had his hand on his weapon and nervousness poured off him like the reek of cheap aftershave. In truth, Deputy Deel probably wasn't cut out for this. Jim sensed he might have realized that eventually had things not collapsed and left him stuck as a cop for the duration of it. Perhaps he would have sold insurance or installed satellite dishes.

"I'm not one of *them*," Deputy Deel said with contempt.

Buddy turned slightly, a question in the quick glance he shot at Jim. He turned back to the Deputy. "What do you mean?"

"We're not all at the superstore," the Deputy said. "Neither is Ford. Not everybody thought that was the right thing to do."

"What did the sheriff do?" Jim asked. "Is he with them at the superstore?"

"Nah," the deputy responded. "We all probably would have gone if it hadn't have been for the sheriff. He didn't think it was right to take over a resource like that and not share the supplies. We all had to make the decision whether we were going to side with him or go with the other guys that took over the store."

"What was the ratio?" Jim asked.

"The what?" the deputy asked.

"How many went, how many stayed?"

"Oh, more went," Deputy Deel replied. "There's probably a dozen cops at the superstore right now. Deputies, town cops, even a few staties. There's just a couple of us left that didn't go."

"Those guys at the superstore still helping out?" Buddy asked. "They still answer calls?"

Deputy Deel looked at Buddy like he was an idiot. "There ain't no more calls. We just try to patrol and see what help we can offer folks, which ain't much. And no, those guys ain't helping at all. I don't know what they're doing anymore. I'm not sure I want to know either."

Jim nodded at that. He didn't know what to think. It was good to know that there were cops who weren't part of that group at the superstore. At the same time, it was disturbing to know that the group at the superstore had given up acting in any official capacity. They were nothing more than another force. They were armed and trained men. If for any reason he had to fight those men, he would probably lose.

Ahead, he saw Deputy Ford smiling and extending a hand to Pops. They shook and Pops patted the man on the back. Jim was sure that Pops knew the man in some capacity, but certainly they'd passed on the road a lot with the man's office being close to their house. When Deputy Ford started back, Pops folded himself into the UTV again and Pete started it up.

"We done here?" Jim asked when the deputy reached his window.

Ford smiled at him. Jim was surprised at the change in demeanor.

"Yeah, you can go," Deputy Ford said, stopping at the window. "Glad to hear that things are going well in the valley."

Jim couldn't hide his shock and that clearly amused Deputy Ford. The deputy tipped his hat at Jim. "You have a good day now." He walked off, having clearly enjoyed the moment.

"My dad told him," Jim said after they were gone.

"Your dad doesn't think like you do," Buddy said. "I'm sure he didn't realize there was an ulterior motive to their questions."

"I'm sure he didn't either," Jim said. "I think we probably don't need to bring him out into town anymore. He's too social. He doesn't keep secrets well."

"Too late to worry about it now," Buddy said, propping his arm up in the window.

Ahead of them, Pops leaned out of the cab of the UTV and gave them a thumbs up to see if they were ready to leave. Jim waved back at him, a bitter smile on his face.

CHAPTER SIXTEEN

Town

Back in their cruiser, Deputy Ford picked up the car radio's microphone and hit the transmit button. "Unit Sixty-One to One."

The reply was almost immediate. *"One here,"* the sheriff said. *"I was waiting on you guys. Had a bad feeling about this one."*

Before the sheriff could say anything else, Ford began spilling the details. "The son wouldn't tell me anything but the old guy spilled it," Ford said. "Those guys came up with a tanker of diesel somehow. He said it's still nearly full."

"Do not say another word," the sheriff said.

"You *know* we're about out of diesel," Ford said. "If we run out we lose power, communications, everything."

"You're on an open channel, you idiot," the sheriff spat. *"You come directly to my house now and do not use your radio again until you've talked to me. Unit One out."*

Deputy Ford looked sheepishly over at Deel. "Hell, I was just excited. You think he would be too. A tank of diesel could hold us for a while. We could start driving that MRAP around again."

"The others, at the superstore could be thinking the same thing," Deel said.

Only then did Ford's mistake hit him. He'd essentially done the same thing the old man in the UTV did. In his excitement, he'd inadvertently shared vital information with people competing for resources. His mind raced. The other group would no doubt be interested if they'd intercepted the transmission.

"Let's get to the sheriff's house," Ford said.

As Ford started the vehicle and accelerated toward town, that very group of officers they'd been concerned about was scrambling just as fast. Like many communities, Russell County gave money to support a local amateur radio club. This funding helped assure that there would be people capable of building and supporting a communication network in a disaster. The group of former law enforcement officers holed up at the superstore in town had understood the critical nature of communication networks early on.

For that reason, they reached out to one of the members of the local amateur radio club soon after moving into the superstore. His name was Hugh and he was a wizard when it came to radios. The cops residing at the store helped him seize the club's equipment and move it into their compound. They erected a series of antennas on the roof of the building and ran the wiring down through a roof hatch. In exchange for regular meals and a roof over his head, Hugh moved in with them at the store and worked the radios all day long and through much of the night. He seemed to derive an energy from the work that left him requiring little sleep.

Hugh set up a pop-up awning in the middle of the store. Beneath it he established a semi-circle of plastic folding tables and covered them with an impressive looking array of radio gear. He sat on a rolling office chair in the middle of it, shuttling from table to table when something caught his attention. He worked with the intensity of a man single-handedly running a spaceship.

The radio operator was a person that at first glance no one would suspect of being capable of the operation of complex electronics. He had a scraggly beard that hung to his belly and matted black hair that hung just as far down his back. His blue eyes appeared to be too large and made him look a little crazy. He was tall and thin, with lanky limbs, and an intense, unblinking gaze that further contributed to the idea he may be a little off center. He wore a Vietnam-era boonie hat and a camouflage jacket that made people wonder if he'd served in the military but no one could ever get a straight answer out of him as to whether that had been the case or not. Despite appearances, he was a hell of a radio operator.

He seemed to effortlessly understand the obscure and mystical formulas behind antenna design and placement. He required no manuals or references, spouting computations and data off the top of his head. He could play knobs, dials, and buttons like a piano to pull in distant signals and clear garbled transmissions. He operated with a headset on most of the time, which made faint signals easier to hear. Even though people couldn't hear what he was listening to, there was usually an audience watching him, drawn irresistibly by the intensity of Hugh's focus. He sat there all day most days, picking up snippets of information about the world at large and the situation locally. Unfortunately for them, most of the information was useless.

When Hugh picked up Deputy Ford's transmission to the sheriff, he knew he had something. His audience knew he had something too, seeing the already large eyes swell to even larger proportion. Hugh's eyes began racing frantically within their sockets, processing the information he was hearing. Some of his audience rose to their feet, sharing in the frenetic energy of his excitement while still having no idea from where it was borne.

At the end of the transmission, Hugh slid his headphones down until they hung around his neck. He turned to a young boy of around ten who was standing nearby, anxious to hear what had taken place within the confines of the headset.

"Get your dad," Hugh said. The words came out slowly and with tremendous gravity.

The boy raced off, arms pumping, feet kicking, as if lives hung in the balance. Shortly, he returned with his dad, a deputy named Barnes. Early in the disaster, Barnes had been assigned to guard a large gas station in a remote section of the county. Aware there weren't many witnesses around to what took place there, Barnes began his own black market, trading fuel for food, weapons, and any other goods he thought he could use.

There were two of them guarding the station in shifts and Barnes soon got the other deputy in on it. Eventually word leaked out about the sweet deal Barnes had going. The sheriff pulled him out of the station, threatened his job, and gave the duty to another officer. Barnes was fine with it. He'd nearly exhausted the station's fuel supply anyway. He was already looking for a new angle to take advantage of. As far as losing his job went, Barnes thought the sheriff must have been the only one that hadn't noticed that trying to maintain law and order was a lost cause now. They couldn't keep people safe with ten times the force they had.

The sheriff ended up stationing at Barnes at the superstore after his failure to secure the gas station. The sheriff hoped that he had enough men working at the location that they'd exert a little pressure on Barnes to operate in an honest, above-board fashion. The super-store was still trying to conduct business but maintaining order required a tremendous effort on the part of the four officers stationed there.

Without power, the loss detection equipment didn't work. People were carrying goods out every door, right under the noses of the cops. They couldn't cover every exit all the time. When their frustration boiled over at being powerless to stop the stealing, Barnes put forth the idea that maybe they should just take the store for themselves. After all, they couldn't provide any security for the town if they didn't have food and gear. They couldn't concentrate on keeping the peace if they were worried about their families' safety. The only reasonable avenue left to them was to take over the store and the remaining supplies, move their families in, and establish a secured compound where they could weather the storm.

"What is it?" Barnes asked when he reached the crowd assembled around the radio operator. He was anxious to hear what the man had found. While the radio operator had shared bits of information with them he'd gleaned from the airwaves, he'd never demanded their immediate attention for an item of news.

Hugh brushed his beard thoughtfully, staring Barnes in the eye. "I picked up a transmission from one of the other cops. They just had a contact with someone who they suspect had a tanker of fuel."

"Who?" Barnes barked.

"No idea," Hugh said, shaking his head. "There were no names used and the sheriff made them shut down the transmission before they said anything else."

"Was it someone they'd pulled over?"

Hugh shrugged. "Not enough information, but it did sound something like that."

Barnes turned away and scanned the crowd, looking for someone in particular. "Sword!"

"Right here," replied a man in camo hunting overalls, throwing a hand up.

"Get that drone up over the center of town," Barnes said. "I need to see if anything is moving out there. If they pulled over someone with access to a tanker of fuel, I want to know who it is."

"You got it," Sword said, jogging away.

"Stay on that radio, Hugh," Barnes ordered. "If you hear anything else, you let me know immediately."

Hugh gave a casual salute, slid the headphones back over his ears, and immersed himself again in his radios. Barnes strode through the building, lit only by the bright sun pouring through the skylights. At the front of the store, the automatic doors were jammed open and Barnes hit the parking lot about the same time Sword backed away from the suitcase-sized drone he'd placed on the asphalt, operating controls on the remote hanging around his neck. The drone began to whine with increasing intensity, then shot upward with surprising speed.

Barnes moved to the lowered tailgate of a sheriff's department pickup and joined a group of men watching a portable LCD monitor. The screen displayed images broadcast from the cameras on the drone. All eyes were on the screen as Sword put the drone high over the small town. He rotated it, catching scenes from the only two streets that ran the length of the town.

"There!" Barnes jabbed the screen with his finger.

"Where?" Sword asked, his eyes still on the drone.

"By the drug store."

Sword turned the drone in that direction.

"Angle down," Barnes ordered. "Can't see shit."

Sword slowed the drone and angled the camera.

"You got it," Barnes said. "Don't move."

"What is it?" asked one of the bystanders.

"Looks like a truck and side-by-side ATV," Barnes said. "Pull back, Sword. Don't spook them."

Sword did as he was told, pulling the drone back and taking it up. Barnes and the men beside him watched the screen in silence, tracking the movement of the two vehicles through town.

"I think they're coming this way," Barnes said. He lifted his radio to his mouth. "Rooftop, this is Barnes."

"Rooftop here," replied the sniper Barnes had stationed on top of the building. He rotated through several positions over the course of the day, monitoring the surrounding roads, fields, and parking lots through rifle scope.

"I've got a truck and a UTV that may be headed this way. They're travelling together. We've got the drone tracking them and I want you to keep an eye out. If they pass by, get tight on them and tell me what you see."

"Roger that," Rooftop replied.

"They're definitely coming this way," said another of the men. "They're going to pass right by the store."

A tone sounded from the radio, then a voice. It was Rooftop. *"I have visual."*

"You want me to keep on them?" Sword asked.

Barnes nodded. "Hang back a little but don't lose them."

"I have a Kawasaki Mule," Rooftop said. *"Two occupants. An older man and a teenager. Behind them I have a big Chevy diesel with two occupants. Both male. Both vehicles are hauling trailers packed full of crap. Looks like someone is moving."*

"Recognize anyone?" Barnes asked.

"That's a negative," Rooftop replied. *"I can get you a tag number on the truck."*

"Lot of fucking good that does," Barnes said. "You know the system is down."

"They're turning off the main road. I'm losing them. They're headed down the creek road."

"You hear that, Sword?" Barnes asked.

"I'm on them."

"Get in closer," Barnes ordered. "I don't want to lose them."

"I'm not going to lose them," Sword said. "Does it look like I'm losing them?"

"Shut your mouth and do your job," Barnes barked.

Barnes kept his eyes glued to the portable monitor, watching from above as the vehicles followed the winding road, moving in and out of shadow, getting lost beneath trees for fractions of a second.

"They must not live down that road," said another of the officers. "If they did, they'd know the road had been blown up."

Barnes shrugged, continuing to watch.

"They can't go much further," the other man said. "They're less than a quarter mile from where the road ends."

"They slowing down!" Barnes said.

The vehicles slowed, then turned left through an open gate. Both vehicles pulled through, then the passenger of the rear vehicle got out and closed the gate. The man walked briskly back to the truck and climbed in. The Kawasaki Mule proceeded on, fording the shallow river. The Chevy began to move too, then its brake lights flashed and it stopped.

Both doors on the truck flew open and the men sprang out.

Barnes looked confused. "What the hell?" Flashes indicated that rifles were being fired in the direction of the drone.

"Get that thing out of there!" Barnes yelled. "Pull back! Pull back!"

The microphone on the drone picked up the whizzing sound of bullets narrowly missing the drone. Sword worked the controls, managing to maneuver the drone out of danger before it was hit.

"We lost them," Sword said.

"That's okay," Barnes replied. "We know where they're going and how they got there. We'll wait for things to cool off and send the drone out exploring again later."

"I'll recharge it," Sword said.

"Rooftop?" Barnes said, speaking into his radio.

"Rooftop here."

"If you see any of those other cops heading toward the creek road, take them out," Barnes said.

"Cops?" Rooftop asked. *"You want me to take out cops?"*

"Yeah," Barnes replied. "That a problem?"

There was a hesitation before the response. *"No sir."*

"Let me remind you we're on an open channel," came a voice from the radio. It was a Hugh. *"You can be overheard by other local law enforcement monitoring this frequency."*

"I hope they did hear that," Barnes said. "Maybe it means they'll stay the hell away and we won't have to kill any of them. If there is a tanker, it's ours."

CHAPTER SEVENTEEN

The Valley

Buddy had gotten out of Jim's truck to shut the gate when he heard the high-pitched whine. For a moment he thought he'd stepped on an underground yellow jacket nest. Then the whine changed pitch and Buddy knew it was one of those drones. He didn't know much about them, but it was a noise you didn't forget, kind of like a flying weedeater. He tried not to react, continuing on to shut the gate just as he'd planned, but as soon as he got back in the truck he told Jim.

"We're being followed," he said. "There's a drone hovering behind us."

"Shit!" Jim said. "Grab your rifle. Let's see if we can shake them up a little."

The two men burst from the cab of the truck and raised their weapons. Jim had the little AR pistol but it had a thirty-round mag. He shouldered it, placed his red dot on the drone, and began dumping the mag as fast he could pull the trigger. Buddy was carrying his lever-action and sent several carefully aimed rounds at the drone but neither managed to hit it, although they did succeed in driving it away. Jim figured it might be hard to get replacement parts for the device. The owners wouldn't want to see it damaged.

"Who do you think sent that?" Buddy asked.

Jim shook his head. "I don't know. The regular cops, the bad cops, or some other group that we got no fucking clue about. Let's get the hell out of here."

They returned to the truck, secured their weapons, and climbed in. Jim put the truck in four wheel drive, going as fast as he could, which was not very fast at all. The farm road they were travelling was meant for tractors and ATVs. It was not meant for speed. Behind them, the trailer bounced and rattled.

In a few minutes, they reached the gate that took them to Jim's house. Pete had left the gate open and Jim drove through, shutting it behind them. Pete and Pops had stopped in front of the house and were waiting on Jim and Buddy.

"What were you shooting at, Dad?" Pete asked.

"A drone."

"Really?"

Jim nodded.

"What the heck is a drone?" Pops asked.

"It's like a toy helicopter," Pete said. "The good ones have cameras and can fly a long way."

"Why is the drone following us a big deal?" Pops asked.

"Someone might have heard that we have a tanker and is trying to find it."

Pops frowned. "I mentioned the tanker to that young man that pulled us over. You think he might have mentioned it to someone?"

Jim took a deep breath. He didn't want to get frustrated with his dad. He let the breath out. "That tanker is probably the most impor- tant secret in town right now. If word of it spreads, we'll be having company on a regular basis."

Pops looked concerned now. "I didn't think I was giving away anything important. I was just making small talk with the man."

"We have to be very careful what we say from now on," Jim said. "Even small talk can be dangerous if you say the wrong thing. People will kill us to take what we have."

"I'm sorry," Pops said.

"It's okay," Jim said. "We've all done things we shouldn't. This is new territory for all of us. Let's just make sure to maintain operational security in the future."

"What's that?" Pops asked.

"It means keep your big mouth shut," Pete said, grinning.

Pops reached over and clouted Pete playfully.

"How about we see if we can fit these trailers in the barn for now," Jim said. "It looks like it might rain and I'm not ready to unload all of this now."

"I miss those weather apps," Pops said wistfully.

"I miss video games," Pete said.

"I miss pizza," Jim added.

"I miss the Frostie Bossie," said Buddy.

Pops snorted. "They've been closed for thirty years."

"And I've missed them for all thirty of those years," Buddy said. "I can still taste their chocolate milkshakes."

"While you all reminisce, I'm going to back this trailer into the barn," Jim said. "Then I'm going to run to Gary's and get this mattress off the roof. While I'm gone, you all stick your trailer in the barn."

"You want us to unload the Mule while we're at it?" Pete asked.

"Go ahead and unload it in the house," Jim said.

"You need me to go with you, Jim?" Buddy asked.

"Nah, I'm just going to unhook and run. I don't want this mattress to get wet if it starts raining."

CHAPTER EIGHTEEN

The Valley

After helping Pops and Pete unload, Buddy returned to his house to find a half-drunk Randi and a half-drunk Lloyd sitting on the front porch. Two empty mason jars sitting on the porch told the whole sordid tale. Randi worked a rocking chair, her eyes half-closed, the creaking chair having lulled her into a stupor. Lloyd was creaking in another chair, plucking at the banjo with his remaining fingers, easing out some tune in an odd key that Buddy didn't recall ever hearing before.

He'd barely beat the rain. In fact, he could see it pursuing him across the fields of tall brown grass. It moved as a sheet, sweeping toward him as he hurried up his driveway. He reached the shelter of his porch as the first large drops fell on his warm shoulders. It felt good but the deluge appeared substantial enough that it would turn him into a drowned rat in short order if he didn't get out of it.

He scrambled up the steps and the train-like roar of the rain grew. There was no wind so it came straight down, pounding the metal roof of the little house.

Randi nodded at him. "Afternoon."

Buddy smiled. "I might start to think less of you if you don't improve the quality of the company you keep."

Lloyd played on, oblivious to the world around him. His eyes were closed. Wherever the tune had originated, elsewhere in time and place, Lloyd was there.

"I've been here a while but I didn't want to leave until I had a chance to talk with you," Randi said.

Buddy held up his hands. "If you want to file a complaint about Lloyd, there ain't nothing I can do. I tried to raise the boy right and it just didn't take. You know how it goes. They pick up the banjo, make a deal with the devil, and it's downhill from there."

Randi continued to smile. It was the calmest, the most at peace, that Buddy had ever seen her. Or maybe she was just drunk.

"Well, if it isn't Lloyd you want to talk about, what can I do for you?"

Randi looked him in the eyes. "I need your help."

Buddy took a seat on the edge of the porch, leaning back against a support post at the foot of Randi's rocking chair. "At your service. What can I do for you?"

Randi sighed as if resurrecting the story would take some effort. "I tried to make what I thought was the best decision for my family. I decided to let Lisa Cross go and put that feud behind me. I didn't want to get killed and leave my family with no one. They've already lost too much."

"But you can't do it, can you?"

Randi paused, searched for words she couldn't find, then just nodded at him.

"I understand," Buddy said. "No explanation needed."

"I thought you might."

"Did Lloyd tell you what I did?"

Randi shook her head. "He said you had some experience in the vengeance department, but that was it."

Buddy's face sagged, as if the recollection drained him. "There was a man I felt was responsible for my daughter's death. From the moment she died until the moment he died, it was like I didn't have control of my body. I was being driven by outside forces and I couldn't stop them. I knew the only thing that would make the world right again was to kill that man."

"Did you?" Randi asked. "Did you kill him?"

"I did. And I made him suffer. I made him wait for his death. As I walked away from the smoke of his burning house, it was like the fog around me was clearing for the first time since Rachel's death. I came back to my senses and barely knew where I was or how I got there. The Lord shaped me into an instrument of his wrath. Until the full stroke of his fiery sword was complete, I had no control of my body or mind."

"I know completely what you mean," Randi said. "I feel like I'm moving contrary to the forces of the world. Like I'm holding back the rain when all a thirsty world wants is a cool drink of water from the sky."

"How can I help you?" he asked. "You just needed to get that off your chest or you need something more practical?"

She looked at him again. "I've killed people, Buddy. I'm not at peace with it, but I know that I did what had to be done. I've never stalked a human being. I need to know how to get close to this woman and kill her."

Buddy thought this over. "Safest way is for you to shoot her with a scoped rifle. Less of a chance of you getting hurt. She'll die just the same."

"I thought about that," Randi said. "I'm not sure it would ease the burning inside me. I need to look in her eyes when I do it. I need her to see who killed her. Does that make me a shitty person?"

Buddy laughed. "I ain't one to pass judgment and throw stones. That's how I did it too. I talked to him about it. I explained to him who I was and why I was killing him. I listened to his screams as he died and it almost shames me to say it, but I found great satisfaction in those screams."

"That's what I want."

"It leaves a mark," Buddy said. "You kill someone up close and personal, it burns an image into your brain that ain't so easy to erase. You'll have to learn to live with it."

"I need something burned in there that will cover the image of my sweet mother laying there in her own blood. I would rather be tortured by the image of Lisa Cross dying at my hand than to see my dead mother in my head every day."

Buddy nodded. "I can help you. We'll need to find her first, make sure she's still living in the same place. We'll have to gather a little intelligence on her living situation. We need to know who she's living with, what their security is like, how tightly they're wound."

"How do we get all that?"

"We go on a recon patrol," Buddy said. "We could take your horses and maybe set up a camp at your old house. We watch her for a couple of days and figure out her patterns. When we find a vulnerability, we exploit it. That's when you strike."

The volume of the rain decreased abruptly, the tail end of the brief storm passing. It was still raining, but gentler now.

"You'll go with me?"

"We can leave tomorrow if you want."

"No use procrastinating," she said. "I'll be ready in the morning."

"I'll come by first thing," he told her. "Saddle me a horse."

Randi stood and wobbled. Buddy rose, ready to catch her if she tumbled off the porch. She steadied herself, turned to Buddy, and threw her arms around him. "Thank you."

"You sure you're okay to get home?" Buddy asked.

"The horse knows the way," she said. "I'll be fine."

"It's still raining."

"I like it. Maybe it will sober me up a little. I go home drunk and my daughters will give me shit."

She turned to Lloyd, prepared to say good-bye, but found him asleep. She and Buddy had been so engrossed in their conversation they hadn't noticed the tapering and fading of the banjo music. Lloyd's head was thrown back, the banjo cradled in his arms.

She and Buddy both shook their heads in amusement.

"He's one of a kind," Buddy said.

"Thank God," Randi said.

CHAPTER NINETEEN

Alice

Alice had never experienced her family farm in the way she was experiencing it now. Despite the fact that they were all alive and they had some livestock and provisions, the entire place was gray and lifeless. The world seemed to filter the light before it reached them, taking away those colors of the spectrum that imparted any beauty and pleasure into their lives. All that remained was dull and draining. She found herself with no energy and no motivation. She couldn't decide if the problem was with her or with the world. She wondered if she had Post Traumatic Stress Disorder. It would only be logical that she did have some lingering effects from her experiences.

Her son seemed oblivious to the collapse of the way things had been. He quickly adapted to carrying a weapon around all the time and performing farm chores from daylight to dusk. He'd never spent very much time on the farm and he was making up for that now. It was like he was born to do it. Pat was sharing a lifetime of knowledge with her grandson and he absorbed it like a sponge.

Without the convenience of power and plentiful fuel, although

Charlie had to do things the old fashioned way, he didn't seem to care at all. He was just as comfortable digging with a shovel as a tractor. He preferred walking over riding an ATV around the farm. If he had to move two dozen fence posts, he didn't care to put them on his shoulder, one by one, and walk them to where he needed them. It was like he was made to live at this pace.

Maybe everyone in the world was and they'd just forgotten.

Before Alice had made it back to her family, they'd lost nearly half the cattle, pigs, chickens, and goats to thieves. Since her arrival, and with the implementation of a nightly watch, they hadn't lost anything. Several times they'd been awakened by gunshots as whoever was on duty fired at coyotes or trespassers. The shots also had a deterrent effect since anyone who escaped the gunfire spread the word among the underclass of thieves that "those folks shoot back".

One morning, the desperate bleating of a nanny goat woke Charlie. His father was on guard duty so Charlie tried to ignore the noise, figuring that if it were anything important Terry would have dealt with it or asked for help. When the noise persisted, Charlie pulled himself out of bed and looked out the window. From his window, he could see the goat standing in the pen adjoining the barn. It looked like its horns were caught in the fence *again*. They'd been locking the goats up at night but goats were notorious for being able to circumvent the best laid plans of men. Charlie would have to go deal with it now.

He slid on his clothes, grabbed his AR, and went downstairs. His muddy boots were on the back porch where he left them each night. He tiptoed down the steps, hoping that he wouldn't wake his mother and grandmother. Both of their doors were closed and he assumed they were still sleeping.

Each night, the person on guard duty manned a lawn chair in the mudroom, which was a shed-type addition built onto the back the house. It was an uninsulated room with a storm door and several windows. There was a table beside the lawn chair with a big hunter's spotlight on it. The mudroom had a good view of the farm structures so the guard could see if anyone tried to break into them. Then he or she could decide whether to hit them with the spotlight or pop a round off at them.

Charlie knew his dad would be sitting there with his .260 Remington bolt-action with the Nikon scope. It was his favorite gun to shoot, whether he was targeting groundhogs or deer. Charlie stopped off in the kitchen and grabbed a cold biscuit from the covered plate on the stove. He took a bite and continued out into the mudroom.

His dad was in the lawn chair asleep, the gun across his lap. His head was thrown back, his eyes closed, and his mouth open. Charlie smiled. While napping on duty was a breach of their new security protocol, Charlie always enjoyed catching his dad doing something he shouldn't be. It gave him the opportunity to give his dad some crap. Charlie would get some mileage out of this.

He shoved the rest of the biscuit in his mouth and sat down beside his dad to put on his muddy boots. They were heavy rubber farm boots that came up to his knees. He propped his AR up against the door and tugged at a boot while trying to think of some creative way to wake his dad. Charlie didn't want him to wake up in a panic and start shooting so he figured he needed to slip the gun out of his hands first.

He finished putting on the other boot and stood. He attempted to lift the gun from his dad's hands but instead of his fingers falling away, they remained wrapped around the stock of the rifle. Charlie carefully reached down to remove his dad's hands. He found the fingers cold and stiff. He dropped the hand and recoiled, drawing his own hands up in front of body. He felt a flush of icy water run through his veins.

"Dad?" he said. His voice was gentle. *Pleading*. "Dad?"

Charlie reached out, touched his dad on the shoulder. It was cool.

Charlie sagged to the ground, resting his hands on his dad's arms. "Oh, Dad. Please, Dad. Wake up, Dad. Please. Wake up. Nooooo...." He broke down and began sobbing, resting his head against the sleeve of the blue hoodie his dad wore.

"Why, Dad? Mom came home to us. She got medicine for you. Why did you still die?"

Charlie cried for his father for a long time before he felt a hand on his shoulder. He looked up and found his grandmother, her eyes red and filled with tears. "C'mon, sweetie," she said. "We need to tell your mother."

His grandmother led him up the steps to his mother's room. Her consoling voice fell silent as they neared the top. Charlie knocked on the door, then pushed it open. The sun was just coming up, throwing hard, angular light through Alice's window. She was sitting up in the bed as if she were waiting for them.

"Terry's dead," she said, taking one look at them. It was not a question. She felt it.

Both Pat and Charlie wished they could tell her that her assumption was wrong, but they couldn't. Alice lowered herself back to the bed, her head resting directly against the tall oak headboard. She stared ahead. Charlie went to her and lay down beside her, instantly four years old again. He wrapped his arms around her and sobbed with the unbridled pain of his loss.

Alice shed no tears. She thought of the things she'd gone through since leaving for Richmond. She thought of her trip with Rebecca and the imprisonment in Boyd's basement. She thought of the men she'd killed to get medicine for her husband. Those deaths had bought her husband less than two weeks. One week of life for each she'd taken to get those medications.

She held her son tight, clutching him to her chest. She could feel his pain, the ache of his grief. She hoped he didn't look into her eyes. If he did, he might see that the blackness inside her left no room for new grief.

CHAPTER TWENTY

Alice

With her daughter and grandson at a loss for how to handle a death in the home, Pat led them through how it was done when she was a child. They laid Terry's body out on the kitchen table. They worked together to wrap his body in a burial shroud made of an old sheet. It was somber work that pained their hearts and soured their stomachs. None had any words for what had happened. In a world of impartial and boundless cruelty, this seemed a particularly nasty and unwarranted outcome.

When he was wrapped in the sheet, Pat and Alice began stitching the edges shut.

"I guess I need to dig my daddy a grave," Charlie said. "Any idea where?"

"Near the pond," Pat said without hesitation. "He liked to fish there. He enjoyed that spot."

Alice nodded but didn't say anything, just continued to crudely stitch the edges of the shroud together. With the Terry that she loved gone already, she was not too concerned about the fate of this empty husk. It seemed pointless to go to much bother about it. Had it just been the two of them, she'd just plant him off in the woods where it wouldn't foul their water supply. Apparently her mother and son needed a little more from this. They needed it to be *right* somehow, though she knew there could never be anything right about it.

"When I was a little girl my daddy always helped folks dig graves," Pat said. "He couldn't much tolerate funerals but he felt like he did his part by digging the grave. He took a lot of pride in it. He had this old broad axe with an offset handle and he'd get in there and shave the walls of the grave smooth. He'd clean up the corners, square them off, and make them look real nice. People always wondered why he went to so much trouble for a hole that was just going to get filled back in, but when it was one of their folks being buried they understood. It was about paying your respects and everybody has to do that differently. For some, that happens in the chapel. For others, it comes from doing the little things that need doing."

"I need to get a shovel," Charlie said. He started off, then turned back to them. "Can we have... some kind of ceremony?"

Pat started to answer but looked at Alice, realizing it should probably be her place to make that decision. Alice was caught off-guard by the question but there was a pleading in Charlie's voice. If he needed a ceremony to close this out, then she'd do her best to provide one.

"I suppose we can," she said. "That would be nice." On the inside, she knew it would be anything but nice. It would only keep the wound fresh that much longer.

"If we're having a ceremony, then there should be a minister," Pat said. "To make it official and all."

Alice had no feelings on this, either. "Fine. If you can find one still willing to speak over the dead."

"Do you know one, Granny?" Charlie asked.

Pat could see the hope in his eyes. She could not bring his dad back to him but maybe she could help him feel better about what had to be done today. "I haven't been to church since people started trying to steal the livestock. It's a shame that people would steal them while a Christian woman was in church, but they did."

"Did they keep having church after things got bad?" Alice asked.

"Reverend Jenkins did," Pat said. "He even offered a meal every night for folks that didn't have anything. People with canning and provisions would donate things, and we'd try to find some way to stretch it into a meal. It wasn't much but a lot of folks came. Like I said, I quit going after people started stealing the stock. I haven't even seen or heard from any of those folks since. People don't visit much anymore."

"So you'll ask him?" Charlie asked.

"If your mother will lend me her car, maybe I'll drive down there when we're done and see if he's still around. The parsonage is right behind the church so unless he's out visiting he should be around there somewhere."

"Unless he's dead," Alice blurted out. "Or found a safer place to hide."

Pat looked at her daughter and tightened her lips into a frown.

"I'll go with you," Alice conceded. "It's not safe to go anywhere alone."

"Surely I'd be safe going no further than that," Pat said. "It's just a little piece down the road."

"Nothing is sure now," Alice said. "Nothing is safe."

"Can I stay here?" Charlie asked. "The grave is going to take a while. I'd like to try to finish today."

Alice nodded. "Keep your gun handy and your head on a swivel."

"We'll see if the preacher might be able to come by in the morning and say a few words over your father," Pat said. "Would that be good?"

"Thanks, Granny," Charlie said, hugging his grandmother awkwardly. He paused as if he was going to hug his mother, but hesitated. When she didn't give any indication a hug was welcome he retreated. He picked up his AR and clomped out of the kitchen, the screen door clacking shut behind him.

Pat's mouth was screwed tight. She kept sewing, her pace picking up until she was stabbing the cloth frantically. Alice watched her mother, noticed her hands were clutching the needle so hard they were turning white. They began trembling. Pat straightened and laid her face in the palm of her hand. She shook her head slowly.

"Mom, are you okay?" Alice asked. She wanted to reach out and touch her mom on the shoulder but she couldn't do that any more than she could open herself to a hug from her son. Her hands wouldn't move, wouldn't stop sewing.

"This is tearing my heart out," she said. "I'm not sure I can take this."

Alice didn't feel that ache. She wasn't sure she felt anything anymore.

CHAPTER TWENTY-ONE

Alice

With their immediate task done, the grim seamstresses climbed into the car and left the farm. As was her practice now, Alice placed her revolver under her right thigh. Her mother looked at it, then at her daughter, then back at the road. The stress of the world was wearing on Pat. She appeared at the brink of what she could deal with. The world had come so far from the place she knew. She came from a day when kids went to the movies on Saturday and church on Sunday. Entertainment was pouring a bag of salted peanuts down the neck of a cold bottle of Coke. This was a world of dark, and death, and car trips with a gun at the ready. It felt to her like a world without meaning. She remembered movies she'd seen over her life where people ended up in a strange land with the road back home having disappeared behind them. This world felt like that now, like the road back to the world she knew was gone and would never return.

They drove silently for ten minutes before pulling into the gravel parking lot of the Sugar Springs Church. From all appearances, it was indistinguishable from thousands of other small country churches just like it: frame construction, whitewashed exterior, and a tin roof with a bell tower. There was a little parsonage behind the church of similar construction. It was the only church Pat had ever gone to, though she'd been through several different pastors. The current pastor, Reverend Jenkins, seemed to have his heart in the right place but he was a little too modern for some of the traditional congregation, including Pat.

She was used to pastors who dressed up in a suit and tie when they went places. This man seemed to think a polo shirt and khaki pants was formal enough most days. He'd also instituted a policy of having a casual day the first Sunday of each month. This did not sit well with the women who'd dressed up in their best clothing every Sunday of their entire lives. Casual day was something that those fancy TV churches did or those big non-denominational churches with their sound systems and interpretive dancers. Little country churches did not have casual Sundays. In fact, they did *nothing* casually.

Alice expected the parking lot to be empty but there were several vehicles. "There must be something going on here," she said.

"Maybe it's a special service," Pat said. "It could be a religious holiday but I'm ashamed to say I've lost track of the days."

"It could be a funeral," Alice said, recalling the reason for their own visit.

The parking lot contained a few vehicles, several tractors, bicycles of every manner, and even a few horses tied up to a nearby fence. Alice noted that there was a pile of manure behind each horse, making her wonder how long they'd been there. They parked the car and got out. The horses acted skittish, shuffling and pulling at their tied reins.

"I wonder how long they've been tied up here." Pat asked. "Should we get them some water?"

"We need to figure out what's going on first."

The horses became even more agitated. Pat stared at them, her fear rising with their unease. She was a country woman used to the ways of livestock. Horses didn't act like this for no reason. She heard a loud, metallic click and jerked her head, startled. Alice had cocked her revolver and was holding it at the ready. Pat looked up from the revolver to Alice's face. Alice gestured toward the white double doors of the old church.

"Let's go."

They walked together, side by side. A crow cawed from a tree to the side of the church. Another landed on a fence and watched. The pair climbed the seven stone steps, Pat holding to the rail to steady herself. Her knees felt weak, as if she'd been squatting in the garden for way too long. Alice held the revolver up, both hands wrapped around the grip. Her eyes were wide. Sweat ran down her face.

They reached the top and stood outside the closed doors, listening. Things weren't right. Every indication was that the church was occupied but it was way too quiet. This many people could not be this quiet. Pat swallowed hard, her mouth a thin line, and looked at Alice for support. Alice nodded at the door, pushing Pat with her will, encouraging her to open the door. One of them had to open it and Alice wanted to be ready to shoot if she needed to.

There must have been fifty layers of paint on the front door. Pat had never noticed that before. She found it hard to make her arm move. Tension stiffened her body.

She raised a hand and placed her spread fingers on the thick white paint, pausing as if she could sense something through the door. With her other hand, she clasped the handle, her thumb pressing down on the worn brass latch. There was a loud click from within the workings of the door. Pat shoved and the door swung inward with a groan.

The older woman immediately sucked in air, her mouth opening, lips curling. A scream rose but was strangled. Alice watched her mother with horror, then pushed her aside to see for herself. Pat staggered backward and doubled over the porch rail, choking and dry heaving.

Alice burst through the door of the church, waving the revolver in search of a target. Her brain raced between mechanically assessing for threats and processing the horror that was in front of her.

Sweep left. No target. No threat.

Pews of dead people.

Sweep right. No target.

A man, arms thrown backward, head hanging over the back of the pew. Vomit running from his mouth and up his face. Into his eyes. Into his nose.

Checking the corners. Gun moving. Eyes moving.

Children sprawled in the aisles. Mothers laying across them.

Glassy, unseeing eyes. No targets but also no one alive. No one alive at all.

There was the scuff of a step behind her and Alice spun, levelling her gun on the frightened face of her own mother. Alice froze, afraid to move, remembering how she'd fired at Gary in the stairwell of her old office building. She'd known it was him but couldn't stop her finger in time.

Alice got control of herself and held her fire. "What the hell happened here? What have they done?" she croaked.

Pat wandered around, hand covering her mouth, eyes wide. "I don't...." She was moaning, sobbing. "Good Lord, *why?* I've known some of these people all of my life."

Alice moved up the center aisle, stepping around bodies, stepping over bodies. The smell was overwhelming. Not the rot of corpses but the stench of *sickness* – vomit and emptied bowels. Alice stepped on a red plastic cup, crushing it. The sound echoed. She noticed more red cups. Cups everywhere. How had she missed them?

"The cups?" she said. She was not sure if she was voicing a question or just processing what was going on in her head.

"Communion, maybe?" her mother asked, pointing toward the front of the church, plastic cups lined up along the altar. A cart held pitchers and more cups.

Alice walked all the way to the front of the church and found the minister there dead, a red plastic cup just beyond his hand. It wasn't communion. They did this on purpose. Except for the children, they had all chosen this. Alice turned back to the pews, imagining the dozens of families who'd sat there and made this decision. What had it been like?

"Why?"

She didn't know why she asked it out loud. She didn't even know why she asked it at all because she *knew* the answer. Considering what lay outside those doors, why wouldn't you do it? Why would you want to be alive in this world? Why would you want your children to stay alive in it? It could get better in a few months or years but it could get a lot worse. Could you watch your children starve? Worse yet, what if you died and left your small children to fend for themselves in this cruel world?

"I've seen enough," Alice said.

When there was no response, Alice looked for her mother and found her crouched at the altar rail. She'd blended in with the bodies, partly due to the low profile of her kneeling form, partly due to the red cup she now held in her hand. She was staring at the liquid, but Alice saw the cup inching closer to her mother's own mouth, as if she were fighting the urge to resist but was losing.

"MOTHER!!!" Alice screamed.

Pat raised the cup to her mouth and tossed the liquid back as if she were a drywaller sucking down a shot of Jack Daniels at the neighborhood bar.

Alice screamed, dropped her revolver, and ran to her mother, grabbing her by the sleeve. "Spit it out!"

Pat stared blankly at her daughter but made no move to spit the liquid out. It was gone. Swallowed. Pat opened her mouth to show Alice.

Alice could not stop herself. She slapped her mother hard across the face. Then she jumped on her, forcing her back onto the carpet. She grabbed her mother by the cheeks, held her head back, and tried to force a finger into her mouth. Maybe she could make her throw up? Maybe it wasn't too late. If she could just get it out of her.

Pat bit down on her daughter's fingers. "Nooooo," she hissed between her locked jaw. "Leave me...alone."

"Mom!" Alice pleaded. "No. *No!*"

Pat's eyes glassed over and her face flushed. Her body began to seize, mildly at first, then more violently. Alice had a hand on each of her mother's shoulders now, staring at her, trying to come up with something she could do, but there was nothing.

Alice began crying, her tears rolling down her face and dropping onto her mother's. Pat's eyes were watering, but Alice couldn't tell if it was from the poison or if she were crying too. When her mother began throwing up, Alice rolled off her and curled into a fetal position. She cried harder, violent sobs that rose into curses and screams.

She laid that way for a long time, even after her mother quit choking, then quit breathing. There was complete silence within the church. Alice felt like gravity was trying to pull her limp body through the wooden floor and down into the core of the Earth.

She thought there was nothing left that could be done to her but she was wrong. She thought her feelings were so pushed down within her that they were unreachable. That too was wrong. That one might reach a place where pain couldn't hurt you was only a fantasy. Pain was infinite, inescapable, and sometimes as big as all the world.

Alice stood, feeling as if she were waking from a long, uncomfortable nap. She found her pistol and tucked it into her waistband. She looked around that gallery of death, then realized she was only torturing herself more by committing those scenes to memory.

She managed to pull her mother into sitting position on a pew, then maneuver her up onto her shoulder, staggering under the weight. The pressure of her shoulder pushing into her mother's midsection made the body emit noises and gurgles that made her sound alive. Alice carried her out the double doors and onto the porch. She spun and kicked the door of the church closed, pushing with her foot as you might prod some vile thing that you didn't want to touch with the flesh of your hand.

Alice's chest heaved and she looked about wildly. She had a fleeting thought to burn the church to the ground. She knew that's what needed to be done. What took place there needed to be cleansed from the Earth's memory. She let go of her mother and quickly patted her pockets with her free hand, but could not find a lighter.

Groaning, she staggered down the steps, nearly losing her mother before she reached solid ground. She felt lightheaded, her knees wobbly. She got to the car and tried to lower her mother into passenger seat. The body was too heavy and she fell as she tried to slide her into the seat. She landed on her mother's body, finding the contact both familiar and repellent at the same time.

She maneuvered herself back out, straightened her aching back, and sucked in air. Her heart was racing and she wiped sweat from her face with the tail of her shirt. She closed the door and felt her pocket for the keys. When she started the car, she drew the revolver and put it beneath her thigh. She stared at it for a moment, realizing more profoundly than ever that there were some acts of violence for which no vengeance could be taken.

She punched the gas, slewing the car around and heading for home.

CHAPTER TWENTY-TWO

Alice

When Alice made it back to the farm, she parked in front of the house and looked over at her mother. She lingered there staring at her, imagining that she was just asleep and she would wake her up so they could go inside. The moment passed with the hard realization that no one was waking up from what was going on. Not the dead, and not the living. Alice got out of the vehicle and found her muscles stiff from having carried her mother to the car. She went inside the house and called for her son but he didn't answer. He must not have finished with the grave.

After a short walk, she found him there, only his head showing above ground as he slung shovels of dirt into a pile. He was into the clay layers now and it was especially hard digging, the material clinging to the shovel when he tried to pitch it out. He was shirtless and his body was streaked with dirt. His hair and muddy jeans were drenched with sweat. He dug with unrelenting fury, gasping for breath because he refused to slow for any purpose. His hands, still not used to constant manual labor, were blistered and raw.

Alice approached and her shadow fell across him. He stopped then, leaning forward against the wall of the grave, his head resting on his forearm.

"I wanted to make it better," he croaked. "I wanted to smooth the walls and square the corners."

Unable to find words for what she needed to convey, she awkwardly spit it out, her voice breaking. "It will need to hold two."

He raised his head and stared at her uncomprehendingly. The absence of his grandmother eventually told the tale and he uttered an exhausted wail. He sagged down into the hole, the clay and mud smearing his face, caking his hair.

"How, Mommy?" he asked. "How?"

"It doesn't matter," she said. She was back to being numb again, so battered by the world that a crust had reformed around her, a shell leathered by abuse and hardship.

Charlie was in a place where she couldn't help him now. She was unable to share in his emotions, unable to empathize. She left him there, sobbing in the hole, while she drove the car to the graveside. It dragged on the farm road, scraping dirt as it straddled ruts. They found an old quilt in the back of the car and used it to wrap Pat. Alice had no more tears but Charlie sobbed and moaned in a manner she'd not seen since he broke his arm as a child.

Once Pat was settled into her resting place, they returned to the house for Terry. Alice had tried to load him when she'd gone for Pat but she'd been unable to budge his larger body. Even with the two of them it had proven nearly impossible. Charlie was scrawny, still child-like in his appearance. They'd been forced to drag Terry onto the porch, then use a wheelbarrow to get him to the car.

Halfway between the house and the grave, the car died.

"Tank's empty," Alice said. "It's been beeping a warning for a while. Do we have more gas?"

Charlie shook his head. "The tractor is diesel and it's empty. The gas cans are empty. Everything with gas or diesel on this farm has already been siphoned."

"There are a few vehicles at the church," Alice said after a moment of thought. "Maybe we should check them for fuel."

"That's a long walk," Charlie said. "Hours."

"Where else do you have to be?"

They geared up and walked in mostly silence, reaching the church in around two hours.

"Are there people here?" Charlie asked upon seeing the horses and vehicles.

"It's best we don't talk about that," Alice said. "To even tell you what happened in there will put images in your mind you'll never get rid of. You've been through enough today."

Charlie appeared to accept that. With all he'd gone through today, it was not like he was intent on subjecting himself to even more torment. When she told him there were things in there he didn't want in his head, he yielded to her judgment.

"You didn't mention horses," he said.

"I didn't think to mention them," Alice replied.

They searched but none of the vehicles had keys. Alice found that odd. If you knew you were coming here to die, why would you bother taking the keys in with you? It had to be purely habit. Alice could not make herself go inside and go through the pockets of the dead trying to find them.

"Hand me the hose," Alice said.

Charlie had a section of water hose they'd cut off. Each of them had brought an empty gas can. Alice took the hose, opened a gas cap, and tried feeding it into the tank. Something was blocking it.

"Damn it," she said. "I can't get it to feed in there."

"Dad said that some vehicles have anti-siphon tanks," Charlie said.

Alice quickly grew frustrated and tried another vehicle. There were only a few there and she quickly discovered that she couldn't get the hose into any of them.

"We could try puncturing the tanks," Charlie said.

Puncturing the tanks was a failure. She could tell from tapping them with her pocket knife that there was little gas in any of them. Only one had a plastic tank. She had Charlie find a cup for catching the gas while she twisted her pocket knife for several minutes, drilling a hole in the tank.

The only cup he could find was a Styrofoam cup with the name of a local convenience store printed on it. When Alice finally penetrated the tank and slipped the cup under the stream, it began to dissolve into a gooey mess. She tried to plug the stream with her finger while Charlie looked for something else to catch the gas. The gas ran down her arm and soaked her shirt. The vapors burned her eyes.

The more uncomfortable she became, the more she yelled at Charlie to find something. When he couldn't, she let go of the hole and let the gas run into the ground. She rolled from beneath the car, cursing. She yanked her shirt off and tried to wipe the gas from her arm and back.

"I'm sorry, Mom," Charlie said. He was upset, feeling like he'd screwed up.

Alice was still feeling numb and not completely in tune with her emotions. She understood, though, that she needed to comfort her son. "It's okay. It wasn't enough gas to make a difference anyway. Where would that much gas get us?"

Charlie didn't answer. He was looking at the ground.

"It's pointless. There's probably not enough gas in there to even get the car started," she spat.

"I'll go inside if you want," he said. "I'll look for keys. We'll find something we can drive."

"Fuck the keys," Alice said. As numb as she was, she'd shocked herself using profanity that way in her son's presence. She took a deep breath. "Let's see if we can get the horses. They are probably of more use to us, anyway."

"At least we can grow their fuel," Charlie said.

"They're a little agitated," Alice said. "Hungry, dehydrated, and sore from having these saddles on for who knows how long. They smell the dead. It may take a little while to calm them."

"There's water in the ditch by the road," Charlie said. "Maybe a drink will make them feel better."

It was early evening by the time they got the horses in a state where they could be ridden. Neither Alice nor Charlie had much experience with horses.

"We're going to run out of daylight," Alice said. "We need to get a move on."

Seeing that neither of them knew anything about horses, they each selected a horse based on no particular criteria at all. They led the others, tying them in line.

"When we get home and finish our work, these horses will need care," Alice said. "Put them in the barn so no one will be tempted to steal them."

"Once we finish with... with Dad, I'd like something to take my mind off things. I'd rather be busy than laying around thinking about how bad this day sucks."

"There are things we need to talk about. While I know the farm has come to mean a lot to you, I'm not sure the two of us can protect it."

"What meant a lot to me was being there with Dad and Gran," Charlie said. "Then you, when you got there. Without them, the farm just seems like a lot of work for nothing."

"It's easy to feel hopeless, Charlie. Trust me, I know," Alice said. "You probably don't care if you live or die right now, but remember we've got each other. That's a reason to live. You're the reason I'm alive. You're the reason I fought to get home."

"Fought?"

"Yes, fought. I'm not ready to talk about it now." She didn't know how he thought she got home but she assumed that he understood it had been a dangerous, violent trek. Maybe he didn't. Maybe he thought it was just a long walk, like walking home from the school bus.

Charlie accepted her explanation with no questions. "Mom, whatever you want to do, I'll do."

"Even if it means leaving the farm?"

"Like I said, without Dad and Gran it's just muddy fields full of animal shit."

Alice couldn't have agreed more.

CHAPTER TWENTY-THREE

The Valley

Dinner in the valley was a social event most evenings. In fact, it was the only social event that occurred on a regular basis anymore. Everyone had work to do at their homes during the day, trying to prepare for winter or trying to make their powerless homes more comfortable. Dinner with the tribe was a chance to relax and share information as well as food. While winter still concerned them, the semi-trailers loaded with supplies that had been obtained from the interlopers from Glenwall had eased some of the immediacy of that concern.

The group of men had been part of a security force that protected an elite golf course community over in Wallace County. Somehow they got the idea that Jim's valley was going to be their new bugout location. Jim had considered the group to be invaders and they'd been dealt with harshly. There were no survivors from that group. The trailers of food and supplies had been intended to get those men through the winter. Now they would serve the same purpose for Jim's people.

Tonight, each family remained at home. After an initial downpour, the rain had slacked off some, but had now returned with a vengeance. It pummeled the roofs, sounding even louder without television to drown it out. There were bolts of lightning that flickered in the dramatic gray sky followed by thunder echoing down the valley in a way it only did in the mountains, sounding like boulders rolling down a sheet of tin. The families spoke on the radio and decided that none were eager to venture out into the wet evening. Everyone would stay home and take their meals with their own families.

Jim and Pete were setting the table. Jim did the plates, Pete the silverware. Napkins and paper towels were used sparingly now, with bandanas and handkerchiefs taking the place of table napkins.

"I hadn't realized how much I missed this," Jim said.

"Missed what?" Pete asked.

"Having a family night with just us."

"Weren't you the one preaching that group dinners were a more efficient use of resources?" Ellen asked.

"They are," Jim said. "Doesn't mean I like them better. That's just a sacrifice I made to help the supplies last longer."

The evening was much quieter than when the group was there eating. There was no banging of the large kettles they had to use when they were cooking for so many. There was no hum of a dozen different conversations. Kids were not yelling, or crying, or playing loudly through the house. Jim didn't feel like he had to play host. Tonight it was just his family.

His mother's mood had been brightened by the arrival of more of her own personal things. Like any good husband, Pops was in a better mood for having put Nana in a better mood. She now had her craft materials, her sewing box, knitting and crocheting supplies, and all of the other things that kept her entertained since she retired.

As befitting a damp and inhospitable evening, they were cooking chili made with freeze dried beef. Nana used a cast iron griddle on a camp stove to cook johnnycakes, a cornmeal flatbread she'd grown up eating. Ariel helped her make the batter and was scooping it out onto the griddle while Nana carefully flipped the cakes when they were ready. Pops was sitting in the living room by candlelight, scratching his dog behind the ears while Jim and Pete finished setting the table.

With no wind, the rain was still coming straight down. When he finished his task, Jim stepped onto the back screened-in porch to watch the rain. He felt like he was in a jungle hut watching the monsoon rains pour on the dense greenery. In the dark evening, the sound of the rain was powerful and began to make Jim powerfully sleepy. He eased down into an Adirondack chair and started to close his eyes for a moment when something caught his attention. He sat upright. He saw it again, a flicker of light in the distance. He only caught it for a moment, coming from a gap between two hills, and partially obscured by trees.

He pulled his radio from his pouch. Buddy and Lloyd were manning the watch tonight. The post on this side of the valley was not within sight of Jim's house but was closer to the Wimmer farm. He was pretty sure they couldn't see in the direction he was looking.

"Buddy, you read me?"

After a moment, the radio chirped and Buddy's voice came back. *"I'm here."*

"You guy see anything out of the ordinary?"

"We can't see shit," Buddy said. *"Besides the dark, I think a cloud has settled in right on top of us. Not to mention this shelter was kind of thrown up in a hurry. The top is waterproof but water is running back in on us from all sides."*

While Buddy talked, Jim scanned the fields behind his house. The farm road that they used to go in and out of this end of the valley ran back there. It was the way they'd come in after their trip to town today. Jim caught a flicker of light there again. It was yellow, like a headlight.

"Buddy, I definitely have something coming in back here. I'm pretty sure I'm seeing headlights. I hate to ask this, but I may need you and Lloyd down here. After seeing that drone today, this may not be a coincidence."

"Roger that," Buddy said. *"On our way."*

Jim stood and went to stash his radio but it chirped again.

"I heard your conversation. Need another hand?" Gary asked.

Jim smiled. Gary always had his back.

"Might be a good idea," Jim said.

"Got it. Out."

Jim shoved the radio into his pouch and went back inside.

"We've got company," he announced. "I don't know that it's anything serious but we can't take chances. I want Ariel and Nana in the basement. Ellen, Pops, and Pete – I need you guys to gear up. Have rain gear handy just in case."

As much as everyone may have wanted to moan and groan at the disruption of their evening, they all knew this was not the time. The seriousness of their new lives was made clear to them nearly every day in some manner. They quietly and efficiently began preparing for whatever was coming their way. Cooking was set to the side, gas stove turned off, lights were doused, and headlamps distributed.

"I'm going to teach you to crochet," Nana said to Ariel as the two of them made their way into the basement. Ellen shut the door behind them. The basement windows had been boarded up long ago. They could use a lantern or headlamps down there with no worries.

The gun safe sat empty and idle most days. Guns were kept around the house, leaned in corners or hung on hooks. They needed to be handy and ready to go. The kids understood the rules just as Jim had when he was a kid. Guns had always been accessible but you kept your hands off.

"Where do you want us?" Pete asked.

"Stay together and monitor your radios," Jim said. "Buddy, Lloyd, and Gary are all on their way down here so I don't want any shooting unless you're crystal clear who's on the receiving end of the round. I just want you to be ready in case I need you."

The entire time Jim was talking, he was slipping on gear. He threw on a black rain slicker, pulled his load vest on top of it, and checked his weapons. The Beretta was on his hip, ready to go. With visibility gone and dark upon them, Jim grabbed his Remington 870 tactical shotgun. With a shortened barrel and buckshot, aim would not have to be as exact.

"Be careful," Ellen warned.

"Always," Jim replied, leaving out the front door. He jogged in the darkness, his feet splashing with each step. In seconds, he was wet from the knees down and rain trickled in around his collar, running down his chest and back. He couldn't see much but after nearly two decades on this property he didn't need to. He ran about seventy-five yards and went through a gate, turned right, and ran along a fence line. He had to make himself slow down there. Cattle walked that fence line and had worn deep ruts into the ground. The muddy ruts made for an easy place to wipe out.

Jim could hear engines now. Not trucks but ATVs, like his father's Kawasaki Mule. There was one gate between Jim and those machines and he wanted to reach it first. He had the advantage of knowing where he was going and whoever this was did not. They were driving slowly. They probably didn't have windshield wipers and farm roads could be confusing. There were no directional signs and there was no way for these people to know if they were following the main route or some offshoot that would lead them to a barn or a watering trough.

When he reached the gate, Jim was the first one there and he was panting from exertion. He slipped behind a fallen tree, hoping that he would be both hidden and afforded some protection if this turned into a fight. The vehicles were closer now, the headlights completely visible, their twin beams cutting into the mist, illuminating raindrops that ran through the beams like static on a television screen.

There were two of the machines and Jim could see that each held two rows of seats. He couldn't see inside the machines but knew that could potentially mean eight men, or even more if they'd jammed in there. The lead machine stopped inches from the gate. A ratcheting sound indicated the parking brake was being set. The plastic side-door popped open and a dark figure stepped out. When it reached the gate, the headlights illuminated the reflective lettering on the raincoat: *Sheriff's Department*.

"Shit," Jim whispered to himself.

CHAPTER TWENTY-FOUR

The Valley

Jim couldn't see everything the figure was doing but heard the rattling of the rusty gate chain and knew the man was trying to unhook it. He didn't want to let that happen.

"Don't fucking move!"

The man jumped, startled at the voice from the darkness, but he obeyed the command. He dropped the chain he was working on, straightened, and turned toward the voice in the darkness. Jim knew his position was probably illuminated by the ambient light from the headlights but hoped that he didn't present enough of a target to take a shot at.

"I'm Deputy Barnes," the man said. "I'm here on police business."

"What kind of police business?"

"That's none of your concern," Barnes replied.

"Everything that happens beyond that gate is my concern," Jim countered.

"You sure you want to be on the wrong side of the law?"

Jim had the short barrel of his pump shotgun leveled at the man over the top of a log. His head was low. He was pretty sure he could drop the man before he could draw his weapon but he wasn't so sure about the rest of those men. He had to cycle the pump, which would require him to move the weapon between shots.

"Which side of the law are *you* on?" Jim asked. "Are you on the side that's out there working to keep the peace or are you on the side that took over a shopping center and turned it into a private fort?"

"Again, I'm not sure that's any of your fucking business," Barnes said.

"If you've got police business here, get the sheriff on the radio and let me speak with him," Jim requested. "I'm sure he can clear this up for us."

"That's not going to happen," Barnes replied.

"You coming through that gate isn't happening either," Jim said.

"I'm tired of this bullshit," Barnes muttered. "MEN! Roll out!"

The doors to the UTVs opened up and his men clambered out.

"You going to shoot all of us?" Barnes asked. "One man?"

With a flicker of red light a red laser beam formed a dot on Barnes's chest. Another red slash cut through the night and a dot landed on another deputy's chest. The men shifted uncomfortably. Another laser flickered from the darkness, playing across the cluster of deputies. Then suddenly there were three more.

Jim was running the numbers in his own head. He knew Lloyd and Buddy weren't the laser type. Who else was out there? The deputies were talking among themselves, clearly not comfortable with how this was going. They hadn't anticipated these odds.

"Maybe we should just call this a draw," Jim said. "You guys go on back home before somebody gets hurt."

"You've crossed a line," Barnes said. "Ain't no backing up from it now. I see you outside of this valley, you're a dead man."

"You speaking as a deputy?" Jim asked.

"Take it however you like. We're not done, though."

"I expect we're not," Jim said. "Now go on home."

The grumbling deputies climbed back into their UTVs, slammed the doors, and awkwardly negotiated turns on the muddy road. As they crawled away, Jim sat there in the dark, the rain pattering on the hood of his slicker. He stood and looked off into the darkness.

"Who the hell is out there?" he asked.

"Me and Will," Gary responded.

"Lloyd and I are here," Buddy said.

Jim clicked on a headlamp and began walking back toward the house. He dug out his radio and informed his family that things had deescalated and he'd be up in a few minutes. He encountered the men crouched a short distance from where he'd been. "Where the hell did all those lasers come from?" he asked. "It looked like there was a fucking SWAT team hidden out here."

"Will and I both have lasers on our rifles," Gary said. "Will's Glock also has one."

"I saw more than three," Jim said.

"The last couple were cheap laser pointers that I carry in my tac vest. I got them at a convenience store," Gary said. "They're not attached to a weapon, but whoever you're pointing them at doesn't know that."

Jim nodded in approval. "Cool idea, but I guess this is another good day gone to shit."

"Why can't things just be cool for a few days?" Will said. "Why does this stuff keep happening?"

"It's the tanker," Jim said. "They know about it."

"How?" Gary asked.

"They got it out of my dad today," Jim said, shaking his head. "Somehow word must have spread to the cops at the superstore, although I'm not sure you can even call them cops at this point." Jim hadn't had the opportunity to tell Gary about his experience with the cops on the road today so he went into that.

"A bad cop can be a bad problem," Gary said. "This could get serious."

"Maybe we should just give them some of the fuel," Lloyd suggested.

"If we give them some fuel then they'll want all the fuel," Jim said. "No matter what we give them, it won't be enough. Then they'll start wanting other stuff, and there's no telling where it will stop."

"But it wasn't our fuel to begin with," Lloyd said. "Speaking from a business standpoint, it's not like we have anything invested in it. Maybe it's better to just give it to them and look at it as the price for keeping the peace."

"If it *would* keep the peace then I'd be fine with that," Buddy said. "People like that don't work that way. It's like Jim said. While they're in here poking around, they'll want to see what else they can take. Next it will be cattle and crops. Then it will be our homes. I'm with Jim — we draw the line at that gate right there."

"You think we should hide the tanker?" Will asked.

"I'm not sure we have a barn big enough," Jim replied. "And if we did, that's the first place they'd look for it."

"Maybe we hide it in plain sight," Will said. "We park it in a field and stack round bales of hay around it until it looks like a plain old stack of bales in a field."

"That's a good idea," Gary said. "You think we could do that, Jim?"

Jim nodded. "We'll get the Wimmers to help with that. They have a bigger tractor and it has a hay spike mounted on the loader."

"What about these guys?" Buddy asked. "They might come back."

"There's no telling where they'll come from next," Jim said. "Maybe we warn every family to keep watch on their own places tonight. Tomorrow we'll come up with another plan."

CHAPTER TWENTY-FIVE

Alice

Alice and Charlie worked late into the night. Unable to move Terry's body with the car, they were forced to roll him out onto a tarp and drag that with a horse. It was primitive and Charlie, already heartsick, stiffened each time his dad's body was pulled over a rock or slipped into a rut.

By flashlight and lantern they arranged the bodies. It took hours to refill the grave. They passed the time with their own improvised memorial service. They told stories of the people they placed beneath the earth. In a different world, it may have been a spooky scenario, standing beside a half-filled grave in the pale splash of lantern light. In this world, after this day, it was as natural as being anywhere else.

When they humped the last shovelful of dirt atop the grave, they patted the mound with the backs of their shovels. They were sore, sweaty, and dirty in the cool air of the late summer night. They had blisters that had opened and were ringed with dirt. In the distance they sometimes heard indecipherable shouts or voices that made Alice touch the handle of her revolver for reassurance. Nothing ever got close, but the smell of smoke hit their nostrils when the wind came from the right direction. It was a reminder that despite feeling alone in the world, there *were* other people out there. For the moment, they wanted no part of them.

"You think that smoke is from a campfire or a house?" Charlie asked.

"I don't know," Alice said. "But we should probably get on home."

"Are we going to take turns keeping watch each night?" Charlie asked. "Just us?"

"I'll keep watch," Alice said. "I won't sleep anyway."

"I don't know if I've ever felt this tired," Charlie said. "I'm almost too tired to sleep, but I'll try to find a way."

They had one horse with them, the one they'd used to drag the tarp. Leading it, they walked home. They left the digging tools at the graveside, carrying only their lanterns and guns.

"If we don't stay here, where will we go?" Charlie asked. "Are we going to stay with your friends from work?"

"I don't know if I'd call them friends or not," Alice said quickly. She considered the things they'd been through. The offer that had been made to her was not casual, nor was it meaningless. She didn't care about her own life anymore, but the offer they'd extended to her could mean a better life for her son.

"I guess they *are* friends," she decided.

"We could go there?"

"We could probably get there in a day on the horses," she said. "We could pack our gear on the extra horses. It wouldn't be easy. We would have to be on guard. It's dangerous out there, Charlie."

"It's dangerous *here*," he said. "What about the stuff we can't take? People will steal it."

"I've been thinking about that," Alice said. "There's an old cistern. It's empty now. We could use that."

"What's a cistern?"

"A concrete box in the ground. There was an old house on the farm that burned down. This cistern collected rainwater from the gutters and they could pump it out when they needed water. I saw the cistern the other day and slid the lid off to check inside. There's a little water in it but we could siphon the water out, seal the inlets, and it should stay dry. I'd cover the lid with a tarp and some dirt."

"So we do that tomorrow and leave the next day?"

"I don't see any reason why not."

Charlie nodded. "Maybe one day this place won't make me sad but it sure does now. I don't want to stay here."

CHAPTER TWENTY-SIX

The Valley

The next morning Jim was sitting on the porch with his M4 pulling guard duty. He'd relieved Pete at 4 a.m. and was now pondering what he might do about last night's visitors. Pissed off cops were never good neighbors. He'd always found cleaning guns helped clear his head and help him think. He had the Beretta disassembled in front of him for that very reason. Rain had soaked his weapons last night and he wanted to make sure they were thoroughly cleaned and oiled.

The rain had quit during the night but left the valley humid with patches of fog. Through that mist strode a figure in camouflage hunting clothes. Jim could tell from the walk that it was Buddy. As he neared, Jim could see that he wore a faded Army-issue pack and had his lever-action rifle slung over his shoulder.

"What are you up to?" Jim asked. "Lloyd drive you out of your own house?"

He reassembled the Beretta, double-checking that the slide, safety, hammer, and trigger all functioned correctly before reloading it.

Buddy stopped and stood close to the porch but didn't take off his gear. "I'm headed to Randi's house."

Jim wasn't aware that the two of them were all that tight. "Everything okay?"

Buddy nodded. "I hate to run off and leave you to deal with that problem from last night on your own but I made a promise to that girl. She didn't want me to tell you about it but I can't hardly run off and not tell anyone where we're going."

"She going after that Cross woman?" Jim asked. He popped out the takedown pins on his M4 and stripped it to the basic components. Once they were laid out, he examined each carefully.

"She is."

"I knew it," Jim said with resignation. "I knew she couldn't let it rest."

"I knew it too," Buddy said. "She didn't even have to come out and say it."

Jim took an oily rag and polished the bolt. "When you coming back?"

"A few days probably. Depends on when the opportunity presents itself."

"Keep an eye on her," Jim said. "Try to get her back here alive. She's got kids and grandkids." Jim held the M4 up to the light, examining the components of the lower receiver.

"I'll do it. You all be safe too. Don't let Lloyd lose any more fingers."

"I'll try," Jim said. Satisfied with the condition of his weapon, he deftly fit all the components back together and checked function.

Buddy gave a wave and started to walk away. "I'll be seeing you."

"Buddy!" Jim called after him.

Buddy turned around.

"If you were in my shoes, what would you do about last night?" Jim asked. "What would be your play?" He respected the older man and hoped he had some insight that might steer Jim in the right direction. Sometimes he reacted with a violent finality. Maybe that wasn't the best response here.

Buddy scratched the stubble of his chin while he thought. He nodded slowly until the gears engaged. "There was a kid I grew up with. Scrawny fellow named Carter. He did something to get on the wrong side of a bully named Kent. Kent would catch Carter on the way home from school nearly every day and either kick his ass or embarrass him in some way. Carter knew it would be pointless to stand up to the bully because he was about a foot taller than Carter and outweighed him by nearly sixty pounds."

Buddy shifted, hooked a thumb under a pack strap. "Then Carter finds this other kid at school who's bigger than Kent, a guy who's been held back three times and already had a full beard in sixth grade. Carter tells the guy that he'll give him a dime to walk him home every day. This was when a dime could actually buy something. So the guy takes the job and walks Carter home every day. Eventually, the guy even takes the initiative to tell Kent that he'll kick his ass from one end of the building to the other if he ever messes with Carter again."

Jim nodded. "You're telling me I need to find a bigger bully?"

"Or someone that this deputy will respect."

"What if he doesn't respect anyone?"

"Maybe it doesn't matter if he respects them as long as his men do. He may be willing to cross lines that they don't want to cross, like killing local folks. In the end, as long as you knock some of his people out of the fight, it doesn't matter if you do it by killing them or by making them not want to engage in the battle."

"Any thoughts on who I should start with?"

"I'd start with that sheriff," Buddy said. "Those other deputies might not be so quick to fight him. They may have more respect for his authority."

After the older man left, Jim pondered what he'd said. He confirmed that the rest of his gear was squared away, then went to the kitchen and refilled his coffee cup from a thermal carafe.

He kissed his wife. "I need you all to keep an eye on things this morning. I'm going to town."

Ellen regarded him, trying to gauge his state of mind. "You're not about to do something stupid are you?"

"No."

"You're not going to pay this Deputy Barnes a visit?"

"No, I'm going to try to find the sheriff and talk to him about this," he said. "Buddy gave me an idea. Maybe there's a way to ease this back a notch without anybody getting killed."

Ellen nodded as if she didn't exactly believe him. "Shouldn't you take someone with you?"

"I'm not taking anyone. I don't want to have to look after them. Just give me a few hours and I'll be back."

He went to the bedroom and threw his load-bearing vest on over a flannel shirt, lamenting the fact that he hadn't bought any body armor over the years, despite looking at online catalogs dozens of times. He'd been wanting the new type of polyethylene body armor. It produced class III chest plates that would stop a rifle round and weighed less than three pounds. He'd been too cheap to spend the money and now it was too late. He could have borrowed Gary's but he didn't like borrowing other people's gear.

He took off his drop leg holster and stored his Beretta in the holster on the vest. It was easier to reach when he was driving. He checked the .22 mini-revolver in the ankle holster and confirmed it was fully loaded. He stuffed his vest with 30 round mags for the M4 and 15 rounders for the Beretta, confirmed that the Microtech LUDT was clipped to his pocket and his ESEE 4 was in position on his belt. He didn't know what you'd call this kind of mission but it definitely felt like a mission.

He started out of the bedroom and caught his reflection in the mirror. Something was off. He examined himself from head to toe and determined it was the hat. It was from a local heavy equipment company that he'd once used to repair a machine. The hat didn't mean shit to him. He took it off, hung it on the bedpost, and looked for another. He found one from his high school baseball team. He hadn't played baseball but the hat had been a gift from a friend who died of cancer over twenty years earlier. The hat was so old that it crackled when Jim put it on. He didn't care. He needed all the luck he could get and maybe the hat held just a little.

He hugged his family, topped off the fuel in his truck, and drove down the valley toward Gary and the Weatherman homes. There was another farm road on that end of the valley. He was afraid to leave by way of the road he'd used yesterday, thinking the deputies may have posted a watch on it. That's what he would have done had he been in their shoes. He might have driven into a trap.

This road took longer than the other route and put him about ten miles on the wrong side of town. From there, he took a circuitous route across several back roads. He didn't want to go through the middle of town because he was afraid that might draw the attention of the cops. He also didn't want to take any of the smaller side roads because he was afraid he may encounter roadblocks or traps of some sort. After a tense forty-five minute drive he found himself on the road by his parents' house. A few minutes later, he was parked directly in front of the 911 center.

He killed the engine and sat there for a moment. The large building had originally been built as an office before being picked up by the county after the business went belly-up. He stared at the dark lobby, the sunlight making it difficult to see through the reflective coating on the amber glass. In a moment he picked up movement – two figures easing up to the glass and staring at his vehicle. It was the two deputies from the other day, just as he'd hoped.

Jim pushed open the truck door and slid out onto the ground. He left his rifle propped up in the passenger seat. The deputies watched him curiously, each with a hand on their holstered weapon. Jim threw a hand up in a wave that, if not friendly, was at least non-threatening. He went up the full glass double doors and tried the handle.

Locked.

"Open up!"

Deputy Ford came and stood in front of the doors. "What the hell do you want?"

"I want to talk," Jim said.

Ford frowned at him. Jim imagined it was the same look the man gave when he sat down with a cheeseburger and got a radio call before he could take the first bite. He clearly thought Jim was an inconvenience, but Jim didn't care; he'd been regarded as worse.

Ford twisted the thumb latch and shoved the door open, stepping out onto the sidewalk. Deputy Deel was not far behind him. Both adopted the same stance, a hand resting on the butts of their weapons. It was the kind of stance that said, *"Okay, let's hear your bullshit story."*

"So talk," Deputy Ford said.

"I need to talk to the sheriff."

Ford bobbed his head, shaking it like he couldn't believe the nerve of this guy. Who the hell did he think he was? "Why?"

"That's between the sheriff and me," Jim said. "At least for starters."

Ford rocked forward on his toes, shrugged, and shook his head. "If that's your fucking attitude, you can forget it. You can tell us what you want and we'll decide if it's worth the sheriff's time or not. Otherwise, pound sand."

Jim sighed heavily. He looked at the concrete. He flipped through his personal inventory searching for whatever diplomacy skills he had at his disposal. "I need to know where he lives," Jim said.

Ford forced a laugh. "Yeah, that ain't happening, either. You have some fucking nerve. All the attitude you gave us yesterday and now you're here expecting us to bend over for you."

"Maybe we could let him talk to the sheriff over the radio," Deel offered.

"You stay out of this," Ford snapped.

"The radio isn't secure," Jim replied. "You can't mention anything sensitive on it."

"Yeah, the sheriff told us that yesterday," Deel replied.

Ford shot Deel a glance that told him he'd said enough. Jim couldn't help but notice.

"You guys didn't mention what my dad told you over the radio yesterday, did you?"

Ford's lips tightened and he shifted uncomfortably. "Police communications are none of your damn business."

"I'm asking because those other cops showed up in my neighborhood last night," Jim said, his voice rising. "That's why I'm here. That's why I need to talk to the sheriff."

Ford looked away and didn't reply. "Look, we don't know that they heard anything," he said. "We got caught up in the heat of the moment and *maybe* a few things may have slipped out before the sheriff reminded us that the frequency wasn't secure."

Out of the corner of his eye, Jim saw Deputy Deel gesturing at Deputy Ford and rolling his eyes in that direction. Obviously, Deel wanted to make it clear to Jim that he was not the one who disclosed the existence of a fuel tanker in Jim's valley. Ford saw Jim looking and turned in time to catch Deel's gesture.

"Okay, it was me, damn it," Ford spat. "I'm not apologizing. I was just doing my job. Guy has a fuel tanker in these times he can't expect to keep it a secret for long."

Jim looked Ford in the eye. "I'm not here for an apology," he said with utmost sincerity. "Those guys are going to be back and I don't want it to turn into a bloodbath. I don't want anyone killed. On my side *or* theirs."

"I don't know what you think the sheriff can do," Deel said. "Those men wouldn't listen to him. That's why they're in the store and we're out here."

"I don't care if they'd listen to him or not," Jim said. "Do you think if it came down to it, they would be willing to shoot him?"

"The *sheriff?*" Deel asked. He clearly thought the idea was too incredible to be a possibility.

Jim nodded.

"I think that son-of-a-bitch Barnes would," Ford admitted. "I'm not so sure about the others. I don't think they're that far gone. I think they still have some respect for the badge. Some of them are just good men trying to make the best of a bad situation. Barnes, on the other hand, is trying to profit from a bad situation."

"But even if they would listen to the sheriff, I'm not sure he'd be willing to help you," Deel said. "He don't hardly come into town anymore at all. He's got an elderly mother at home and she's doing poorly. He's got a wife and kids. They're just barely scraping by."

Jim stared at the sidewalk. The conversation wound down. Jim wasn't sure about what he was about to do but sometimes you just had to dive in.

"What about you two men?" he asked. "You all have family?"

"I had a wife but we split up," Ford said.

No surprise there, Jim thought, but he kept the smartass comments to himself. "Deel?"

Deel shook his head. "I live in an apartment in town by myself," he said. "My family lives on a farm in Tennessee. I'm sure they're doing fine."

"Here's the deal. What I'm about to tell you is between you, me, and the sheriff," Jim said. "I'm not threatening you, but I'm willing to kill to maintain the confidentiality of what I'm about to tell you. This is strictly for your ears only."

"That sounds like a threat," Ford said, bristling.

"Yeah, it *is* a fucking threat," Jim said. "But hear me out."

Ford and Deel were both silent, watching him.

"I have a group. We have the resources to get through this winter. I'm not talking about a life of luxury but I am talking about surviving. I'm personally inviting you two, the sheriff, and his family to come join us. There's an empty home for them and I know of a mobile home you two can share. Both have wood stoves and access to water. You understand, though, that if you don't accept my invitation then I have to ask that you don't mention it to anyone."

The two deputies stared at each other, then back at Jim.

"Why would you invite all of us to move back there with you?" Ford asked.

"I'm not giving up the tanker and I'm not giving up our supplies," Jim said. "If those cops come back, it's going to turn into a war. They've got a lot of guns but we do too. We also have a lot of women and children. I don't want anyone injured or killed. I just want to be left alone."

"I'm not sure I'm willing to kill cops in exchange for food and a place to live," Deel said.

"I'm not asking you to kill cops," Jim said. "It's like we talked about earlier. The sheriff's presence may deter some of those other cops who are supporting Barnes. If they find the sheriff is on our side, they may not be so willing to start killing us indiscriminately."

Ford was staring off into the distance now, lost in thought. He turned back to Jim slowly. "Let's go talk to the sheriff."

"I'll follow you in my truck," Jim said.

CHAPTER TWENTY-SEVEN

Jim

Jim followed the Ford Escape across several desolate side streets, then on a narrow highway out of town toward Crow Town Mountain. When they hit the base of the small mountain they turned off into a farming community. After a couple of miles on the twisty back road, they turned onto a farm and eased across a sagging cattle guard that rattled beneath their vehicles.

A tall, thin man stood by a poorly-built construction of old lumber and used wire. He appeared to be trying to cobble together a pen of some sort, though it seemed unlikely that it could even hold back the frailest of the animal kingdom. From the amount of farming equipment scattered around and the size of the structures, Jim could tell that this farm had once been the pride of an agricultural family.

It had clearly fallen into disrepair in the hands of the current generation. Clusters of barns and sheds sagged sideways like hump-shouldered old men gathered to tell their lies. Fruit trees stood gnarled and overgrown, broken limbs trailing the ground like dogs pulling along their fractured hind legs. Fields scratched from the earth by horse-drawn plow were returning to forest and would not turn back without a fight. The farm told the story of a man who'd inherited a farm he didn't want but could never escape, bound to it by the blood of the dead relatives buried in its soil.

The man whom Jim recognized to be the sheriff wore faded work clothes but carried his duty pistol. Jim parked behind the Escape, got out, and followed the other men. The sheriff did not seem to be very pleased to have visitors but Jim felt the same way when people showed up at his house. He could relate to this man and wasn't offended by the reception.

"Who the hell is that?" Sheriff Scott asked, nodding in Jim's direction.

Ford took the lead. "One of the men we pulled over yesterday. I think you need to hear what he has to say."

The sheriff sighed. "I guess I might as well since he's already here." He turned around and pitched his hammer underhanded toward his project.

Jim suspected that had the hammer struck the pen, it would have totally collapsed. "That some kind of pen?" he asked.

"I was trying to make a pen for some rabbits and chickens," Sheriff Scott said. "I traded for them this morning. I'm hoping they might put some food on the table. I'm embarrassed to say that we weren't as prepared for this kind of thing as we should have been. An ice storm we could handle. This is like the ice storm that just won't end."

"No one is ever as prepared as they'd like," Jim said.

"We pretty much weren't prepared at all," the sheriff admitted. "We took most of our meals in town anymore. With the hours I kept, my family would meet me in town for dinner and I'd go back to work afterward. They'd come back home without me. Pretty shitty life now that I think about it."

"I might be in a position to help," Jim said.

Sheriff Scott raised an eyebrow at him dubiously, as if he'd heard this line before. He knew that nothing came without a price.

"I live in the far end of the valley on the back side of town," Jim said. "One of my neighbors, Henry, had a son that worked in your 911 operations center."

"David," the sheriff said. "I remember him. Haven't heard from him a while."

"You won't," Jim replied. "One of those inmates you turned out of the jail killed David and both his parents."

Sheriff Scott flinched, stung by the remark. Jim fully intended the remark to have that effect. Releasing those inmates was a stupid move and almost got members of Jim's family killed.

"We didn't just turn everyone out," the sheriff said. "We made the hard calls on some of the more violent people. We took steps to make sure they'd never walk the streets again. It wasn't an easy thing to do. My conscience is still burdened by it."

"You made the wrong call with that one," Jim said. "He almost killed my mother and son too, before I put a bullet in his head." Jim was curious if his admission at murdering the ex-convict would prompt any reaction but there was none.

"Well, if that's what you're here to talk about, you're wasting your breath," Sheriff Scott said. "It's done now and you can just join the long list of people who think I'm doing a shitty job. If the world ever gets back to normal you can vote my ass out. I'm praying for the day."

"That's not what I'm here to talk about," Jim said. "I'm sorry I got sidetracked. The reason I'm here is that we had a run-in last night with a group of cops that I assume come from the superstore. A Deputy Barnes?"

Ford nodded. "He's one of them. He's in charge of that bunch."

"He's a son-of-a-bitch is what he is," the sheriff spat. "He never was a good cop. I should have fired him years ago."

"We turned him and his men away at gunpoint," Jim said. "I expect he'll be back. They were in UTVs and there were about six or seven of them, though I couldn't be sure in the dark. They all seemed to have his back."

"He stole those UTVs from the department," Ford said. "That and a bunch of other stuff. That's gear that's supposed to be used for enforcing the law, not breaking it."

"We've fought off a lot of men," Jim said. "Each time, we take the risk that we're going to lose people we love. Fighting these men would be bad. I worry about the risks."

The sheriff shook his head in disgust. Not just at what Jim was telling him, but at the whole sorry state of the world. "Well, if you expect me and my last two deputies to come over there and save the day for you then you're shit out of luck," the sheriff said. "I can barely feed my family and that's pretty much all I care about right now. I don't care about you, I don't care about Barnes, and I don't care about this county. The only things I care about in this world are in that house back there."

Jim smiled at the sheriff's singlemindedness. It was much like his own. "Then we speak the same language. And no, I'm not here to ask you to fight our fight for us. Someone just gave me the idea that your presence might shake some of the other men with Barnes. They might not be so quick to shoot if they knew another cop could be on the receiving end."

"I'm not in the private security business either." The sheriff shook his head in disgust and turned to walk off. "Your fight, your problem. Now I got work to do."

"They want us to move into the valley with them," Deel called after the sheriff. "They're offering housing and food. You can bring your family."

The sheriff froze in his tracks for a moment, then turned around skeptically and regarded Jim. Then he turned his eyes on his men. "You all are buying his bullshit?"

"I think he's being honest with us," Ford said. "What he's saying matches up with what the old man told us yesterday."

"Which you manipulated him into telling you," Jim said accusingly.

Ford shrugged. "It's part of the job."

"Who's in this valley of yours?" Sheriff Scott asked.

"Some of the people who lived there originally and weren't run off, like the Wimmers. A few people from work. I tried to make it alone originally, but it was hard without having people around I could trust. One man can't guard a place all the time *and* raise food *and* fix everything that breaks. You have to have help. We've all formed a group and we look after each other. We try to keep our neighborhood safe, whatever it takes. Picture a neighborhood watch on steroids."

"I guess having a fucking tanker of fuel helps, doesn't it?" the sheriff said. He said it with an edge to his voice as if Jim had no right to keep such a resource to himself.

"That's apparently a hard secret to keep," Jim said. He felt no need to explain or defend how he'd come to have that resource.

"And what would our role in this group be?" the sheriff asked. "We have to start working for you? We the new hired guns?"

"No, nothing like that," Jim said. "We're all just individual families working together. We share guard and security details because it's less of a burden if you have several people sharing it. Some of us work together more than others but it's just because we get along. There're no rules, really. I don't like a lot of rules."

The sheriff smiled. "You and I might get along after all."

"Don't get ahead of yourself," Jim said. "I can be a dick sometimes."

"I'll need to talk to my family," the sheriff said.

"How long you need?" Jim asked. "You need me to come back later?"

"I'll do it right now. You guys sit tight. You'll probably have your answer in a few minutes."

Jim and the deputies stood around awkwardly while Sheriff Scott was inside his house. They discussed the weather and if the coloration of caterpillars had indicated what was in store for them this winter. The men asked about the valley and what other families lived there. The deputies recounted their visits to the valley over the years and what trouble had brought them there.

In a few minutes the screen door banged again and the sheriff was back with them. He walked up to Jim, his face giving away nothing. The sheriff regarded Jim for a moment as if making some final assessment.

"We're going to take you up on your offer," the sheriff said.

Jim nodded. "I think you're making the right choice."

"I have no choice," the sheriff said. "My family is on borrowed time."

"When do you want to leave?" Jim asked.

"My wife is ready to leave now," the sheriff admitted. "She thinks we're going to die here in this house. She thinks the children are going to starve. My mother had a stroke. It's been hard taking care of her without help."

Jim nodded with understanding. "My truck is empty," he said. "You can pack stuff in it. Do you still have a running vehicle?"

Sheriff Scott nodded. "My department Tahoe still has fuel. We'll pack it full first. It may take an hour or so to get everything gathered up." The sheriff turned and headed off toward the house.

"Can I be of any help?" Jim asked. "I can at least carry loads."

"Sure," the sheriff said without even turning around.

Jim looked at the deputies. "Are you all still interested in coming along?"

Both men nodded.

"Then go pack," Jim said. "We'll meet you at the 911 center when we've got everything loaded."

CHAPTER TWENTY-EIGHT

Jim

Two hours later Jim pulled into the 911 center, his truck jammed full of items belonging to the sheriff's family. The sheriff led the way, his own vehicle packed with gear, children, a nervous looking wife, and his frail mother. While his wife may have wanted to escape their barren farm, she didn't seem comfortable not knowing what lay ahead of them. Jim hoped that the other wives might pitch in and help her unpack, which would do a lot to dispel some of her anxiety. The sheriff's mother, disabled by a recent stroke, lay propped up in the back seat. Her face was pale and drawn, her eyes accepting the events of the day with the resolution possessed by one who has already experienced very bad things and has no expectation that life will get better.

Deputies Deel and Ford were waiting on them. They had two police vehicles this time – the Ford Escape and an older Chevy Blazer with sheriff's department markings. Both vehicles were packed to the point of having gear tied onto the top.

Jim rolled down the window and called out, "You guys ready to go?"

Ford and Deel looked at each other, shrugged, and went to their respective vehicles.

The sheriff whipped his vehicle around until his driver's window was aligned with Jim's. "Which way we going?"

"I'm going to drive right through town," Jim said. "

"To send a message?" the sheriff asked.

Jim nodded.

"What if it provokes a reaction?"

"I can't control what other people do."

"I guess you're keeping a weapon handy?"

"Always," Jim said.

The sheriff nodded. "Lead the way."

"We'll have to take a diversion onto a farm road before we get to the valley, so don't be surprised when I turn off through the creek," Jim said. "The main road was damaged."

"Damaged?" the sheriff asked. "How?"

"No idea."

Jim backed his vehicle around and shot out of the parking lot, setting a quick pace. He chided himself for habitually using a signal light to turn from one empty road onto another but he did have a cop behind him. He ran a dead stoplight where the secondary road joined Main Street and continued through town.

Some people came into their yards to watch, a moving vehicle having quickly become a novelty. A woman tried to run toward the convoy of vehicles, her intentions unclear. She stumbled and collapsed in her yard. A man shuffled up one lane of the road, a garbage bag in his hand, sagging with some small item. He didn't move for their vehicles and they swerved around him.

In one yard, two bodies lay covered with sheets, the corners weighted down with old bricks. In another, a deer carcass hung from a tree beside a tire swing. The muscles had been crudely hacked into cuts of meat, leaving much to waste. The organs were still present and strands of intestine hung from the cavity like bluish garland. Flies formed a dark and moving crust on the exposed flesh.

Businesses along the street had all been looted. Few windows had escaped the stones of the angry and starving. Trash and discarded packaging, flattened by feet and weather, was everywhere. There was so much debris that the four lanes of traffic in this section of town were reduced to one passable lane. Jim removed his pistol from its retention holster and kept it in his hand, resting on the center console of the truck. He expected any minute that a crowd armed with sticks and rocks would surge from an alley and surround his truck like in some futuristic movie.

As he passed the courthouse, Jim noticed that the flag had been taken down and re-hung upside down. The windows of the courthouse had been shattered and papers scattered everywhere. It looked as if people may have been taking the opportunity to try and expunge their court or tax records in hopes that the electronic version might not be accessible again. It was also possible that the scattered papers were just the products of bored teens and done with no intention at all other than spreading mischief.

Past the courthouse was a cluster of older buildings that had all been remodeled into law offices. Someone had apparently seen this lawless period as a time to settle scores against perceived injustices. All that remained of the various offices were scorched foundations and the occasional brick wall precariously balanced against collapse.

Two miles later, they were passing the shopping center with the superstore. Their drive took them on the frontage road along the parking lot. Jim slowed a little, actually wanting the attention of the residents. He wanted them to see what was happening, wanted them to know that he'd upped the ante and an attack on him would also now be an attack on one of their own. He knew there were people inside who didn't care, but he hoped that there were at least some who *would*. Every one of them inside there who might question what they were doing and choose not to be involved would be one less person trying to kill him; one less person *he* would have to try to kill.

Jim caught the flash of a scope on the roof and knew they were being glassed. He also knew it was an amateur sniper who didn't understand what a killflash was, which would have prevented that reflection off his optic. A few people were milling around outside the main doors. A grill was smoking and a man he recognized from the Mexican restaurant was cooking. There was still a wall of parked cars blocking off most of the parking lot. Jim noticed a lot of broken windows in those cars now.

In seconds, they were past the shopping center and less than a mile from where they'd dynamited a chunk out of the road. Jim knew the road a little better than the men following him and had gotten ahead. The cops also seemed to drive slower than he did when passing by the superstore. Perhaps they hadn't seen what their former colleagues had constructed there.

Just before the point where he would turn left through the creek, Jim rounded a curve and found a police car blocking the road. He couldn't get past it to reach his turn. He checked his rearview to see if the sheriff and the two deputies had caught up with him but he couldn't see through the items packed into the back of his truck. He checked his side mirror and found the road behind him to be empty.

His eyes going back to what was ahead of him, Jim found one man sitting in the cop car. He wasn't wearing any uniform but he had on the sunglasses. Cop sunglasses. The man made no effort to get out. Jim flipped his truck into four wheel drive. The three-quarter ton diesel truck would push the small car out of the road easily. Hell, he could probably drive overtop of it if he wanted but decided he'd wait and see what the sheriff thought. He didn't want to start this partnership out on the wrong foot.

It seemed longer but it was probably less than fifteen seconds before the sheriff and the two deputy vehicles rolled in behind him. Jim threw his driver's door open and got out. He knew the door provided no ballistic protection but it at least provided some conceal-ment while he stood waiting on the other men. Deel was the first to reach him, though his vehicle was the last in line. The sheriff had not gotten out of his Tahoe yet and Ford stood at his window talking with him.

"I don't think we should sit and powwow too long," Jim said. "This could be a trap."

Deel dismissed him. "Bullshit," he said. "They're not going to do anything with the sheriff here." Deel went around to the front of Jim's truck and stared at the other cop who sat in his car about twenty yards away.

Jim heard a door shut behind him and saw that the sheriff had gotten out of the Tahoe and was approaching with Ford.

"Hell, that's Deputy Browning," Deel said. "He rode with me when he was training."

Deel stalked off toward the car.

"Get back here!" Jim said.

He saw the man in the car raise his radio to his mouth and talk into it.

"What the hell is this?" the sheriff asked.

The sheriff and Ford bypassed Jim's door and walked toward the patrol car. They were barely past Jim's bumper when two quick shots rang out. Deel flinched, grabbed his midsection, and crumpled to the ground.

The sheriff threw a hand out and screamed. "NOOOO!"

The engine in the patrol car roared to life. Jim drew his weapon just as Ford drew his. Ford began firing through the window of the patrol car. Jim hopped onto the running board of his truck, dumping more rounds into the driver. The shots must have had some effect because the driver's foot slipped off the brake and the car began rolling slowly forward.

Ford and Jim quit firing. The car eased toward them, then veered to Jim's left, getting a tire stuck in the ditch and blocking most of the road.

"He probably called for backup!" Jim shouted. "We have to get out of here *now!*"

Ford ran and checked the driver. "He's dead!"

The sheriff was at Deel's side, feeling for a pulse.

"There's no time!" Jim yelled. "We're not even a minute away from the shopping center. Throw him in my truck!"

Jim pulled his passenger door open while Ford and Sheriff Scott dragged the unconscious and heavily bleeding man to his truck. He helped them heave the dead weight into the vehicle and then ran back to the driver's side. If he took off, maybe they would get the picture and follow him. They seemed to be in shock at the loss of a friend. They weren't used to these things. They were rural cops, not soldiers, not patrolmen from cities where gunfights were common. Jim could understand their feeling but knew that there was no time for it now or they'd be carrying more than one dead body out of there.

The cruiser blocked a portion of the road. Jim eased into it, using his four-wheel drive and solid steel winch bumper to push the car to the side. When it was out of the way, he hit the accelerator, dropping over the embankment and fording the creek. On the opposite side, he opened the first of several gates and pulled through. The gate wouldn't stop any determined vehicle so there was no point in waiting around to close it. He kept going, all four wheels spinning on the grassy road.

He looked in his side mirror and saw the other vehicles behind him, easing through the creek and up onto the bank. Deel's vehicle was in the very back and would provide a temporary roadblock but not for long. The keys were probably still in it. Thinking of the man's vehicle caused him to look over at his passenger. Blood filled the seat and the plastic floor mat.

Jim put his hand on the man's neck. There was no pulse.

CHAPTER TWENTY-NINE

Barnes

Five vehicles shot out of the shopping center at dangerously high speeds, Barnes in the lead. In less than a minute, he rounded a blind curve and found Deel's blazer blocking the road. He slammed on the brakes and tried to skirt around it but one wheel slipped into a deep ditch hidden by the overgrown weeds. Barnes slammed the steering wheel, cursed, and threw open his door. He slid out of the cruiser, his gun drawn.

More vehicles fell in behind him and he heard doors opening, the sound of running feet. Past Deel's abandoned vehicle, he found Browning dead in his car. The windshield was spider-webbed from multiple rounds, the man's face an unrecognizable pulp.

"Son of a bitch!" Barnes hissed.

The sound of a distant engine caught his attention and Barnes looked up just in time to see Ford's vehicle disappear over a hill.

"Should we go after them?" Sword asked.

Barnes' face was red, his heart pounding. "Not yet," he said.

"But they killed Browning!" Sword said. "I never imagined the sheriff would murder one of his own deputies."

Barnes knew there was probably more to the story of why Browning was dead but that didn't matter. What mattered was that these men would be more loyal to him if they thought they couldn't trust the sheriff anymore. Having them lose faith in the sheriff could only help Barnes.

"Let's wait," Barnes said. "They're probably expecting us to charge after them. We need to pick a better time, when their guard is down."

"I can't tell Browning's wife about this," Sword said, emotion rising in his voice. "She's pregnant. "

"I'll tell her," Barnes said. "Then she has to pack her shit and get out."

Sword looked at his boss, stunned.

"She's only there because of Browning. If he's not there, she's just a drain on resources," Barnes explained. "I'm sure she's got family somewhere."

"People aren't going to like that," Sword said.

"Anyone who doesn't like it can come see me," Barnes said, "on *their* way out."

CHAPTER THIRTY

Alice

They day after they buried half their family, Alice and Charlie accomplished very little. They kept a haphazard watch over the farm, both of them silently hoping that someone would stray onto their property. They wanted to kill someone. They wanted to avenge Pat's and Terry's deaths, even though there was no one to blame. No murder would ease their hearts, but both silently wanted to try.

Except for feeding the remaining animals, they spent most of the day sorting their possessions into piles. There were things they would take with them, things they would bury on the farm, and things that didn't matter to them. They would take what guns and ammunition they could, but some would have to be cached. It was the same with clothing, farm tools, kitchen stuff, and family mementos.

They packed storage totes with photo albums and family photos. When they were full, the used duct tape to seal them tight. They lowered these into the abandoned cistern and stacked them. Kitchen goods were placed in garbage bags and stacked on top of the storage totes. Unsure of how else to store them, Charlie used lithium grease from the barn to coat the weapons they couldn't take with them, then wrapped them in plastic. Adding a layer of tape, he stored those in the cistern as well.

"Are we taking the livestock?"

Alice was sorting clothes, deciding what to take and what to store. "I had thought we might but I think it will just slow us down," she said. "I don't want to die for a pig."

"We can turn them out in the back pasture," Charlie said. "It's fenced and you can't see it from the road. Maybe they'll be there when we come back. Maybe they'll have babies and there will be more of them when we come back." Charlie swallowed. "We will be coming back, won't we?"

Alice was folding a flannel shirt. It had been her dad's. She was taking it with her, both for warmth and for emotional support. "I would say so. Things will get back to normal one day."

"Can we live here?" he asked. "I like this place better than our old house."

"Sure," she said. "It's practically yours now anyway."

"Really?"

Alice nodded.

Charlie looked around, seeing it all differently now. "When are we leaving?"

"I had hoped tomorrow," she said. "I don't know if we'll be ready or not."

CHAPTER THIRTY-ONE

Randi

When Randi first moved her family from her parents' home to Jim's valley, the trip over had taken longer because of her grandchildren. With nothing to slow them down but old bones and soft posteriors, Randi and Buddy made good time on horseback. Randi also had the opportunity to correct a few navigational mistakes she'd made on the first trip that caused her to add miles and lose time.

Despite the grim nature of the journey, it was a beautiful day to travel through the country. The sky was clear and the first leaves were beginning to turn yellow and drop. No one mowed anymore and previously shorn patches of ground were returning to wild. It was as peaceful a day as she ever remembered. It was the perfect preamble to the mission she had planned. When she returned this way, she hoped to do so with the blood of her enemy beneath her fingernails and a burden lifted from her heart.

They reached the shell of her family's old home by late afternoon. She thought she'd come to terms with much of what had happened. At least it felt like she had while living in the valley so far away from the source of her pain. Yet returning here reopened the wound in the most violent of ways. It was like the tearing away of a bandage glued to a wound with blood and fluid. Upon sight of her home, a sob forced its way from her and she relived the whole experience in a flash. She saw the worst day of her life running before her eyes in a rapid loop that she could not turn away from.

Buddy, no stranger to pain and loss, allowed her the dignity of her grief. When the worst of it subsided, she looked at him. He took the cue and rode alongside her, throwing an arm over her. She cried into his shoulder for a long time, until the horses shifted, forcing them apart.

"We can sleep in the barn," she said.

While Buddy rode over to it and tied his horse off, Randi went to the spot where they'd buried her parents. She slid from the horse and tied it to a fence post. She had cigarettes again from the bounty found in the Glenwall trailers. She lit one, finding a small degree of peace in the ritual. It was too soon after their deaths for grass to have begun growing on the graves. In a yard already scarred by the burned-out shell of her home, the dirt patch that marked their graves was yet another reminder of why she was here.

She settled into a thick patch of grass at the edge of the graves and let flow what tears still needed to come. When she ran out, she talked to her parents and told them where they were now and how their children, grandchildren, and great-grandchildren were doing. She told them she was sorry about not finding her brother's body but that she hoped he was with them now. She apologized for what she was about to do because she knew they wouldn't approve of her putting herself at risk. She reminded them that if they understood her at all, they would understand why she had to do it.

When she was done, she walked her horse to the barn and tied it alongside Buddy's. She found an upright bucket that had filled with rainwater, put it in front of the horses, and let them take turns drinking. When they'd emptied it, she went to the spring and brought back more.

Hearing the sounds of life returning to the mountain farm, a chicken came from the woods, perhaps hoping someone had finally returned with grain for it and that the chicken's days of scrounging for bugs were over. Randi stared at the bird for a moment before snatching it up and wringing its neck with a rubbery snap. She looked over at Buddy and found him staring at her wide-eyed.

"Something wrong?" she asked.

"No," he said. "I guess for some reason I just thought you were going to pet it."

"I'm hungry. I need to eat a chicken more than I need to love on it."

Buddy shrugged. "Me too."

Randi plucked the bird while Buddy built a small fire. The feathers didn't come loose as easily without having scalded the chicken but Randi didn't care. It occupied her mind. When she was done, they singed the remaining feathers off in the fire. Buddy gutted the bird, stuck it in a pot of water, and hung it over the fire.

"How far is that girl's house from here?" Buddy asked.

"Their land joins up to the back of our place," she said. "Probably takes thirty minutes of walking through the woods to get to their house. It's rough ground."

"She got other kin in the area?"

Randi nodded. "Some. She's also got a bunch of druggie friends that she might take up with."

"We need to figure out if she's still in her house or moved in with someone else. That's the first step."

Randi watched the fire. "I'd like to see her spitted over my camp-fire," she said. "I'd like to burn her alive."

"We'll see what opportunities present themselves," Buddy said. "You'll just have to keep yourself open to what you can get away with and not expose yourself to undue risk."

Randi scrounged around in the garden and found a few remaining potatoes, which they sliced and threw in the pot with the chicken. When it was done, Buddy sliced off some of the meat and put it on a plate with the potatoes. While they ate, Buddy described to Randi some of the basics of observing a target. His training had been in the jungles of Vietnam but he felt it was still relevant to the jungles of the central Appalachian Mountains.

"Can we start tonight?" Randi asked. "I hate to be this close and not be doing something."

Buddy shook his head. "I'd prefer we didn't. If we go at first light, we can learn the path. We can clear it of sticks so stepping on them doesn't give our position away. Then we can find our hide. Once we've established the hide and learned the trail, going at night won't be a problem. We'd be stumbling blind tonight."

The light faded around them, color leaving the world. Birds changed shifts, the day birds tagging out and going home, leaving their night brethren to send their strange sounds out into the darkness. The small fire crackled and the pair stared at it, each lost in their own thoughts.

"We should turn in," Buddy said. "I'll get us up before dawn. We'll head out then."

Randi took up a bucket of horse water and tilted it over the fire. It hissed and popped, faded, and left them in darkness. The two clicked on their headlamps and made their way to the hayloft.

CHAPTER THIRTY-TWO

The Valley

Jim drove like a madman over the short distance between the creek and the gate that entered his property. The road was really just a path through the field. It was full of ruts, rocks, and bumps. Jim drove way too fast, wanting to get to his home and arm up in case he was being followed by Barnes and his men. He didn't have to worry about Deel at this point. He was pretty sure nothing could be done for him. Even if the guy still had a pulse he needed emergency surgery and that wasn't happening.

He pulled his radio out of his vest. "Pete!" he said, ignoring any attempt at call signs.

"Yes, Dad?" came the reply.

"We're coming in hot, little buddy. I've got the sheriff with me and a deputy named Ford behind him. I need someone to open the gate for us. I also need you guys to arm up in case the bad cops are following us."

"Got it," Pete replied. *"I reopened Outpost Pete while you were gone. I'm up there and on the rifle."*

"I'm on the gate, Jim," Pops said. *"I'm heading there now."*

"Gary, you hearing any of this?" Jim asked into the radio.

"Affirmative," Gary replied.

"You guys be on guard," Jim said. "This went south in a big way."

Jim knew Gary would want to know what that meant but now wasn't the time.

"Will do," Gary said.

Jim came within sight of the gate and Pops was there holding it open. Jim shot through it, barely slowing down. Pops kept it open and the other sheriff's department vehicles pulled through behind Jim's truck. Pops shut the gate and relocked it, tucking the key in its hiding place under a rock.

They kept up their speed until they reached Jim's house. When Jim got there, he slid to a stop on his lawn, springing out the door of his vehicle. He ran around to the passenger door and flung it open. Deel's body sagged toward him and Jim caught it, lowering the man to the ground and stretching him out. The round had caught him below his body armor, obviously hitting an artery. There were massive amounts of blood soaking the man's shirt and pants. He didn't have a chance. Regardless, Jim felt again for a pulse.

There was none.

He rested his hands on his thighs, his head sagging. Deel's attitude had pissed him off the other day but he'd come to like the man. He was smarter than Ford and cool-headed. Jim heard the other vehicles stop, doors opening. He paid them no attention until he was blindsided, a body slamming into him and knocking him over. His head struck the open truck door.

Jim grunted from the impact, too stunned to even curse as he went down. Then a fist connected with his head before he could even piece together what was happening. Jim's eyes focused and he saw it was the sheriff, his face a bright red mask of fury.

"You son-of-a-bitch, what the hell did you drag my family into!" the sheriff said, spit flying into Jim's face.

Jim was still reeling from the blows to his head. His first thought was to go for his gun but it was mounted to the vest and he couldn't reach it with the man sitting on him. The sheriff drew back for another blow but Jim got a hand free and throat-punched the man. The sheriff's eyes bugged out and he grabbed at his throat with both hands, his breath not coming. He started to fall backward and Jim helped him with a stiff shove.

The sheriff's wife bolted from the Tahoe and dropped to her husband's side, calling his name over and over. Staggering to his feet, Jim moved toward the sheriff, actually planning on checking his well-being but he didn't make it.

"Freeze!" It was Ford and he had his service weapon leveled at Jim.

Jim did freeze and in the silence heard the click of a revolver's hammer being drawn back. It was not Ford's gun. Jim and Ford both looked sideways to see Pops training a shiny magnum revolver at the deputy. The hammer was cocked, his finger on the trigger. Ford was a hair away from dying too.

"You sure you're up to this, old man?" Ford spat at Pops.

"I haven't shot anyone during this whole mess," Pops said. "I kind of feel like I'm not pulling my weight. I've got catching up to do."

In the midst of their standoff, Ellen stepped out onto the porch, an AR levelled at the deputy. A red laser beam bounced on Ford's brown shirt. "Pete radioed me. He's got his .270 and he has a clear head shot on the deputy."

Ford screwed his mouth up in anger. He was mumbling to himself, unsure of what to do.

A gasp from the ground interrupted them, the sheriff finally sucking in a lungful of air. His wife was still stroking his hair and repeating his name. The sheriff began coughing violently.

"Put your gun down, Ford," Jim said. "You all chose to come out here. Deel confronted that man on his own. I told him not to go. He didn't die at my hands. He died from trusting one of you, from trusting another deputy."

Ford angrily shoved his Smith & Wesson into his holster. "I still say his death is on you."

Jim probed his swelling cheek. That sheriff packed a punch. "Think what you want, but it doesn't matter either way now. We're on the wrong side of a bad cop and we need to figure this out before someone else gets hurt."

"Jim, a little hospitality goes a long way," Ellen spoke up. "How about we show them to the houses where they're going to be staying? If they want, we'll help them unpack. Then everyone can rest a little bit and cool off. You folks can come back here for dinner tonight if we can eat together without guns coming out."

The sheriff's wife looked at her coughing husband with uncertainty. She looked like she was ready to jump back in the vehicle and go back home. The sheriff couldn't speak but he met his wife's eyes and nodded.

Jim stepped toward the sheriff and reached down to grab his hand but Ford pushed him to the side. It was an assertive but not necessarily aggressive gesture.

"He don't need your help," Ford grumbled. "You're the reason he can't stand up on his own anyway."

"Did you miss the part where he jumped me?" Jim said in his own defense. "Or the part where he punched me?"

Ford didn't respond. He helped his boss toward the passenger seat of the Tahoe and the sheriff's wife slipped behind the wheel.

"Pops, you and Nana stay with Pete and Ariel," Ellen said. "Radio us if you see anything unusual."

"Will do," Pops said, only then lowering the hammer on the revolver and tucking it back in the pocket of his vest.

"I can show them to their house," Jim said, rubbing his temple.

"No," Ellen replied. "I'll show them to their house. You and the other deputy there can give your friend a decent burial."

Jim looked at Deel's body, realizing that in all the chaos he'd forgotten the dead body lying in their midst. He nodded groggily.

"Not sure you're fit to drive anyway," Ellen said. "You look a little addled."

CHAPTER THIRTY-THREE

Randi

Randi had a hard time going to sleep there in the loft, dropped back into the midst of her old life and the loss that was still too fresh. She must have eventually dropped off, because she was dead to the world when Buddy shook her awake. She jerked up, disoriented and briefly terrified, but calmed at the sound of his voice. Things came back to her.

In the light of his headlamp, Buddy removed two sets of camouflage clothing from his pack. They were for turkey hunting and blended well with the local foliage. Hunting turkeys required more stealth and invisibility than hunting people, who were the least observant and situationally-aware animals. When Buddy had changed into his clothes and Randi had slipped into her coveralls, Buddy smudged their faces with charcoal from the remnants of their fire.

They readied their weapons and gear. Buddy handed a chunk of deer jerky to Randi. "Eat."

"I can do that on the trail," she said, starting to shove it in her pocket.

"If you're eating on the trail, you're not ready to fight. A hand is occupied and you're not fully paying attention. If you eat in the hide, the food has an even better chance of drawing animals to us."

Randi shoved the jerky in her mouth and started chewing. She was carrying a pump shotgun Buddy had lent her. Buddy was carrying his lever-action rifle with iron sights. They were a plain-talking, plain-shooting, low-tech hit squad. Buddy slung on his pack and began taping a Gerber Mark II to the shoulder strap with black electrician's tape. The knife hung upside down and would be easy to reach.

"That's a big knife," Randi said.

"I got it in Vietnam," Buddy said. "Lots of the men carried them. I haven't touched it since the war except to oil it occasionally and check the edge. It's not something you use for cutting the twine on a bale of hay. Knife like this only has one purpose really."

"That why you're wearing it now?"

He nodded somberly. "You come to kill, you bring the tools for killing."

They started off, Randi in the lead. She made no great effort toward silence until they reached the edge of her family's property. At that point, she began to draw on the methods Buddy had mentioned to her. She began to watch every step for where her foot would land and what would happen when it did. Would she kick a rock? Snap a twig? Was there something there that would make her stumble? Walking in this manner took much longer.

"You're not walking, you're stalking," Buddy had said. "Once a noise is made, you can't take it back."

It occurred to Randi that they timed this right. In another month, they would not have been able to walk this path without the crackling of dry leaves under their feet. For now, the poplars and oaks still carried their leaves but they would fall soon. After that, the cold nights would come and life would become harder for all of them. Randi needed to get this done before then. She could not spend the winter in a quiet house, staring at the fire and thinking of her failure to avenge her family.

As day broke they emerged on the hill above the Cross family home. It was quiet, but the smell of smoke hung in the air. It appeared someone was there and had built a fire last night. It had died down and the smell was the remnant of a banked fire in a woodstove.

Buddy noticed a fallen cedar tree and pointed them in that direction. The cedar tree had been down for some time, the needles brown, and strands of bark hanging loose in delicate shreds. They made their way in that direction and eased down in the shelter of the tree. It provided a blind that concealed them from the house while allowing them to monitor it. In their camouflage, it was unlikely anyone would have been able to detect them until they tripped over them.

They made themselves as comfortable as they could and they settled in for a day of watching. For the first three hours they saw nothing. Then a door opened and a scruffy man staggered out onto the porch. He wore jeans and a sleeveless t-shirt that said *Life Ain't Easy When You're Fat and Greasy*. He was shoeless and walked to the edge of the porch, unzipping his pants and relieving himself into the grassless yard.

After he went back inside, there was nothing for another half-hour. Then a woman came out and picked her way through the trash-strewn yard to the outhouse. Buddy looked expectantly at Randi, his eyes full of the question. Randi looked back at him and nodded.

They watched until the sun was directly overhead. No one else ever came outside. After another hour of sitting, Buddy tapped Randi on the shoulder and gestured with his hand that they should leave.

He leaned close and spoke into her ear. "Follow me. Stay in the shadows. Watch where you step, and don't move too fast."

She nodded and began stretching her stiff muscles. After so long in one spot, even standing was awkward but she did her best to do it without making any noise. When she was on her feet, Buddy headed out. He moved so naturally through the woods that she could easily imagine him as a younger man doing this in foreign jungles.

They crept in silence, taking a step and listening. At each step they examined their next footfall, looking for anything that might crackle or give them away. In the silence of the hills sound carried a long way. The crack of a limb, the scuffing of leaves, was an unnatural occurrence and drew the ear. They'd gone a great distance before Buddy dared speak.

"I think it's just the two of them. If no one came out to pee, I would assume they might be using slop jars. Since two came outside that makes me think that everyone would be coming outside to relieve themselves. Since no one else came, I would venture to guess it's just the two of them."

Randi nodded. "Any thoughts?"

Buddy walked in silence for a moment, grinding through scenarios.

"I think I'll have to kill the man," he finally said. "He's a big old boy. I don't reckon he'd stand by and let it happen. He's going to have to die first. Then you can do what you need to do."

"I want you to help me think of a way to do it," Randi said. "I want it to be personal. I want her to see me doing it. I want her to know who killed her."

"I'll study on it," Buddy said.

CHAPTER THIRTY-FOUR

The Valley

Later that evening, after the sheriff and his family had settled into their new home, Ellen convinced them to return for dinner. Even Ford came back after moving into a mobile home on a private lot. Both homes had woodstoves, and both had access to spring water which could be gravity-fed into the house with a little work. That would allow them to continue using the inside bathrooms throughout the winter. It was as comfortable and convenient accommodations as anyone might expect to have under the current circumstances, unless they had access to solar power.

The sheriff, with his wife and children, pulled his Tahoe into Jim's driveway and parked by the house. He was hesitant to go in after the episode earlier, standing in the driveway shifting awkwardly from foot to foot and looking for an excuse not to go inside.

"You coming?" his wife asked. Her name was Holly and she was a serious woman. With her husband gone much of the time, she'd had to run the show at home. It required structure and planning, at least to the extent that the mother of small children can plan things.

The sheriff looked around desperately, trying to find an excuse to linger. He heard the sound of an engine and saw Ford's vehicle approaching. "You go ahead," he said with relief. "I'll wait on Ford."

Holly raised an eyebrow at him but went on. She was climbing the porch steps when the door opened and Ellen came out. Ellen hugged her and guided her inside the house.

"You get your mother settled in?"

The sheriff jumped. He hadn't heard anyone come out. He found Jim standing on the porch. Jim had given up the load vest but still wore a sidearm.

"She was asleep when we left," the sheriff said. "I hate to admit it but it's kind of a waiting game with her now. She can't speak, can't feed herself, and can't go to the toilet. She's total care."

"How long since she had the stroke?" Jim asked.

"A couple of months ago."

"And you've been taking care of her the whole time?" Jim asked. "That's a big commitment."

The sheriff shrugged. "I wish I could claim credit for being that good of a son. Actually, she was in a nursing home until the lights went out. I went by to check on her and found most of the patients abandoned. The staff had gone home to be with their families. I moved Mom out and the department tried to get as many of the folks back to family as they could. Not all the families were so eager to have their elderly relatives coming back to them under the current conditions. Most of the families could barely take care of their own needs. I didn't know what else to do."

"I can imagine that was a tough sight," Jim said. "We have a nurse. She may be of some help to you. She's not around right now. She's off... taking care of some personal business." Jim didn't feel a need to mention she left with the intention of committing a murder.

"I appreciate that. I'll talk to her when she returns."

Ford pulled in and killed his engine. He got out and looked at the other two men. "I hope you all weren't waiting on me to show up before you started fighting again."

The sheriff looked sheepish. "No, I think we're good for now."

"Nah, we're good," Jim said. "At least until the tequila shots come out."

Jim said it so seriously that the men looked at him with concern. "Joking," he said. "Just a joke."

Ellen came out the door and looked at Jim. "You going to invite them in or make them stand in the yard all evening?"

Jim waved a hand at the men and they followed him inside. Without electric lights, the interior of the home was dark this time of day. The men stood around awkwardly for a few moments before Jim ushered them out onto the back porch. The men were more at ease there and settled into chairs. Had it not been for the state of the world, the persistent backbeat of violence, this could have been a normal Saturday evening cookout anywhere in the country.

Jim pointed to a nearby hill topped with a fallen tree and a scattering of rocks. "My son has a lookout up there. He's become obsessed with maintaining watch over us."

"Shit, I can't make out anything that looks like an observation post," Ford said, shielding his eyes against the sun.

"It's pretty low key," Jim said. "He built it himself while I was still walking back from Richmond. He kept an eye on the rest of the family from up there while I was gone. I tried to close his post up a few days back and let him pull duty at the other watch posts but he wasn't too excited about it. He feels a strong sense of duty to be up there."

"You let him go back to his spot, huh?" the sheriff asked.

"After what happened last night," Jim said. "Until then, we hadn't been too concerned about people coming into the valley on one of those old farm roads. Most people don't know about them. Then those guys showed up last night in their UTVs and suddenly Outpost Pete is back in business."

"Fucking bastards," Ford spat. "That gear belongs to the county. They looted nearly everything."

"How did they manage that?" Jim asked.

"They pretty much just walked in and took what they wanted," the sheriff said. "A lot of the guys have keys to the places where we store gear because you never know who's going out on an operation. Barnes got to all those guys and rounded up all the gear he could."

"What did he offer them?" Jim asked.

"Food and safety for the family men," the sheriff replied. "Food and loot for the single men."

Jim smiled. "The age old promise that took many a pirate to sea."

"They got a lot of good stuff," Ford said. "They got most of the department-owned weapons that weren't generally issued, like the sniper stuff, the select-fire weapons, and the breaching gear. They got all the grenades, flash bangs, smoke, and tear gas. They got all the MREs and survival rations."

"Don't forget they stole all that amateur radio gear," the sheriff added. "The county provided the amateur radio club with a place to store the gear that the county subsidized. It all went missing. Those guys were pissed."

"The radio gear doesn't do them any good without an operator," Jim said. "That ham shit is complicated. Any of them know how to work it?"

"Oh, they have an operator," the sheriff said. "They scooped up one of the members of the amateur radio club who was willing to work with them. Guy named Hugh. I'm sure they made him the same promise they made the other cops. Food, protection, and a roof over his head."

"I used to work with a ham guy named Hugh," Jim said. "Tall, lanky fellow who always wore a camouflage boonie hat."

"That's him," Ford said, pointing a finger at Jim. "Kind of an intense dude, obsessed with all that radio stuff."

"Yeah, that's him for sure," Jim agreed. "He's definitely intense. We used to work at a radio station together. I was in high school and he was going to college. We got along real well. He was sharp as a fucking tack and understood everything about how the radio station worked on an engineering level. I haven't seen the guy in years."

"Well, we're pretty sure he's in there monitoring everything we say on the radios," Ford said. "We've tried changing frequencies to maintain communications security but he's always a step ahead of us. He's made it dangerous to use the radios at all."

"My guess is that Hugh doesn't really have any allegiance to them,"

Jim said. "He's pretty much a loner. He also gets wound up if people start telling him what to do. He'll be okay as long as they're giving him a long leash. If they get too demanding, he'll quit cooperating."

"You think you know the guy well enough you could turn him?" Ford asked.

"I don't know if I could get him to work for us," Jim said after a moment of thought, "but I'm pretty sure he wouldn't work against me if he knew what was going on."

"That's a long-term play," the sheriff said. "You might not have time to implement that strategy. Those guys could come back again tonight. They could come back anytime. They're probably pissed about one of their men getting killed."

"We lost someone too," Ford spat. "It's their fault. I'm not in too forgiving a mood right now. I don't have any sympathy for them. They chose their side."

"We didn't have anything to offer them," the sheriff said. "Barnes at least offered them something. It's the same thing we've talked about over and over since this happened. If your family was starving, you'd make a deal with the devil himself if it let you put food in their mouths. You'd worry about your soul later."

"Sounds like the problem is Barnes," Jim said. "Those guys wouldn't give a shit about us if Barnes wasn't in the picture."

The sheriff nodded. "That's probably true."

"So maybe we try to lure him out alone," Jim said. "Maybe we eliminate the problem without the rest of that compound feeling like they're under attack."

The sheriff furrowed his brow. "I don't know about that. I'm not sure I could play a role in murdering one of my men."

"I think I could," Ford said. "I'm not volunteering to do it now, but if it came down to it, I think I could."

Ellen poked her head out the French doors to the back porch. "Dinner is ready," she said. "Hope you guys are hungry."

There was a chorus of comments, all supporting that the men were indeed starving.

"We'll be right in," Jim said. He looked at the other men. "Any ideas what we should do in the meantime? We maintain a watch constantly but I have a bad feeling about this."

"Maybe I'll get on the radio and talk to those men later," the sheriff said. "I'll explain what happened."

"It can't hurt," Jim said, knowing that it might not help either.

CHAPTER THIRTY-FIVE

Randi

They made a small fire that evening and heated a few of the canned goods they'd brought from the valley. While Randi cooked their dinner, Buddy removed a multitool from his belt and used it to cut a couple of feet of electric fence loose. It was smooth wire, flexible and strong. He tossed the wire down by the fire, then went to the barn and found a handsaw. He used the saw to cut a four-inch length off of an old broken broom handle that had been propped up against the barn wall.

Returning to the fire, Buddy used his pocketknife to cut a groove around the middle of the broomstick. He wrapped a couple of turns of wire around the groove, then tied it off. He now had a two-foot length of wire attached to a wooden toggle. He formed the length of wire into a snare and tested that the loop closed easily when the toggle was pulled.

"What's that?" Randi asked. "You going to chase down our breakfast with it?"

Buddy shook his head. "It's a garrote. You drop the loop around that girl's neck, then you pull the handle and don't let up until she's dead."

"Just like that?"

"I suspect not," Buddy said. "She'll be kicking and fighting but it's more of a sure thing than a knife fight. With this, her entire focus will be on getting it loose. She won't be able to run. She probably won't even be able to think."

"What if my hand slips off that handle?"

"We can tape it to your hand so it won't come off," Buddy said. "I've heard of assassins doing that with knives."

"What about the man?"

"I'm going to try to lure him off," Buddy said. "Maybe I'll take a shot with my rifle down close to their house. He'd probably want to check that out and see if there's a dead deer to be had."

"You going to kill him?"

"I haven't decided," Buddy said. "Depends on how he acts."

Randi extended her empty hand and Buddy hung the garrote delicately on her fingers. She examined it, pulling gently on the loop to see how it worked. She placed her wrist in the loop and pulled on the toggle. It closed easily. She pulled harder and the wire bit into her flesh. Her hand began to change color, the blood flow cut off.

"It'll cut into her," Randi observed.

Buddy nodded. "You want that. It makes it harder for the person you're killing to get their fingers under it and try to loosen it."

Randi looked at Buddy. "Will it cut her head off?"

"It's not likely you can pull that hard. It will cut into her neck. There will be a trickle of blood. She might lose control of her bowels or bladder so don't get distracted if that happens. Don't let up until you know she's dead."

Randi studied the simple device and seemed to be considering the implications.

"You having second thoughts?" he asked.

She looked him in the eye and shook her head sincerely. He could see that she was telling the truth. "I just don't want any surprises," she said. "I don't want to lose control of my own bowels because her head pops off unexpectedly and rolls across the porch."

Buddy understood that this was how Randi processed things. The humor, the sarcasm, were all part of her dissecting a plan and learning it. Everyone had their own way of dealing with combat, and this *was* combat. It was no different than many of the actions and operations Buddy had taken part in back in Vietnam. Well, it was a little different. There were fewer rules now. There was nobody second-guessing your decisions like they had in the war.

"What happens afterward?" Randi asked.

"I'll circle back to her house and cover you," Buddy said. "Once we confirm she's dead, we'll return here. If there's any reason we get separated or everything goes to hell, then we meet up back here."

"So when do we do this?" Randi asked.

"I think we should do it early in the morning," Buddy said. "Maybe around 7 a.m.. If they're not morning people, they won't be on top of their game. It may give us an advantage."

They bedded down early that night with plans to be up at dawn. It was a clear, warm night and they moved their sleeping bags outside of the barn, stretching them out on an old tarp. Randi thought of how the world had changed and taken her life with it. She missed her grandchildren. Part of her wanted to just roll everything up and go back home to them but she couldn't. Her children wouldn't understand. They were too *modern*. That was why she had asked Buddy to help her with this. Despite the difference in their ages, he was of the same world. He understood blood for blood. He understood that some people had to die to make things right in the world.

It took her a long time to go to sleep. She stared at the stars, wondering what her grandchildren were doing. She imagined her parents looking down at her. She knew they'd be telling her to change her mind but she wouldn't.

She couldn't.

CHAPTER THIRTY-SIX

The Valley

Around dark, the sheriff went out to his Tahoe. His wife was settling their children into bed in a strange house that did not feel home. They'd already settled his mother in for the night. It was not an easy thing to do. Without the availability of home medical supplies they had to improvise everything. They were out of adult diapers and absorbent pads for the bed. They couldn't get any kind of disposable wipes for cleaning her. They'd even been out of soap until they'd moved to the valley and Jim had been able to set them up with some, although he hadn't said where it came from. The folks in the valley obviously had some resources that they were keeping tight-lipped about.

He climbed into the vehicle and turned on the radio. He selected the standard sheriff's department frequency which he knew those guys would all be monitoring. He'd tried to come up with an inspiring speech but had been unable to find the words. He was just going to wing it.

"This is Unit One, Sheriff Scott," he said into the microphone. He added his name just to make sure they knew he was the *real* Unit One, the man who had given them their orders until recently. He waited a moment but there was no response. He didn't really expect one.

He keyed the mike again. "This is Unit One addressing the former law enforcement officers sheltering at the superstore. I want to speak to you about the tragedy that took place today. This department has not lost a man in the line of duty in over sixty-five years. Today we lost two, although I am forced to question what *duty* Deputy Browning was performing when he shot Deputy Deel. The attack was unprovoked and resulted in myself and several other men having to return fire. Deputy Browning was killed in that exchange."

The sheriff paused, waiting to see if there was any response. None came. The sheriff knew that Ford and Jim were listening. Beyond that, he didn't know if anyone heard his words or not.

"I'm not questioning why you men made the decisions you did. Everyone has had to make hard decisions to try to protect their families. I will, however, question the integrity of any man who attacks another law enforcement officer for the purpose of stealing resources. I will question any man who loots from the citizens of this county to try to better their own situation. If that's what you're doing, you no longer deserve the badge and I won't recognize you as law enforcement. If you do still consider yourself a servant of the public, I ask you to recall the meaning of your oath."

The sheriff stopped, took a deep breath, and continued. "Although I'm not saying that you have to leave the compound you established to keep your families safe, you cannot continue bullying the folks of the county. You cannot steal resources under the authority of the president's executive order when you are giving nothing back to the people in return."

The sheriff released the mike button and sat there in the dark evening. The radio crackled.

"*Nice speech,*" Barnes replied. "*We no longer recognize your authority. It's clear that you've simply moved to a better spot and seized the same resource we were after. That's not an appropriate action for a public servant either.*"

"I moved into this valley to help protect these folks," the sheriff said. "They were concerned about an attack from rogue law enforce-ment officers. They invited us in."

"And there's nothing in it for you?" Barnes asked.

"They offered to help my family," the sheriff replied. "We need the help."

"You're going to need help," Barnes said. *"We're coming into that valley. If we find this tanker we've heard about, we're taking it. If anyone gets in the way, we'll kill them. That includes you."*

The sheriff let Barnes finish, then began to address his former deputies directly. "Any of you listening, you don't have to be part of this. I do not question you trying to help your families but if you declare war on citizens of this county, there's no coming back from that."

"No one here is interested in what you have to say," Barnes replied. *"Save your breath."*

The sheriff felt his blood pressure rising. "You may think I'm nothing more than a politician, Barnes, but I didn't keep this office for twenty years by hiding behind a desk. If I was you, I'd watch my ass."

The sheriff slammed the microphone onto the dashboard and cursed. In truth, he *was* kind of becoming a politician these days. The job turned you into one whether you liked it not. There were always meetings to go to and budgets to deal with. He hadn't always been this way. In the early days, he'd knocked heads together when it needed to be done. He'd turned his back a few times on what may have technically been crimes but served the greater justice. Under his polished veneer was a redneck farm boy. That boy was about to come out.

The sheriff went inside and told his wife he'd be back shortly. He confirmed she had her weapon and that it was accessible, then he drove to Jim's house. Jim and Ford were still standing in the dark outside Jim's house talking. After he turned into the driveway, the sheriff killed his lights and drove in using the park lights to avoid ruining the men's night vision.

He piled out of his truck and ambled over to the Jim and Ford. "Guess you all heard that?"

The men mumbled assents.

"So much for appealing to their sense of duty," the sheriff said. "I don't know if anyone besides Barnes heard a damn thing I said."

"This shit makes me a little edgy," Ford said. "You say you got men on lookout?"

"I've got my friend Lloyd up there in Pete's outpost," Jim said. "He ain't much use sometimes but he can keep a lookout. I've got him set up with a cheap night vision monocular. It will at least let him see a little bit. I've got another guy with a thermal scope watching one end of the valley and a guy with a night vision scope watching the other. It's not perfect but it's about the best we can do."

"And you said you blew up both roads in?" Ford confirmed.

"Yep," Jim said.

"That's a felony," the sheriff said. "We'll let it pass under the circumstances."

"There's still a lot of ways in," Jim said. "Men on foot have unlimited options. I just got lucky last night because the dumbasses came in riding machines with headlights."

"We can't defend an open, accessible location like this," the sheriff said. "We need an advantage."

"We definitely need something," Ford agreed.

Jim looked at Ford, really not much more than an outline in the moonlight. "If you leave your radio with me I could try to talk to Hugh. Maybe I could get him to give me some information. We used to be kind of tight. Is there a frequency I can use that he might be monitoring but none of the other cops would be listening in on?"

"You could switch over the state police frequency or even one of the frequencies used by the adjoining counties. I can show you how to change it on the radio. Those are all stations that the other group could pick up but it's unlikely they'd be using them. Even so, you've got to be discreet until you know he's the only one listening. You don't want to put him at risk," the sheriff said.

"I agree," Jim replied.

"Well, I'm going home," the sheriff said. "If you need me, I'm assuming someone will come get me or something."

"We'll set you up with one of our radios tomorrow," Jim said. "They're nothing fancy, just family band radios, but they do the job.

That's how we all keep in touch. I would recommend keeping a gun handy."

Ford and the sheriff departed, leaving Jim standing in his dark driveway. He now had Ford's handheld radio. He didn't know anything about radios but it was less than two miles to the superstore as the crow flew. Maybe he could get through.

Jim raised the radio to his lips, took a deep breath, and hit the transmit button. "This message is for Hugh. If you're listening, please don't react. Just key your mike twice and I'll continue." Jim let up off the button and waited.

Nothing.

"Come in, Hugh. If you're listening, we need to talk. Do not draw attention to our conversation. Do not react. Just key your mike twice so I know you're listening."

When there was no response after several minutes, Jim set the radio down on the hood none too gently and raked his fingers through his hair. He was getting stressed out, which led to him making bad decisions. He didn't know where it went from here except that it was bound to get worse. Then there was a burst of static on the radio and two pronounced clicks.

Jim grabbed up the radio. "Hugh?"

Two clicks.

"Is this secure? Is anyone on your end listening?"

No clicks.

"Can you talk?" Jim asked.

"*Yes,*" came the hushed reply. "*Who the fuck is this?*"

Jim smiled. He knew that voice. It was Hugh for certain. Jim could imagine him there huddled in the glow of radio LEDs, headphones clamped down over his boonie hat. It was exactly how he remembered him looking as he worked the control board at the radio station.

"Think back to your first job. It was mine too. We traded issues of *Soldier of Fortune* magazine."

"*I think I know who this is,*" Hugh replied.

"Don't use my name," Jim insisted. "I used to have a magazine that we laughed over quite a bit. It suggested that winos had a particular purpose after the collapse. Do you remember what it was?"

Jim waited. If the man on the other end responded correctly, it was definitely Hugh.

There was a chuckle. *"It suggested that winos would make good jerky because they were already marinated."*

Jim sighed with relief. It was his old friend for certain.

"Now tell me, what the hell are you doing on my radio?"

"I'm one of the people you all are trying to kill," Jim said.

"Repeat that."

"The people you're working for seem to think I have something they want," Jim said. "They came for us the other night but we turned them away. Things are escalating."

"No shit," Hugh said. *"They're pissed because you killed one of their men."*

"He fired first," Jim said. "He killed a deputy."

"I'm not sure it matters who fired first," Hugh replied.

There was a dead air for a moment as Jim thought about what to say. "Do you know if they're coming tonight?"

Silence.

"Hugh?"

"You're putting me in a position," Hugh replied.

"I completely understand that," Jim said. "I'm in a position too. My entire family is in danger. My friends and neighbors are in danger."

"I don't think they're coming tonight," Hugh said. *"Everyone is out in the parking lot. They have a bonfire made of pallets and they're just hanging out."*

"Can you let me know if you hear anything?" Jim asked.

"No promises," Hugh said. *"But I'll try. For old time's sake."*

"Thank you," Jim said.

"I have to go."

"Is this a good frequency if I need to reach you again?" Jim asked.

There was no response.

CHAPTER THIRTY-SEVEN

Alice

Alice and her son traveled across the broad farms at that end of the county. They passed large herds of cattle and pushed through dense hardwood·forests. They avoided public roads, except to cross them when forced to. Alice carried bolt cutters on her saddle and cut fences when they stood in their way.

It was not a neighborly way to conduct oneself, but Alice was losing touch with the nuances of how people conducted themselves. She did not care about the people whose lands they crossed. She thought nothing of their troubles and situations. She did not care if their cattle wandered off through the openings she left. Her only concern was anyone might try to prevent their passage. She was ready for that. If they tried, she would kill them without argument or discussion.

At a place called Raccoon Branch they found a dead child in a weedy ditch. Charlie was in the lead and thought the thin, pale limbs belonged to a baby doll. A comment on the lost toy was already forming in his mouth when it went sour with the realization that the figure was indeed a dead child.

"MOM!" he cried, his voice rich with fear.

She nudged her horse and was at his side in a moment. She regarded the body without comment.

"It's a little girl," Charlie said, his voice almost a plea. He needed to hear something from his mother. As mature as he'd become over the last few weeks, there were times he needed reassurance. Having spent most of his time on the isolated farm, he hadn't seen as much of the world as she had and needed that reassurance now more than ever.

"Let's go," Alice said, jostling past him and continuing on her way.

Charlie stared at the body for a while longer, feeling like he should do something but not sure what to do. When he saw his mother putting distance between them, he trotted on, pulling his packhorses along.

"Mom," he called after her, "shouldn't we try to find her family and tell them? Somebody has to be worried about her. Somebody is missing her."

Alice said nothing and she did not stop. She wore sunglasses against the light of midday and her eyes were hidden. He could see nothing of what was going on inside her head. She was a total blank, a mystery.

"We could at least bury her," he mumbled.

Alice stopped her horse and sat it for a moment. She looked at her son. "That girl is nothing to us. We have our own problems. The world took that girl. Her problems are over. What's left behind back there is of no use to anyone. It doesn't matter if you bury it or leave it for the coyotes."

Charlie scowled. He couldn't take any more of his mother's attitude.

"What happened to you!" he yelled. "You used to care about people. Everyone always talked about what a nice person you were and how you helped the people at your office. You're not nice anymore and you don't care about anything."

Charlie made a clicking sound and nudged his horse forward. In a moment, Alice was at his side.

"I care about you," she said. Her voice was flat and emotionless, as if she were choosing between two mediocre and unappealing items on a menu.

"I'm not so sure, Mom," he said. "Do you *really* care or are you just trying to care? I get the feeling all the time that you're trying to care but you can't make yourself do it."

Alice thought about that. She wasn't sure she knew how to answer such an accusation, especially when it held so much truth. A year ago, she would have lied to Charlie to make him happy, because sometimes you had to lie to your children to protect them. Now, she couldn't make herself lie. She couldn't protect his emotions.

"I'm trying," she said. She opened her mouth to say more, to offer justification or explanation, but she could find no way to soften it.

"You never had to try before," Charlie said. "It was just the way things were."

"Things happened on the road, son," she said. "Things I can never tell you about. It changed me. I feel like a shell sometimes. It made me different."

"No *shit!*" he yelled.

She could tell he was angry now but she was so emotionally blunted that she didn't understand it. Nor did she know how to fix it.

"I know I love you," she said. "It may not seem like it and I may not be good at showing it anymore, but that never changed. It's why I didn't give up when every part of me wanted to lie down on the road home and die."

Charlie was riding ahead of her at this point. Only five feet separated them. She knew he heard her even if he was choosing not to respond. The coming hours would be silent between them. The five feet between them would swell into a vast emotional chasm that neither would ever make it back across.

Ever.

CHAPTER THIRTY-EIGHT

Randi

In the early morning, fog lingered in the wooded furrows of coal country. It was always late in the day before the sun got high enough to penetrate the narrow valleys and burn off the moisture. Randi crouched in the wet grass at the edge of the Cross family's yard. Not realizing that her late brother had used the same trick to distract the Cross dogs, Randi had brought food. It was the universal language of dogs and single men. She used chunks of stew meat to pacify the scrawny beasts, quickly becoming their new best friend.

Buddy was hunkered in a thicket of rhododendron nearly half a mile away, where the family's driveway met the dirt county road. At any moment, he was supposed to fire a shot and she nervously awaited it. If luck was on their side, the man living with Lisa would leave the house in an attempt to figure out what was going on. That would leave Lisa for her.

Randi looked down at her hand. Her right, her strongest, clutched the wooden toggle that served as a handle for the garrote. It was bound to her hand with several passes of duct tape. The toggle could not be pulled from her hand. No matter what happened, she would not let go. Were every finger on that hand broken, she would still be able to pull on the toggle and accomplish her task. Only amputation would stop her, and she hoped it did not come to that.

She watched the house, wondering what had happened to all of the people that had once lived there. Had they all died at her brother's hand or had natural causes taken them? Had they all left and moved elsewhere? There had once been a houseful of the evil creatures. It had probably been the meanest single houseful of people to be found anywhere in the whole count—

BOOOOM!

The rifle shot startled her and she nearly jumped out of her skin. It was happening. It was happening now. The sound of the shot rang away, the echo taking a while to fade completely. She focused all of her attention on the front door of the house, waiting for it to swing open. Her anxiety skyrocketed. She tried to use the force of her will to make the man come outside but nothing happened. Maybe he ran out the back of the house? Maybe no one was home?

BOOOOOM!

There was a second shot. Had Buddy been forced to fire on some-one? Was he in trouble? Or was the second shot only added incentive?

It worked.

This time the door of the house flew open. A man in jeans and unlaced boots came staggering onto the porch, a black pump shotgun in his hands. He didn't appear completely awake yet. He clambered down the steps and studied his surroundings, then decided that the shots must have come from down the driveway. He loped off, the shotgun clutched in one hand.

When Randi returned her eyes to the porch, she found Lisa Cross standing there. Lisa was scanning her surroundings, trying to figure out what was going on. She did not appear to have any weapons and had her arms crossed in front of her body as if she were chilled from the morning air. At one point, Randi almost felt as if Lisa was staring at her but the woman gave no reaction that indicated she'd seen anything amiss.

Lisa rubbed her arms against the chill, then backed into the house. It was Randi's cue to get moving. She got to her feet and scrambled through the weeds, skirting the house.

At one side, the weeds came close to the house and there she eased out of them. She ran, quickly crossing the open yard, and flattened herself against the peeling wood siding. The garrote hung from her right hand. In the back of her waistband, she had her pistol as backup. If all else failed, she had a knife in her pocket. At this point, Randi didn't care how Lisa died as long as she got to cause it, as long as Lisa got to watch her do it, and as long as it hurt.

She had to make her hurt.

A dog reappeared, sniffing at her, hoping for a second round of treats. She passed him one, buying a few more moments of silence. She moved to the corner of the house, reaching the edge of a porch that spanned the entire front of the house. It was not as grand as it sounded, rippling and slouching, as if it were balanced of the backs of tired men of irregular heights. It was made of a poplar gone gray and soft as a brushed wool sweater. Some boards and most railings were missing. Trash and debris covered the porch, eventually yielding when new trash pushed the old over the edge.

Randi tried to climb up onto the porch but was not tall enough. She turned her back to it, rested a hand on each side of her, and boosted herself up in a sitting position. She spun and slid back against the house, her heart pounding. She listened. There were no sounds from inside the house.

She looked down the driveway to make sure that Lisa's new friend was not returning. Thankfully he was nowhere in sight. She edged sideways to the door, still not sure how she was going to make entry. The dog came back up the steps at this time, wagging his tail and smiling at her. She cursed under her breath. The dog was going to give her away. Its happiness shone like a beacon on the dark and accursed property. Joy was an unnatural thing there.

She held her breath, terrified as the dog approached her and began licking her face. If Lisa saw the dog's tail wagging through the screen door, she might investigate and find Randi sitting there. Just then,

Randi saw a Folger's can of clothespins sitting nearby. She leaned and retrieved one.

"I apologize for this," she said, and then she clamped one on the hound's ear.

The dog howled and bolted for the steps. Randi shot to her feet and flattened herself against the wall. The screen door flew open and Lisa Cross ran out.

"What the hell?" Lisa yelled.

Randi made a swipe at Lisa's head with the loop of the garrote. From the corner of her eye, Lisa caught the movement and ducked, ramming an elbow into Randi's midsection. It knocked the air out of Randi and threw her back into the wall. Lisa spun to face her opponent, aiming a jab at Randi's face. It connected and Randi's head bounced off the wall. Instead of stunning her, the pain fueled Randi's fire.

Lisa tried to knee Randi in the stomach but Randi crossed a knee in front of herself, deflecting the blow. Undeterred, Lisa immediately threw a forearm up to Randi's throat, pinning her against the wall.

Randi's mind was racing. She was amazed at how fast Lisa had been even when caught off guard. Then she realized that her breathing was completely cut off and she was being choked out. Next she noticed that her hands were still free and that she should still make them do what she came here to do. She whipped the loop of wire around Lisa's neck and jerked it tight before the woman had a chance to understand what was happening.

Both of Lisa's hands instantly flew to her neck and she began clawing at the wire but could not get a finger under it. Randi realized she did not have enough tension on it and Lisa might get a finger under it if she didn't remedy that. Randi moved to her right, yanking her hand and pulling the garrote tighter.

A croaking sound came from Lisa's throat. Her eyes widened in a panic that revealed she knew the seriousness of what was happening. She was in deep shit. She tried to kick at Randi but Randi was behind her now, hauling backward on the toggle. She stumbled down the steps, dragging Lisa with her.

Lisa fell but got back on her feet. She gave up trying to loosen the wire noose and began to focus on Randi. She tried punching at Randi but Randi kept moving. She took some blows but they were rushed and imprecise. Randi kept moving to Lisa's back, yanking on the toggle, throwing Lisa off balance. The wire was cutting into Lisa's neck. Blood began to flow from multiple cuts made by the wire. Lisa staggered and Randi took advantage of it, yanking the toggle firmly, and pulling Lisa to the ground.

Randi quickly sat down above Lisa's head, putting her feet on Lisa's shoulders, and pushing with her legs. It yanked the garrote tight, making it easier on her cramping arm. The load was no longer on her biceps, but on her legs.

"I'm killing you bitch," Randi hissed. "I'm killing you for my brothers and my parents."

Lisa's mouth came open like she was going to say something but she could not. Randi pummeled her with her free hand for even trying to speak. She kept the pressure up with her legs, hoping the wire wouldn't break. She pulled as hard as she could.

The wire was completely buried in Lisa's neck now. Randi gritted her teeth. Her legs and arms were both cramping now. It was only pain and it wouldn't stop her. Something popped within Lisa's neck. Her eyes were open and went glassy. Her mouth was locked open, waiting for a breath that would never come. Randi sagged backward onto the grass, keeping the tension, closing her eyes with the effort. She muttered incoherent and disjointed curses, tugging, afraid to let up.

A shadow fell across her face and she opened her eyes, blinking. "Buddy?"

"I ain't your fucking buddy," came a man's voice.

He raised a rifle and pointed it at Randi's face. She was too spent to even protest.

"Just fucking do it," she whispered. "I've already done what I came to do. I killed her." She couldn't help but give a weak smile as she said it.

His body jerked violently and he staggered. Only then did Randi hear the shot. There was the mechanical sound of a lever action rifle cycling, then another shot hit the man, knocking him to the ground. He arched, kicked, and scrabbled at the ground but he was done.

Buddy came running up, breathing too hard so speak.

"Took you long enough," Randi said.

"Thought ... I was ... breathing too ... hard to ... shoot straight," he gasped.

He sagged to the ground beside Randi, and then lay back in the yard, staring at the sky.

"You dying?" Randi asked.

"I don't think so," Buddy said. "You?"

"No. Me neither."

They each lay there for a few moments, simmering in their own thoughts and emotions. After several minutes passed, Buddy raised up. "We best be going."

Randi sat up. She shoved her left hand in her pocket and came out with her knife. She'd never opened it with her left hand before but fumbled around until she got it, then set about cutting her hand loose from the garrote. She slipped once, drawing blood from the side of her hand, but she saw it as a small price to pay.

When she was free, she stood and regarded the ghastly countenance of Lisa Cross. There was no doubt she was dead, her face purple, her eyes and mouth still open. After regarding her for a moment, congratulating herself on a job well done, Randi bent and grasped the toggle again. Her hand was sore and her muscles screamed but she towed the dead woman across the yard.

When she reached the porch steps, she made it two steps before running out of steam.

"Buddy, can I get a hand here?"

Buddy shrugged, knowing that there was no point in asking what this was about. He started up the steps, grabbed a handful of Lisa's shirt, and helped drag the dead woman onto her porch.

"What are we doing?" he asked.

"Get an arm," Randi ordered.

Buddy grabbed one arm and Randi the other. Following Randi's direction, they stood her against a porch post, where Randi lodged the garrote's toggle into a brace nailed between the porch post and a support beam. When they released the body, it hung there, supported only by the wire around its neck.

"That's a wicked greeting to leave for an unsuspecting visitor," Buddy said. "I pity the poor soul that walks up on it."

"This place is cursed," Randi said. "This ground produced nothing but devils and hate. It's a service to mankind to warn away the unsuspecting."

CHAPTER THIRTY-NINE

The Valley

When Alice and Charlie made it to town, they chose to quietly skirt around it rather than take the shorter and more direct route through the center. They were tired, exhausted really, and knew their horses and the goods packed on them would make a tempting target for anyone looking to steal. They were armed and willing to shoot, but understood that someone in the dark recesses of a Victorian townhouse could shoot them from a window. They had no defense against that other than to avoid civilization as best they could.

They led their packhorses through an outer orbit of subdivisions, crossing yards and suburban hayfields when the roads ran out. They saw many signs of death, hunger, and violence but did not stop. Alice would not let her focus waver. Her mission was to reach Jim's valley and find safety for the two of them. She would not stop for anything. At this point, it was almost animal instinct.

By dusk, they'd reached the same spot where the men had set the trap for her by pulling the dog into the road. She wasn't sure the men she'd fought had been dead when she left them but they were certainly dead by now. There was no treatment available in this world for a bullet wound to the gut or for a traumatic impact with a fencepost.

She paused at the spot and recalled the experience. When she'd left Jim's valley she'd thought the hard times were over and that her bad experiences would be relegated to memory. It had not happened that way. She continued to rack up bad memories the way truckers rack up miles. Had those men she met on this road had their way, they'd have robbed and killed her before she ever learned the fate of her family.

In some ways, it might have been a more merciful end for her. She'd have been spared the deaths of her husband and mother. She'd have been spared the scene in the church. What if she hadn't made it to her mother's farm, and those things had still happened to her family? Charlie would be there all alone and dealing with these things without her. Maybe that would have been better for him in the end too, to not have seen her like this, to not know what she'd become.

The "what ifs" were overwhelming to consider sometimes. It was incredible that each life could be so altered by the impact of minor and completely random events. The decision to not go out for a drive with friends could cause someone to miss a car accident that would have taken their life. The decision to go to a concert with friends could lead to meeting the love of one's life, and inevitably, to the children that were the greatest experience they ever had.

Alice sometimes thought that she was nothing more than a steel ball in a pinball game. God had drawn back the plunger and threw her into gameplay. Now she was bouncing from bumper to bumper with no control.

"Mom, are you okay?" Charlie asked.

It was only then that Alice realized she'd been sitting there immobile in the middle of the road. She had no idea how long she'd been lost in thought. Her horse shifted under her and snorted.

"It'll be dark soon," she told Charlie. "I don't want to go into the valley at night. They're a jumpy bunch and they have a lot of guns. They might shoot visitors on sight."

They'd only been riding for a day, though it had been a long one. They hadn't talked much since arguing over the dead child's body. Now she was drained emotionally and physically and they needed to settle in somewhere. They had camping gear and would stay in the woods.

"We should get off this road," Charlie said. "Back in the woods."

"Definitely," Alice said. "Nothing but bad memories."

Charlie looked at her curiously but she did not elaborate.

She turned her horse down a well-worn trail off the left shoulder of the road. There were tire marks leading into the creek. She didn't know the area well enough but she considered that it could even be a back way into the valley. The road seemed to go in that direction.

"It stinks here," Charlie said.

There was the smell of rot in the air. Having grown up on a farm where dead livestock were pulled off to a sinkhole to rot, she knew the smell of decomposition and death. She did not look too closely into the ditch or the brush on the shoulder of the road. There would be a body somewhere and she didn't want to see it. It could have been one of the men she encountered here or it could have been someone else. She doubted that she was the only one who'd been forced to take a life on this road.

Once they were across the creek, she left the rutted farm road. It appeared to receive some traffic and she didn't want to be close to it if someone came through. They found a path off to the side that may once have been a logging road and followed it into the woods. It was nearly full dark when they found an isolated clearing that might hide them if someone came along.

"As much as I hate to do it, we should probably get the loads off those pack horses," Alice said. "They've had a hard day. They've earned a break."

They unpacked the animals and tied them to long leads. The horses appeared grateful, dropping and rolling around in the dry grass despite their tethers.

Alice spotted Charlie gathering twigs and stacking them. "No fire," she said. "People can see it or smell it. We're in blackout. I don't even want to see a flashlight."

Charlie sighed. "Then I'm probably just going to bed." He sounded a little disappointed.

"That's just as well," Alice said. "We'll spread a tarp out, put our sleeping bags on it, and just sleep like that. Do you need something to eat?"

"No," he said. "I'm more tired than hungry. I'll eat in the morning."

Although Alice hadn't had much of an appetite either, food was important to keeping up their strength. She would have to make sure they ate well tomorrow.

"What about bugs and snakes and stuff?" Charlie asked as he rolled out the blue tarp. He'd camped his whole life but never out in the open without a tent.

"There are worse things out there," Alice said. "Trust me on that."

He knew better than to ask what.

She wondered if she should have said that to him. While she didn't want to expose him to all of the horrors of the world, neither did she want to isolate him. He needed to realize the dangers. He needed to know that he could never assume he was safe and that he should never trust anyone until they'd earned it. What a disappointing world it had become.

"Do we need to keep watch?" Charlie asked.

"I think we'll be fine," Alice said. "The horses will let us know if something comes around." Still, she would sleep with her revolver in her sleeping bag and a rifle beside her. She advised Charlie to keep his AR handy as well.

It took them very little time to settle into their sleeping bags. They could see stars through the trees above them. There were frogs peeping somewhere below them. Night birds called. The horses tugged at grass and chewed.

Soon they were both asleep. Despite their grief, leaving the farm had lifted the yoke of sorrow from them. They were sad and devastated, stripped of two people who had helped define their family and their world, but they were free now of the constant reminders of their loss. They would not notice each day the shut door to Pat's empty room. They would not see Terry's sweat-stained John Deere hat hanging on the coat rack. When they awoke, it would be the first day of a new life. It had to be better than the one they'd left.

It had to be.

CHAPTER FORTY

Jim

Ellen was still on night watch when Jim woke up in the morning. He made coffee and joined her on the porch. They sat in the swing with warm mugs in their hands, the support chains creaking as they rocked.

"It's cool," Ellen remarked. "Feels like fall."

"I used to like fall."

"You don't like it anymore?"

"It's hard to enjoy anything with all the crap going on."

"It does seem like something bad is always happening," Ellen said. "I keep waiting for things to level out but they don't."

"Just so we're clear, I *don't* enjoy this," Jim said. "I'm not sure I ever did, even though you seemed to think so. I'd gladly go back to my boring job now. I'd gladly go back to the security of knowing that you all were safe. I worry constantly and there's no relief from it."

"We could move back into the cave until things are worked out," Ellen suggested.

"I thought about it," Jim said. "I don't think there's room for everyone. How could I move you all back in there and leave Gary's family and Randi's family out? Not to mention Lloyd and Buddy."

"The dampness is hard on your mother too."

Jim nodded. "About killed her last time."

The screen door flew open and Pete came out. He was dressed in camo and had a pack full of gear with him. He was also carrying an M1 Garand. Jim did not own one of those.

"Going to my outpost," Pete said. "Have to relieve Lloyd." He started down the porch steps.

"Where did you get *that*?" Jim asked.

"It's an M1 Garand," Pete said, holding the rifle out for Jim to see.

"I know what it is, but where did you get it?" Teenagers seemed never to give you the straight answer you wanted. You had to pry everything out of them.

"Mack Bird," Pete said. "He told me if I was going to have an outpost, I needed the right rifle. He lent me this one."

"Your .270 was pretty accurate," Jim said.

"This is accurate and I can do fast follow-up shots," Pete countered.

"Just be careful," Jim said. "It takes a while to get used to a new gun. Be safe."

"I'm already used to it," Pete said. "Mack let me use it every time we did watch together."

Jim and Ellen watched Pete go, walking off toward Outpost Pete with his man-sized strides. He was Jim's height now. How that had happened, Jim had no idea. One day he was a child with a toy tool belt and a rubber hammer pretending to help build things, and in the blink of an eye he was wearing the same size clothes as Jim. It was too heartbreaking to dwell on. The passing of time could hit you like that sometimes, like a brick to the head.

"So what are you getting into today?" Ellen asked, breaking the downward spiral of Jim's thoughts.

"Pops, Gary, and I are going to offload as much fuel as we can from that tanker. That way if we do lose it, they're not getting everything. We'll have some in reserve."

"Where can you store it?"

"I have several old fuel tanks from oil furnaces," Jim said. "We're going to mount one on a hay wagon and use that to refill all of the old in-ground tanks at houses throughout the valley. Some people also have tanks they use on the farm for fueling tractors. We're going to fill all those too. All of those little tanks are easier to hide than a big shiny fuel tanker."

Ellen was concerned about the fuel but more concerned about food and staying warm over the winter. The food they'd obtained from the Glenwall trailers had been helpful but it was hard to feel comfortable when they had no idea how long this event was going to last. She didn't serve a single meal where she didn't wonder how she was going to replace the ingredients she'd used.

Jim rose from the swing. "I guess I better get to work. Sitting here worrying isn't accomplishing anything."

Ellen wasn't far behind him. "I've got stuff to do too. The list never ends."

Jim went back in the house, threw his load vest over his shoulder, and grabbed all of his every day carry gear. He found his truck keys and took up his M4. On his way to the truck, he saw his dad's Kawasaki Mule sitting in the barn. The two-person utility vehicle was diesel-powered and they'd been using it to do perimeter checks. Usually the team pulling guard duty would load up at random points in their shift and do checks. They'd been stretched thin the last couple of nights. Re-opening Outpost Pete, mostly manned by Lloyd, Pete, and Buddy, had reduced the number of men available to do random patrols.

Jim decided that it might be a good idea to do a lap around the valley before getting started on the fuel deliveries. It was still early and Pops wasn't even up yet. It usually took about an hour to make a pass around the valley. He had the time.

He'd improvised a floor-mounted rifle rack in the UTV similar to what cops used in their patrol vehicles. He confirmed there was a round in the chamber of the M4 and slapped the bottom of the mag to make sure it was seated firmly. As he started off in the vehicle, he realized he hadn't told anyone what he was doing. He pulled his radio from its pouch. Moving around outside, regardless of the threat level, was not something you did without making people aware of where you were going.

"This is Jim, heading out for a perimeter check," he said into the radio.

He didn't wait for a reply, nor did he even notice that he didn't get one. He shoved the radio back in the pouch and patted the Velcro flap back into place. Ellen, the intended recipient of that message, was getting Ariel up at the time Jim tried to reach her. Her radio was sitting on the kitchen counter and the volume had been lowered to keep from waking up everyone who was still asleep. She never heard him.

Pete usually heard most of the radio transmissions. He had good signal at the outpost and was hypervigilant. At the moment, he and Lloyd were admiring the M1 Garand. Lloyd was telling Pete a story about his grandfather using the M1 Garand in World War II. That led to more stories about the other things his grandfather saw in the war and finally a dirty little song sung to the tune of *Whistle While You Work* that involved Hitler and Mussolini.

They, of course, missed the transmission. They heard the radio chatter but dismissed it as part of the everyday chatter between residents of the valley that went on all day long. They both assumed that if it was important, there would be a retransmission.

The diesel Mule was slower than a truck but its tires and suspension handled the farm terrain much butter. It practically floated over bumps and ruts. Jim left his farm and shot down the farm road toward the creek crossing. They hadn't blocked this route because they needed it, but he had put several branches and tripwires in place as tells that should let him know if people had driven in this way. Although none of them were disturbed, there was no comfort in that. They would still be coming at some point. It was inevitable.

He had a cheap set of binoculars with him and he used those to glass the creek crossing where Deel had been killed. All of the vehicles that had been left there were gone now and no others were in sight. Jim retreated and headed north to another farm. He drove along the fence line until he reached a gate and crossed. From there, he drove to a high knob that allowed him to check the perimeter of that property for any places where the fence had been cut to allow vehicle access. He didn't see anything out of place.

It crossed his mind that if he didn't dwell on the reason he was out here doing this, it was pretty enjoyable to just be out here riding through farmland on a sunny morning. He descended from the high open field and followed a logging road through a hardwood forest. Some trees were already starting to change color, an indicator that colder days would be on them soon and life would become even harder.

He came upon a tree that had fallen across the logging road. It was common enough and didn't raise any alarms. The woods were full of dead trees that dropped without warning or healthy trees that uprooted in high winds. This one was a small maple about eight inches in diameter. Jim got out to put the winch on it. When he looked off toward the base of the maple he noticed a pile of fresh sawdust at the base of the tree. It took a second to settle in but the tree had not fallen on its own.

It had been cut.

The hair on his neck stood up, issuing a warning even before his brain caught up. He grabbed for his hip but his Beretta wasn't there. He recalled too late that it was holstered on the vest which had been lying beside him in the seat of the Mule. He went for his backup but never had a chance to draw. There was an explosion of sound behind him, a sting on his back, and a staccato burst of electrical discharge.

Taser!

It was the last thought that passed through his brain before the signals got scrambled. His limbs stiffened and he toppled over, falling like the tree across the road.

"Hit him again!" someone yelled.

There was another series of crackles and his body went rigid. Then a rifle butt came down on the side of his head and the lights went out.

CHAPTER FORTY-ONE

The Valley

Alice woke early but remained in her sleeping bag. The night hadn't been cold but had been chilly enough that the warmth of her bag was comforting. She was eager to bolt out of the sleeping bag and head into the valley but Charlie was still asleep. After what he'd been through she would let him enjoy the small peace that sleep offered. She thought about their argument yesterday and felt bad about it. They would have to revisit it again after they were settled. She wanted him to understand her. She wanted him to know that he was loved.

She might have dozed off again herself but at some point she heard what sounded like an ATV headed in their direction. She sat up, wondering if they'd left some kind of trail that was drawing attackers to them. She clutched the revolver, fear clutching her chest. She forced herself to relax. The sound of an ATV didn't mean people were pursuing her.

She slid out of her bag and walked to where she could see the logging road they'd followed through the forest. She was about forty feet from where Charlie lay sleeping. She noticed a flicker of movement in the woods. It corresponded with the sound of the machine and she ducked, watching.

"What is it, Mom?" Charlie asked.

He was awake and looking at her, rubbing the sleep from his eyes like he was three again. She held a finger to her lips and kept it there until he opened his eyes and saw.

Instantly understanding, he slid from his own bag and grabbed his AR. He crouched and crept to where his mother knelt. "What is it?"

"Four wheeler," she said, keeping her voice low out of habit.

Charlie knelt beside her and they watched. "It's a side by side," he said. "A UTV. Probably a farmer. Probably the guy that owns this farm."

Alice didn't answer, just watched intensely. Shortly, the driver encountered a downed tree across the road. Alice remembered the tree from last night. They'd had to walk the horses into the woods to get around it. The horses had that advantage over this wider machine.

"That looks like..." Alice trailed off. "Do you have your binoculars?"

Charlie ran back to his gear and returned with the binos. Alice quickly raised them and focused on the UTV.

"That's Jim!" she said. "The guy we're looking for!"

Charlie grabbed the binos to take a look. Alice stood and was starting to walk down the hill toward Jim when Charlie grabbed her from behind.

"Get down! Don't make a sound!" he said.

Alice started to fight him off, unable to stop herself, but he shoved the binoculars at her. She stared at them for a moment, then took them and studied the scene again. There were more men now and they appeared to be searching a man on the ground.

"There were men in camo hiding," Charlie said. "They tased him."

Alice couldn't believe it. The man was definitely Jim. She hadn't seen these other men. What the hell was happening? Should she open fire?

She couldn't do that, she couldn't tell who was who. She didn't know who to shoot. What if the shots brought more men? Her mind raced.

As she watched, the men handcuffed Jim and threw him into the back of his own vehicle, then drove off.

"What was that?" Charlie asked.

"I think some bad men just took Jim," she said. "We need to let his family know. We need to see if we can help."

"Maybe I should follow them," Charlie said. "I can keep an eye on them, see where they take him."

"No," Alice said firmly. "I'm going to follow them. You gather the gear and take all the pack horses. You go back the way we came until you hit the farm road, then you keep going on that. You tell them who you are. You tell them what happened. Do not raise your gun. These men will be armed and a little jumpy but it will be okay."

"I don't want you to go," Charlie said, even as Alice was running toward her horse.

"Have to," Alice said. "Now do what I said!"

She threw her saddle on her horse and cinched it up. In a moment, she had her rifle on her shoulder, her Go Bag on her back, and was riding off through the trees.

When he was certain she was out of sight, Charlie sank to his knees and began to sob hysterically. "I love you, Mom! I'm sorry."

CHAPTER FORTY-TWO

The Valley

Charlie cried for a long time in the silence of the forest, his anguish quieting the chatter of birds and squirrels. He fell over on his side, his face resting upon thick cool moss. He didn't know exactly why he was crying, but at the same time he knew the tears were shed for every single injustice visited upon him and his family since the terror attacks occurred. When the tears finally stopped, he felt as if a weight had been lifted, even if it was only a momentary reprieve.

He stood and dusted himself off, then gathered up the sleeping gear. When the sleeping bags were rolled into the tarp, he saddled each horse and loaded them. That accomplished, he tethered them head to tail in a train and set out to do as he'd been told.

He left the woods by the trail they'd followed in, then turned left onto the rutted farm road. He hadn't even traveled a mile when he encountered another group of riders. They came upon each other so suddenly that both parties realized there was no avoiding nor hiding. Either they'd pass in peace or they'd fight it out in close quarters.

"Morning," Charlie said as the riders neared. He tried to sound like a man, hoping his voice didn't convey the fear he felt.

The other riders were a woman about his mother's age and an old man. They had pack horses too, and both carried guns.

"Morning," the older man said. "That's quite a string of horses you're leading."

"They're *mine*," Charlie said. "And I aim to keep them."

"Whoa there, boy," the man said. "I ain't after your horses. I'm just commenting that in this day of video games and skateboards it's an uncommon sight to see a young man of your age leading a string of pack horses across the land."

Charlie thought the old man talked funny but he didn't seem to be dangerous. "I was never into video games or skateboards," Charlie said. "And I only recently came to be into horses."

"My name is Buddy," the old man said. "This here is Randi."

Charlie nodded at them. "I'm Charlie."

Buddy pointed to the east. "We live in this valley and we're headed home," Buddy said. "Whereabouts are you headed?"

There were a lot of questions, and perhaps even a warning, buried within that question. Part of Charlie didn't want to admit anything. Another part of him knew that he had to get help for Jim and his mom.

"You all know a man named Jim?" he asked hesitantly.

It was immediately obvious that the name meant something to them. There was a change in the way they looked at him and at each other.

"We know him," Randi asked. "Why?"

She'd already got in trouble once for bringing folks to Jim's house. That ended with her having to watch the execution of two men. She didn't want to make that mistake again. If she brought someone into the valley with her, there better be a damn good reason for it.

"My mom is Alice," Charlie said. "She was on a trip with him with all this happened."

"I know your mom. We work...*worked* together," Randi said. "I was on that trip with her. Is she okay?"

"I'm not sure," Charlie said. "We were on our way to this valley because Jim said we could come stay there if we needed to. My mom thought she saw him this morning driving a UTV through the woods. About the time she figured out who he was, these men in camouflage came out of nowhere and hit him with a Taser. They took him and my mom followed them."

"Shit!" Randi said.

"Shit is right," Buddy said. "Randi, can you take the packhorses and lead Charlie to the valley? You need to tell Gary and Ellen what happened. I'm going to try to catch up with Alice."

"Alice doesn't know you," Randi said. "You run up on her and she'll blow your head off before you can introduce yourself."

"She's right," Charlie said. "Mom is different than she was when she left. She doesn't have the same kind of feelings inside that her that she used to."

"Then you go," Buddy said. "But be careful. If you find him, don't engage the men that took him until we get there. You'll just get yourself killed."

Randi frowned at the way he was talking to her. "I'm *not* stupid."

"I know you're not," Buddy said. "I just don't want to see you hurt."

Randi accepted that without comment. She handed the lead to her packhorses to Buddy and took off in the direction Charlie said they were headed.

Buddy and Charlie moved as quickly as they could with the two strings of packhorses. When they neared the back gate into Jim's farm, Buddy removed a radio from his pocket and spoke into it.

"Valley, this is Buddy. I'm coming in the back way and I've got someone with me. Pete, you up there?"

"Got eyes on you," Pete said. *"Who's that with you?"*

"Best you hear it in person, Pete. Come down to your mom's house. And if you guys are listening, I probably need Gary and Mack to come to Jim's house too."

It was just a moment before Gary and Mack confirmed they were on their way.

Pete was jogging down to the house and arrived at the same time Charlie and Buddy did. Buddy asked Pete to help Charlie get the horses in the barn.

"Should we unload them?" Charlie asked.

"Go ahead and toss the packs off," Buddy said. "Get them some water. Then come inside so we can get a plan together."

Buddy left his string of horses with Pete and quickly walked to the house. Ellen saw him coming and came out onto the porch.

"What's going on?"

From the barn, Pete saw Buddy put his hand gently on his mother's shoulder, then lead her into the house. He saw his mother move her hand up to her mouth. It looked like she'd received bad news.

Pete turned to the other boy. "Did something happen to my dad?"

Charlie was tugging at a knotted rope, trying to get a bundle loose from one of the pack horses. "Is your dad Jim?"

Pete nodded.

"We saw some men take him," Charlie said. "They used some kind of stun gun or something on him. Then they took him away."

"He didn't shoot any of them?" Pete asked, his voice rising. "He didn't fight back?"

"He didn't have a chance to. The men were hidden."

Charlie went back to the rope he was struggling with, trying to figure out why the knot wouldn't give. When he looked back up, Pete was gone.

CHAPTER FORTY-THREE

The Shopping Center

Jim regained consciousness as he was being dragged through the back door of a vacant storefront in the shopping center. His shoulder banged against the doorframe as the men struggled to get him through the opening. His hands were zip-tied behind his back. The men carrying him each had an arm looped beneath his biceps. Jim could feel muscles tearing in his shoulders and the pain was excruciating.

They slammed him into a metal kitchen chair. Zip ties were fastened around his ankles, holding them to the chair. The ties around his wrists were cut, then his wrists refastened behind the chair. He looked at the faces of the three men around him. While he didn't know them, he recognized all of them. All were from various branches of local law enforcement.

"This is what you've become?" Jim asked, looking each man in the face. "A bunch of fucking kidnappers?" He had a blinding headache from the blow to his head and it didn't help his mood.

Two of the men looked at the ground and wouldn't meet his eye. The third was more defiant.

"You open your mouth again and I'll put a bag over your head," he said. The same man pointed to one of the others. "Get on that back door. We don't want any of the women or children wandering in here. Barnes doesn't want them to see this."

Jim had no doubt that the man would put a bag over his head. He wasn't sure if that meant a cloth bag he could breathe through or a shopping bag that would suffocate him but he had no intention of finding out. He took the offered advice, focusing on looking around and taking in his surroundings. There were a few mattresses scattered around the room and a lot of trash. There were racks with weapons and stacked boxes containing survival food. The boxes were probably supplies stolen from the county's emergency supplies.

Jim didn't judge the men for taking supplies available to them. He didn't judge them for setting up shop in the superstore. He *did* judge them for doing it under the pretense of it being a law enforcement action and he damn sure judged them for what they were doing now. If they killed him, how would his family make it? He could only hope that his friends would fill in the gap and help them survive.

These men had blown any pretense of official action when they killed Deel. They were willing to kill one of their own, and you couldn't make excuses for that. They were also willing to kidnap one of the citizens they swore an oath to protect. They were not people Jim could ignore anymore, hoping that they'd stay on their side of the fence. They were not fellow survivalists trying to make it through this bout of societal collapse. They were a threat and would have to be dealt with as such.

If he lived that long.

A tall, thin man in camo fatigues came in through the back door. He regarded Jim for a moment, then dropped his cigarette onto the low pile carpet and ground it out. From the way the other men deferred to this man, Jim assumed that he knew who he was. This was the boss.

"You must be Barnes," Jim said.

The man approached Jim and seemed to study him, as if he were trying to place whether the two of them had ever met before. Without warning, he lashed out with a short jab and shattered Jim's nose. He was wearing some kind of tactical gloves with hardened protection across the knuckles. The pain was blinding and Jim could taste blood pouring into his mouth.

Barnes gave Jim a moment to recover and then grabbed him by the hair, wrenching his head up. He stared into Jim's eyes. "I figure that punch saved me at least five minutes of bullshitting with you and listening to your smartass remarks. You should understand now that I'm pretty fucking serious and I won't hesitate to hurt you."

Jim did indeed understand that. He could not remember ever taking such a blow to his nose before. He could feel it swelling and filling with blood, forcing him to breathe through his mouth. If he ever had the opportunity, he would kill this man. He prayed there was the opportunity.

"We're clear," he hissed.

"Good," Barnes said, straightening out. "Then I'll cut to the chase. We hear you have a tanker of fuel. We want it. We need to keep our generators running through the winter. We have diesel vehicles that need fuel. Unfortunately, we're about out."

"I thought you all seized all the gas stations in the county," Jim said. "You should have plenty."

Barnes shrugged. "Unfortunately, we made some short-sighted decisions based on financial need."

"Let me guess, you traded the fuel instead of saving it?"

Barnes nodded. "I'm sure you understand how that might happen."

Jim started to respond but choked on blood running from his sinuses down his throat. He coughed and blood sprayed from his mouth. Barnes backed up, a warning expression on his face. Apparently he didn't want his fatigues to get stained.

"We would be glad to trade you fuel," Jim choked out when the coughing passed.

Through his watering eyes, Jim missed the lightning fast jab coming toward his nose again. He heard the bones crunching in his skull, felt them grinding beneath the man's fist. He nearly passed out from the pain, but could hear the man yelling in his face.

"WRONG FUCKING ANSWER!" Barnes yelled. "Who said

anything about a *trade*? How about you deliver that tanker to me and I let you live? How's that for a trade?"

Jim was unable to respond. He was stunned, the synapses in his brain flooded with the pain, and he could barely breathe.

"Excuse me," one of the other deputies spoke up. He was wearing an earpiece. "The sheriff is on the radio. He's asking for you."

Barnes stared at the deputy who interrupted his interrogation. "He ain't my sheriff anymore," he said, but went and took the deputy's radio anyway.

Jim looked around at the other deputies but none would meet his eye. They looked a little sheepish, but if he was looking for sympathy, he wasn't finding it here.

"Barnes here," the man growled into the radio.

"Killing Deputy Deel was one thing," the sheriff said, *"but now you're kidnapping people? Is this what you've turned into?"*

"Desperate times, desperate measures," Barnes said, his voice lilting almost playfully. "I need fuel and this asshole has it."

"That asshole *is Jim Powell,"* the sheriff said. *"He's a citizen of this county. He's a dad with a wife and two children at home. He's a man who's been helping his neighbors survive. What have you done for anyone lately?"*

"This *citizen* stole that tanker from somebody and now I'm stealing it from him," Barnes said, casting an eye at Jim. "That's how shit works now. There's always a fish one size bigger waiting to eat you and this fucker just got ate."

"Look, these folks don't care about that tanker," the sheriff said. *"They'll gladly give it up to get Jim back, but they can't drive it out of here. They blew the roads up to keep strangers out. They're impassable. You're welcome to the fuel but you'll have to find another way to get it out of here."*

"You can bring it out that farm road," Barnes said. "Same way you and Ford got in there."

"It's too heavy," the sheriff said. *"There's no way a road tractor can pull it through a pasture. It can't get enough traction."*

"Doesn't sound like my problem," Barnes said.

"You let him go!" the sheriff insisted. *"You have my word that the fuel is yours. You get a truck from the farm supply or one of the home heating oil companies. You can haul it out one truck at a time."*

"Your word means nothing to me," Barnes said. "Here's the deal. I want to see that tanker sitting in my parking lot by the end of the day or I hang this *citizen* from a light pole in the parking lot. You got it?"

"You're not being reasonable," the sheriff said.

"Reason is for the mediocre," Barnes said. "I'm done being mediocre." He set the radio down. He was done talking.

Jim knew that the sheriff was right. There was no way the heavy truck could come out of the valley now that the roads had been blown up. They had a road tractor they'd used to move the tanker and the food trailers but it just wasn't made for off road use. It would sink up on the farm road and be stuck forever.

Barnes seemed to know what was going through Jim's head. He stared hard at the man. "You better hope they think of something."

CHAPTER FORTY-FOUR

The Shopping Center

One storefront over, Hugh had listened to the entire exchange between Barnes and the sheriff through his headphones. Not giving any indication of what he was listening to, his only visible reaction was a single raised eyebrow at the mention of the old friend he'd spoken with on the radio the other night. It was the same expression frequently used by Mr. Spock on the original *Star Trek* series and could mean anything from sarcasm to interest to vague amusement. In some ways, Hugh seemed much like the unemotional Vulcan, so unwaveringly focused on his task with the radios.

Hugh had been afraid to talk to Jim on the radio the other night. It was clear that Barnes was unstable and was becoming more unhinged by the day. He couldn't seem to handle the stress of watching the world as he knew it grinding to a halt. Hugh was trying to come up with his next move but he didn't know how to make it. He needed out of this shopping center group but he didn't know where to go. He didn't know of any groups other than the group he was already part of. He'd only recently learned that his old friend Jim had a group but he was afraid their future might be limited if Barnes had his way. Even though he hadn't been invited to join Jim's group, Hugh knew that radio operators such as himself were a highly desirable addition. That would have to be his exit strategy. It was all he had.

From what he heard on the radio, Hugh suspected that they must be holding Jim in the old shoe store next door. He'd only been in there once. Since these men were trying to keep the main superstore space family-friendly, the old shoe store was where they went to drink, where they took women that visited the camp, and where they stored anything they wanted to keep away from the families.

Hugh wasn't in any position to storm in the shoe store and take Jim by force. There were at least a half-dozen cops here and several more men that were associated with them. Hugh couldn't take them all. He was armed with a Taurus 1911 that he appendix-carried in a leather holster. It was concealed in the waistband of his pants and he didn't know if the cops were aware that he carried it or not. He preferred that they not be aware of it. He carried two spare mags in a kydex carrier on the back of his belt.

Obsessed since childhood with edged weapons, Hugh carried several homemade kiridashi, a type of Japanese utility knife with a durable edge and sharp point. He'd made them himself in his home shop from old files and carried them in an assortment of locations on his body. He carried one up each sleeve, fastened to his forearms in sheaths he'd designed himself; one in each boot; one dangled upside down from a case he wore around his neck; and two were attached horizontally to his belt – one at the back, one forward of his left hip.

Hugh sat at his radios trying to decide what to do. He thought of trying the frequency Jim had contacted him on but he didn't know if anyone would be listening or not with Jim apparently out of the action. He couldn't take a chance on the superstore group hearing his transmission. Someone would put a bullet in his head right there at the radio table.

He assumed that at some point there would be an action taken against the shopping center, an attempt to get Jim back. They would have to do it today or Barnes would probably kill Jim just as he said he would. Logic told him that if anything happened, it would probably be later in the day. It was unlikely they could pull something together this quick after talking with Barnes.

Hugh believed the sheriff when he said they didn't have a way to get the tanker out. It made sense. If Barnes was thinking logically, he'd understand that and try to find some way to work with them. By taking Jim, he had their attention and they were willing to do what he asked. It was his mistake to ask for something that was impossible to deliver.

Hugh decided that he'd go up on the roof under the guise of checking his antennas. There was a sniper stationed there and Hugh liked to go smoke with him and talk guns. He could use a break anyway. He could use some fresh air. It would give him time to think and maybe come up with a plan.

He wanted to get out of the superstore more than ever. Now he would have to take his friend with him. He and Jim hadn't been close in years but they had been close once and it had been at that crazy point in their youth when it was important to find people who thought like you did. That shit meant something.

Standing and stretching, Hugh looked around and saw that no one was paying any attention to him at the moment. He grabbed his pack of Winstons off a table and walked to the back of the store. He tucked the smokes in his pocket and climbed the wall-mounted steel ladder. At the top, he unlatched the roof hatch and climbed out onto the rubber roof.

At the sound of the hatch opening, the sniper turned and saw Hugh's lanky frame unfolding onto the roof. "Hope you have a cigarette I can bum," he said.

"Gotcha covered," Hugh said. He shook two out of the pack, tossing one to the sniper and sticking one in his own mouth. He lit his, then tossed the lighter to the other man.

The sniper lit his own smoke then returned the lighter. "Anything going on down there?"

Hugh had a lungful of smoke, but shook his head. He exhaled. "Not a damn thing. Here?"

"Saw a couple of deer and a few groundhogs. Saw a big bird that I think was an osprey. That's about it."

"Who'd have thought the collapse of modern society would be so dull, right?" Hugh commented.

As if provoked by his judgment, the world responded. Gunfire erupted behind the shopping center. Hugh flinched and ducked out of reflex.

The sniper scrambled for his Remington 700 and bolted toward the back parapet wall. Hugh watched as if it were all happening in slow motion. The moment of decision was upon him. He took a deep breath and made his choice.

CHAPTER FORTY-FIVE

The Superstore

Barnes gestured at the man tied to the chair, his face a mass of crusting blood. "Somebody lock this piece of shit in the storeroom. There are too many kids wandering around this place. I can't have them running next door to tell everyone there's a hurt man over here."

Sword went to the chair. Jim was conscious but not speaking to them. Sword slipped a Spyderco from his pocket and sliced through Jim's bonds. "Stand up!"

Jim slowly rose to his feet.

Sword put new flex cuffs on his hands, took him by the arm, and led him toward the back of the store. Jim was slightly disoriented from the pain and swelling in his face, the difficulty in breathing. His eyes were crusty from watering. He had no idea what was in store for him. He looked toward the back of the store. He blinked at the bright light coming through the open back door. He could see the sun shining on an overgrown cornfield. He wondered if it would be the last time he saw the outside. Then something blocked part of his view.

A figure. He assumed it to be one of the cops at first, but it was someone smaller, less bulky. A woman. He had a moment to think that Barnes was going to be pissed about one of the women knowing they had a prisoner over here. The man seemed to be trying to keep that under wraps. Then Jim noticed the woman had a gun.

It was raised and pointed in his direction.

Jim dropped to the floor. With his hands behind his back, he couldn't catch himself. He face-planted on the concrete floor, landing on his already pulverized nose. He didn't even have time to consider the pain before gunfire erupted.

BOOM!

The shotgun blast was deafening in the nearly-empty space. Sword dropped, falling beside Jim. They were face to face, Sword gasping like a fish as thick blood oozed from his mouth. He was a dead man who just didn't know it yet.

Jim rolled toward him, groping awkwardly for the Spyderco clipped to the man's pocket.

BOOM!

Another shotgun blast and there was drywall dust in the air. He didn't see anyone fall. He thumbed open the knife and slipped the blade inside one of the cuffs. It was tricky and he sliced the hell out of his palm when he jabbed the blade into it. He struggled to lever the knife against the plastic restraint, then it went through and he was free.

One of the cops had been behind Jim and was retreating into the store. There were few hiding spots in the large open storefront. His weapon was drawn and held straight in front of him, dumping rounds at the doorway. The figure in the doorway lunged to the side, taking cover from the barrage of .40 cal rounds.

Before their attention turned back to him, Jim grabbed Sword's sidearm from its holster, and put two rounds into the center mass of the retreating deputy. He dropped. Jim knew Barnes was still in there and there could be more. He'd lost track of who was coming and going from the room. He couldn't see them at that moment, but assumed they were hiding behind the boxed-in columns that supported the roof.

Jim rolled to his knees, firing at one column, then the other, forcing the men to stay hidden while he backpedaled toward the door. He hoped like hell that the woman with the shotgun didn't pop back in, blind from the sunlight, and blast a hole in his back.

He heard someone returning fire, caught a glimpse of a handgun hooked around the corner of a column, and firing blindly toward him. Jim focused his fire there, pumping rounds, and chewing up the drywall covering the column. The column had a steel core that he couldn't shoot through, but he could make it pretty damn uncomfortable to be standing there.

When he reached the back door, he had no idea if he was backing out into a friendly or someone who just had a grudge against the cops at the shopping center. His hackles rose and he gritted his teeth against the blast that could be the last sound he ever heard on this earth. When he hit daylight, he moved to the east side of the door, behind the protection of the outside block wall.

Across from him, he saw Alice. He was stunned for a moment, forgetting where he was, and what he was doing. At least until a round sailed out the door between them. Alice stuck her shotgun back around the corner and fired into the room. She tried to pull the trigger again but the gun was dry. There was nothing but a dull click.

"Hunting shotgun!" he yelled. "Just three rounds!"

"Fuck!" she yelled, throwing the gun down. Apparently, she had no more rounds with her. She drew her revolver.

"We have to run," he said. "Over the bank, into the cornfield. I'll be behind you."

Alice wasted no time, she ran for the edge of the pavement. There was about forty feet of open asphalt before it dropped away to a steep embankment. She was nearly to the drop-off when a gunshot snapped her head sideways and she fell.

"*ALICE!*" Jim screamed.

He saw the shooter come off the loading dock at the superstore. The man was fifty feet to Jim's right and carrying a rifle. Jim aimed two rounds center-mass, then fired two more back into the open doorway, hoping it would force Barnes and his men back into cover. Then he ran like hell.

As he ran, he fired behind him, only getting off one round before the slide locked open.

"Shit!" He dropped the empty weapon, snagged Alice by the belt, and tugged her toward the looming edge of the parking lot.

One foot.

Two feet.

A round sang by his head. Then they were rolling down the steep embankment at the edge of the property. Jim tried to protect his face but his hand was tangled in Alice's belt. His face caught the exposed end of a drainpipe, stunning him with a wave of pain.

When they reached the bottom, Jim staggered to his feet, finding Alice's belt again, and dragging her into the concealment of the dense cornfield. He tried to move between rows and not displace any more corn than he had to. He didn't want to leave an obvious trail.

"*JIM!*"

He froze. He was having trouble thinking clearly but he knew that voice.

"Randi?" he choked, breathless from dragging Alice. He still couldn't breathe through his nose and blood was running down his throat, constantly choking him.

She lunged through the corn at him, then spotted Alice at his feet. Randi handed her shotgun to Jim and dropped to her knees, the nurse kicking in.

Jim backed out of the way, crouched, and watched their back. He could hear shouting at the superstore, women screaming, kids crying. He kept the shotgun raised in that direction, scanning back and forth. He couldn't see the back of the store for the mature corn, only the parapet wall at the top. He knew men were looking in their direction, preparing to come after them. They didn't have much time.

"We've got to go," Jim said, his speech garbled. "Can you stabilize her?"

There was no answer.

He turned and found Randi biting her lip. "I said I wasn't fucking crying again," she hissed. "And no I can't stabilize her."

Jim looked down at Alice's face. Her head was covered in gore, a gaping entry wound where her ear used to be, her eyes open and dirt-encrusted. She was lifeless. Dead.

Jim groaned in frustration, wanting to roar and scream but not wanting to give their position away. She had saved his life.

Randi stood. "We've got to go. I hear an engine. Somebody's coming."

Jim ducked and struggled to pull the lifeless body onto his shoulders.

Randi had to help him, then she picked her shotgun up. She watched Jim struggle to balance the weight. "You could leave her."

He shot Randi a look. His grim determination and the rage burning in his eyes gave her his answer.

"Then let's go," she said.

Jim staggered forward across the uneven soil of the field, hauling Alice's body on his shoulders. "She died for me, Randi. After everything we went through."

Randi fell in behind Jim, turning every other step to watch their back. All she could think of was the boy she'd sent on with Buddy. The boy who'd just lost his mother.

CHAPTER FORTY-SIX

Hugh

The sniper set his backpack on a rooftop air conditioning unit next to the back wall. He climbed onto the unit, rested his rifle on the pack, and began glassing the area through his scope.

"See anything?" Hugh asked.

The sniper moved his scope picture in a methodical grid across the field, watching for any signs of movement.

"Got 'em," he whispered.

"What do you see?"

"I got a man carrying a body over his shoulder. A woman behind him. She's armed," the sniper replied.

"And you're positive they're not our people?" Hugh asked. He was standing right beside the sniper and could see a vague disturbance in the cornfield, but couldn't make out any details.

"They're fucking running away," the sniper said. "What do you think?" His voice was full of sarcasm.

Hugh hated sarcasm, especially directed at him. This would make his decision easier.

"Call Barnes on the radio," the sniper said. "Tell him what I told you. Confirm I'm clear to take the target."

Hugh slipped two of the razor-sharp kiridashi from the sheaths on his arms.

The sniper didn't remove his eye from the scope, didn't want to take a chance on losing his prey in the vast sea of green stalks. "Did you hear me?" he said. "Call it in before I lose them."

Hugh held one of the sharp, thick blades in each hand. He had to act before the sniper turned to see why he wasn't making the radio call. He leaned over and struck, burying one in each side of the sniper's neck. He hit both windpipe and carotid artery. The sniper jerked away from his weapon, clutching his neck and trying to speak. He kicked violently, knocking the rifle from the air conditioner unit as he struggled. He would have fallen off himself but Hugh didn't let go of the knives, holding the man pinned in place like an insect specimen.

Hugh twisted the knife that lay buried in the man's carotid, reaming the hole larger, and expediting the blood loss. Soon the man was no longer able to struggle. Shortly after, he was no longer breathing. Hugh extracted the knives, wiped them on the sniper's shirt, and placed them back in their sheaths.

Realizing that he was now fighting against discovery, he went into action. He picked up the sniper's pack and slung it over his shoulders, then did the same with the rifle sling. He stepped to the edge of the roof and looked over. He heard an engine start and saw two men shooting off into the field in an ATV. Hugh assumed Barnes to be one of the men but he couldn't tell which of the two.

He unslung the rifle and tried to spot the ATV in the scope. The machine was bobbing over the irregular terrain of the cornfield. Heavy ears of ripe corn flew in all directions as the machine plowed a wide swath. It didn't help that Hugh's adrenaline was surging and he couldn't keep the rifle still.

He flipped the safety off and aimed for the driver. He centered the crosshairs on what he could see of the man's neck. The vehicle jostled and he struggled to keep his intended point of impact in sight. Then the vehicle seemed to hit a smooth stretch of field. He held his breath and pulled the gun tight against him, trying to still the movement. He squeezed the trigger and took his shot.

The rifle boomed and Hugh's target flinched. The man stiffened and sagged over. The ATV took a rapid swerve to the left and the tire caught a rut. The machine flipped, then rolled violently. Hugh watched it for a moment and saw no movement. Maybe the passenger had been killed or at least trapped beneath the machine. He cycled the bolt and flipped the safety back on, then headed for the roof hatch. It was time to make his escape.

When he reached the open hatch, he slung his legs over, and carefully placed them on the round steel rungs. He made his way down, hoping that no one noticed he was carrying the sniper's rifle.

The room below was chaos. Children were screaming and their hysterical mothers were trying to restrain them. Women were screaming for their husbands. Hugh couldn't see any of the men. He assumed they were all outside, all in the fight.

He trotted to his radio table and grabbed his pack. With one pack and the rifle over his back already, he put his personal pack on his chest and threaded an arm through each shoulder strap. It was awkward but this was about time, not comfort. He would try to come back for the radios if he could but now was not the time to worry about them.

He heard shooting from the back door and knew that was not the direction to go in. He bolted for the automotive section, knowing there was a fire exit he could leave through. Hugh slammed into the panic bar and forced his way through the door, struggling as his packs snagged on the frames. He had not considered that the alarm mounted on the emergency exit was battery-operated and fully functional without electricity. The ear-splitting alarm sounded, its trill only adding to the chaos. If he hadn't attracted attention before, he certainly would now.

Hugh stumbled out into the parking lot and quickly scanned for threats. He had no idea how many of the men were left but none were here. He ran across the back parking lot, bounded over a ditch, and took off into the weeds.

CHAPTER FORTY-SEVEN

Pete

Pete ran from the barn as fast as he could. His brain was firing messages with a machine-like efficiency.

Dad is in danger.

I have to get to him.

I can get to him before anyone else.

Don't trip in that rut.

It's shorter to cross the hill than run for the farm road.

Don't run straight up the hill. Angling up it will conserve energy.

Despite the urgency of his mission, despite his fear, he realized he was not the scared child he'd been when he killed that man on his parents' porch two months or so ago. While others may have seen the changes in him, he had not noticed them himself. He saw it now. He was acting like a man. He was on a mission to save his dad. This was not about being scared. This was about something more.

His lungs were soon burning and his legs weren't far behind. He stumbled a few times, then forced himself to concentrate and pay attention. He had to focus. There was no choice. If he were injured and out of the game, his dad might die.

From his observation post, he'd had time to study the lay of the land. He'd figured out where various local landmarks were as part of learning where to watch for possible trespassers. He'd figured out where the superstore was, where the various roads snaked close to their valley, and what hills were between him and town. He memorized the proximity of local subdivisions and housing complexes. He used all of that knowledge now, cutting through fields and climbing short hills.

When his legs began to fail him, he told himself that he would walk fifty steps to give his lungs a moment to recover. He made it only twenty steps before he was running again, knowing that he'd never forgive himself if he got there too late. He soon found his second wind, hit his pace, and was making good time. He intersected the farm road, his feet raising puffs of dust on the grassless path. Then he was at the creek crossing and hit the water full speed.

The slimy rocks were treacherous and he wiped out before he'd made it halfway across. He barely managed to hold onto the rifle. He was not concerned about it getting wet – the ammo would be fine, but he didn't want to bang the scope. That might impair the accuracy of the rifle and cause him to miss a critical shot. He couldn't afford that. He only had the eight rounds of .30-06 that were in the rifle. He'd brought nothing else with him.

By choosing to hold onto the rifle he had one fewer hand with which to catch himself and he hit hard. There was a blinding pain in his tailbone as he caught the sharp corner of a rock. His eyes watered from the pain but he fought back to the urge to lay there a moment and recover. Before he knew it, he was on his feet again, wading across the water a little more carefully. When he reached the opposite shore, he sloshed up the bank, his shoes making a squishing sound as they squeezed out the creek water.

Then he was on the pavement.

Then he heard the shooting begin.

CHAPTER FORTY-EIGHT

Jim

Jim staggered blindly through the corn. He'd driven by this field often enough to know that it pitched downhill toward the road. If he could reach the road, it would just be a matter of making it the quarter-mile to the creek crossing. Then he'd be able to take the farm road back to the valley.

If he made it that far.

Right now, he wasn't so sure. Sweat poured into his eyes and no amount of blinking cleared the burning. He tried to move a hand to his shirttail. He wanted to pull it up and wipe the sweat away from his face but the body on his shoulders began to slip. He nearly dropped her and made a quick move to try to stabilize himself but it was too late. In trying to move her weight back into the best position, he staggered and fell. Her body ground his face into the dirt, flattening his already crushed nose.

He shoved the body off him, then choked back a scream of rage, emitting a roar that scared Randi. He wanted to brush the dirt from his blood-encrusted face but didn't dare touch it.

"We're almost there," Randi said. "I don't hear the ATV anymore. Maybe they gave up. Maybe they're going back to the store."

Jim got to his feet. Somehow he doubted it was over. He was wobbly and panting.

"Just leave her," Randi pleaded. "We can come back for her."

"No fucking way!" he growled.

They maneuvered Alice's body onto his shoulders, then they were moving again. Jim got into a pattern of sucking air through his mouth, then trying to blow out slowly, hoping to force more oxygen into his bloodstream. He tried to breathe out his nose but it was completely swollen shut and the effort made him feel like the top of his head was going to blow off.

"We still...good?" Jim panted. "You...hear...anyone?"

He was blind again from the sweat and needed the reassurance. He was lost in a tunnel of pain and focus. His senses were useless. Then he pushed through a row of dense, leafy stalks and caught a glimpse of something he couldn't process through his stinging eyes. It was a burst of black movement.

Had he disturbed crows feeding in the corn?

By the time he realized that it wasn't crows, Barnes was already swinging the rifle like a baseball bat and caught Jim in the face.

Jim didn't even have time to process the pain. He twisted, dropped like a rock, and nearly lost consciousness.

Randi was about ten feet behind Jim and her attention was directed to the rear, hoping to catch anyone running up behind them. She didn't realize that Jim had been taken out until she heard the command.

"Drop the fucking gun!" Barnes shouted. "Drop it or I'll shoot!"

Then Randi saw Jim on the ground. She thought he was dead at first but saw his fingers curling and uncurling. One leg tried to straighten. He was alive but out of action. Above him was a man she'd never seen before and he had a rifle aimed in her direction.

Randi immediately knew she was in no position to fire at the man. Her shotgun was aimed completely in the wrong direction. By the time she spun on this man, he could put five rounds in her.

"DROP THE GUN!" he demanded.

She dropped her shotgun before she even knew she was doing it.

"Hands above your head!" Barnes demanded. "Do it!"

Randi complied. The man came up behind her and put his rifle barrel against the base of her skull. The sensation gave her a cold chill, knowing she was a finger twitch away from dying. The man quickly searched her with his free hand. He found her pistol and tossed it to the side. She was awaiting his next command when there was a vicious kick to the small of her back that sent her sprawling. She flew across several rows of cornstalks and fell in a heap, stunned.

"Was it you or the dead bitch that killed my men?" Barnes asked.

Randi groaned in pain and tried to think.

Barnes stomped over to Jim, who still lay semi-conscious in the dirt. He planted a foot on Jim's neck, applying pressure. Jim's face reddened and he choked, the struggle to breathe forcing him into consciousness. He raised his hands to the foot on his neck but he was too weak to pull it away.

Barnes lowered his rifle barrel to Jim's head. "I'll fucking kill him," he said. "I asked you a simple question. Was it you or her?"

"I came up afterward," Randi said, her voice wracked with pain. She turned her head toward him, resting her cheek back on the dirt. Her back hurt so badly. "She was already dead when I found them. What does it matter?"

"Because if it was you, I was going to kill you. Since it was her, I'm going to shoot this bastard and then I'm going to trade you for the tanker."

Randi's mind raced. She could not let this happen. Jim had saved her life. He had gotten her home. She did not want to watch him die. She did not want to have to tell his family that he was dead.

"I'm not from that valley," Randi said. "They're not going to trade to get me back. I mean nothing to those people."

Barnes looked her in the eye and she saw the gears turning. She realized too late that she had played the wrong cards.

"Then you're going to die," he said.

He raised his rifle in her direction and sighted on her head. Randi closed her eyes and was saying a quick prayer for her children and grandchildren when she heard a wet smack. It was quickly followed by the delayed report of a gunshot.

She was waiting for the pain but didn't feel it. Her eyes opened and she saw Barnes stagger, his body arching, then falling onto his side. She didn't know if he was dead but she scrambled toward him, recovering the rifle he'd dropped. She rose on her knees, aimed in the general direction of his head, and put two bullets point-blank into his skull.

She dropped the rifle and crawled to Jim. She was hypervigilant, scared, her heart racing. Where had the shot come from? She had to get Jim out of here before more people showed up. She was at his side, trying to get him on his feet when Pete ran up. Randi was startled and grabbed for the rifle, and then saw who it was.

She took one glance at him and knew that it had been him who saved her life and his dad's. "Help me get him up."

Pete ran to her side, slowing when he caught sight of the dead man, then Alice. Pete had seen dead bodies before but not out in the daylight like this. It was different. It was real in a way that he hadn't experienced before, real in a way he hoped he never experienced again.

"Pete!" Randi ordered, worried that he may go into shock if she couldn't keep him engaged. "Get over here. I need your help."

There was a sound behind them and they both flew to attention, pointing rifles in that direction.

"Don't shoot!"

Had Hugh not emerged from the rows of corn with both hands raised over his head, they'd have killed him instantly. His gesture of surrender gave him just enough time to state his case.

"I'm Hugh," he said quickly. "I'm an old friend of Jim's. I took out the ATV driver. We need to get out of here now."

The sound of a roaring engine drew their attention to the road. Pete could hear that it was Mack Bird's Dodge. The truck was crossing the creek and spinning up onto the pavement.

"Pete!" Mack yelled out the window. "Pete!"

There were other voices too, everyone trying to find Pete.

Randi wasn't sure about trusting the new guy just yet. "Pete, you run to the road and get those guys up here to help us. I'm keeping a gun on Hugh until you get back. I don't feel very trusting right now."

Pete ran the short distance to the road, calling to Mack before he broke cover. "I'm here!" Pete said. "We need help!"

In less than a minute, there was a force of men from the valley surrounding Pete, Randi, and Jim. Mack and Buddy got in a short fire-fight with two men from the superstore. They killed one and the other fled. If there were any other forces remaining at the superstore, they were either hiding or retreating. It seemed the threat was neutralized.

Jim was fully conscious now. Lloyd and Hugh were helping him back to the truck.

"I don't know who gave you that nose job, but it's about damn time you had something done about it," Lloyd said. "It's an improvement."

Jim was too battered to reply.

"You remember how Ariel likes pugs?" Lloyd cracked. "Now her daddy looks like one. She'll be thrilled."

Jim ignored the jab and looked at Hugh. "I appreciate your help. Welcome aboard."

Hugh nodded. "I appreciate that."

The sheriff and Deputy Ford retrieved Alice's body and put it in the back of the truck, covering it with a tarp. When they were all loaded, the two law enforcement officers didn't get in the truck.

"What's the matter?" Jim asked. "Aren't you coming back?"

"Eventually," the sheriff said. "I'm going up to the store. I want to talk to who's left. I want to make sure this is over."

"They may be hostile," Jim warned. "There may be men left. Or even worse, pissed off women."

Both the sheriff and deputy held up M4s.

"We're prepared for either possibility," Ford said.

Jim nodded. "Then we'll see you later."

CHAPTER FORTY-NINE

The Valley

Mack eased his truck down over the bank and crept across the creek. Jim and Randi sat in the front, needing a slightly more delicate ride than the truck bed provided. In the back, the rest of the men watched for threats, their guns at the ready.

As the truck eased out of the creek, Gary reached over and patted Pete on the back. "You did a damn good job, Pete."

Pete smiled nervously. He was still jittery, coming down from the adrenaline dump of the last thirty minutes. "I hope my mom thinks so."

Gary shook his head regretfully. "Not a chance, kid. She's going to beat your ass like she's playing a drum."

Pete's smile disappeared. "I *had* to save my dad."

"I know you did and I'll help you plead your case," Gary said, "but I ain't sure it's going to do you any good."

Pete looked glum. The truck hit a bump and everyone grabbed on.

"Sorry!" Mack yelled, trying to keep a slow, steady pace. It was difficult on the rutted farm road. They started up an incline and Mack crept along. When they topped the hill and came in sight of Jim's farm, Mack lurched to a stop.

"What is it?" Jim asked.

Mack pointed to Jim's house.

Jim saw that there were four Humvees parked around his house.

"Shit!" Jim muttered, shaking his head. "What else can go wrong?"

"What should I do?" Mack asked.

Jim opened his door and slid out of the truck. He faced the men in the back. "I don't know what the hell is going on down there but you all should get out and take cover. If I need you, you'll do me more good up here. I'm going to ride in alone."

"No way," Mack and Randi both said at the same time.

"Look, I don't want to put anyone else in danger today," Jim said. "You all have saved my ass once already. That should be the daily limit for anyone."

"Actually, Pete saved your ass," Randi pointed out.

"I'd rather go in alone," Jim said.

"Fuck that," Mack said.

"Agreed," Randi said.

Jim sighed. "Well, I'm too tired to argue. Let's go."

The three of them climbed back in the truck and Mack started the engine. They continued to the house and parked in the driveway. Jim's wife, his daughter, and his parents were all sitting on the porch. Randi's family was there, as was Gary's. Even poor Charlie, who did not yet know the fate of his mother, was sitting there stoically. Standing among the familiar faces were men with rifles and tactical gear, men Jim had never seen before.

The trio sat there for a moment, taking in the scene. Seated on the porch steps, sipping a bottle of water, was a large man that Jim also didn't recognize. He was dressed in expensive casual clothing and had an AR-15 laying across his lap. He wore body armor, as did the men who were with him.

"Who the hell is that?" Mack asked. "He looks like he just came from a firefight at a golf course."

"Shit," Jim muttered. "He probably is from the golf course. Why the hell not?"

"They better not have hurt my family," Randi warned. "They'll meet a side of me they won't like."

"Just relax," Jim said. "Let me out."

Randi opened her door, the operation of the latch unusually loud in the stillness of the day. She slid out of the vehicle and stepped to the side. Jim was right behind her. He walked around to the front of the truck, leaned stiffly back on the bumper, and regarded the scene before him. Mack and Randi followed, taking positions on either side of him.

Ellen's hand moved to her mouth, alarmed by Jim's condition. Ariel started crying, apparently not impressed that he looked like a pug. All anyone seemed interested in was his damaged face. Didn't they realize there were bigger problems on the table? Yeah, his face hurt like hell but he couldn't do anything about it right now.

"You guys hang back here for a second," Jim said to Randi and Mack, noting that the armed men on the porch had moved to a heightened state of alertness. The rifles they carried were now shouldered, the barrels up but not pointed directly at anyone.

Jim approached the big man reclining on his steps. It was on the tip of his tongue to ask who the fuck the man thought he was, but he bit his tongue and cleaned it up for all of the children within earshot. He would try to keep this civil, though his fuse was understandably short at the moment.

"Can I help you?" Jim asked.

The man regarded Jim's appearance. His mouth hung slightly open as if he couldn't make sense of something. "Son, it looks like someone broke the ugly stick right across your face. Maybe a couple of times."

Jim let out a deep breath, which had to go out his mouth since his nose wasn't working at the moment. "Let's skip the niceties," Jim said. "As you can probably tell, I've had a rough day. I'm tired and there's nothing I want more than to go soak my face in some nice cold spring water."

The man considered this. "Then I'll be short and to the point," he said. "My name is Lester Hurt and I think you have my fuel tanker. I want it back."

Jim forced himself to take another deep breath and let it out. It was supposed to be calming but it wasn't working. The intake of air made his sinuses throb. He was tired of the fuel truck and all of the problems it had brought upon them.

"Do you know what I'm talking about?" Lester asked.

Jim nodded slowly.

"There was a son-of-a-bitch that stole a bunch of supplies from over at Wallace County," Lester said. "That's where I live. Some of us spent our own personal money to bring in fuel, food, and other supplies for our community. Things weren't perfect but we were set pretty good. Then this asshole named Baxter stole our shit and brought it over here. He had plans of setting up his own little camp and using our supplies to do it."

"I'm aware of that," Jim said. "We probably killed him for you."

"No, you didn't," Lester said, smiling. "I had the pleasure of seeing him killed right in front of my own eyes. Our own people took a little payback out on him for stealing our shit."

Jim nodded. "Well, whoever the men with the trailer were, we killed the rest of them."

Lester chuckled. "Those were members of his team and I've got no problem with you killing his people. Just saved me the trouble of doing it. I do have a problem with you keeping the tanker and supplies. I understand why you took them – spoils of war and all that – but they do belong to the folks in my community. We're here to take them back."

Jim shrugged. "Then take them. Those supplies have been nothing but trouble for us."

Lester smiled. He was wearing sunglasses that hid his eyes, making it hard to tell if the smile was genuine or not. "Glad to hear you see things my way."

Jim put a foot on the porch step and leaned forward conspiratori-ally. "I have to tell you, though, we blew up the roads into the valley. It may not be so easy to get them out."

"We noticed," Lester said. "We came in through a logging road. It was on the old maps."

"So how do you plan on retrieving your trailers? We figured road tractors would sink up trying to pull them out on dirt roads."

Lester wagged a finger at Jim. "This ain't my first rodeo, son," he said. "I came up in the mining business. We move trailers around mine sites without trucks nearly every day. I've got a D8 dozer being unloaded from a lowboy trailer right now. It's pulling a tow dolly that will hook right up to that trailer and pull it out of here pretty as you please."

"Good for you," Jim said. "Knock yourself out."

"One more thing, am I going to find my trailers empty?" Lester asked.

"We used some of the supplies, some of the fuel," Jim said. "Most of it's still there."

Lester nodded. "I guess that's to be expected."

"Now you got what you wanted so why don't you get your people off my porch? I'll tell you where your trailer is and you can go help yourself. We won't try to stop you."

Lester lay back comfortably on the steps, splayed out, his foot bobbing. Despite his AR-15 and body armor, Jim noticed that he was wearing shiny penny loafers. He grinned at Jim. "I'd rather keep them here until we're safely out of the valley. Wouldn't want you changing your mind. It could take a few hours to finish up and be gone."

Jim raised his radio to his mouth and looked Lester in the eye. He pushed the transmit button and said, "Water bottle."

There was a distant boom and the water bottle at Lester's side exploded. He jerked but caught a spray of water from the shattered bottle.

"Dammit!" Lester hissed.

His men ducked, looking around frantically.

Jim hit the transmit button again. "Balls," he instructed, saying it loudly enough that Lester would have no doubt as to the command.

Lester flinched, slamming his legs shut. He threw a hand out in Jim's direction. "Okay, okay," he said. "We'll leave. You've made your point."

"Tell your men to get off my porch and get off my property," Jim said flatly. "You can take your trailers and get out of here."

Lester worked his bulk into a standing position, gesturing to his men. "Let's go!"

Jim stepped to the side and watched the men file off his porch and to their vehicles. When they were all off the porch, Ariel and Ellen ran to Jim's side.

"Did they hurt you?" he asked.

Ellen shook her head. "Just scared us. They came out of nowhere on foot and took us by surprise. They only brought the vehicles in later."

"Are you okay, Ariel?" Jim asked.

"I'm fine, Daddy," she said, holding him tightly.

"Where's Pete?" Ellen asked. "Is he okay?"

"He's with the other men," Jim said. "They're hanging back to make sure things are okay here."

"I'm going to tan his hide," Ellen warned.

"Go easy on him," Jim said. "He did exactly what I would have done."

"That's what worries me," Ellen said.

Jim pulled away from his family. "I need to go soak my face in some cold water," he said. "It's a little tender."

Ariel looked at him, her eyebrows raised. "You call that tender?"

"Okay, it's very, very tender."

"What happened to your nose?" Ellen asked.

"Which time?"

Ellen winced and took his hand. "Come on. Let's go to the springhouse. That's the coldest water we have."

CHAPTER FIFTY

The Valley

Charlie took the news of his mother's fate better than anyone expected. Perhaps he only saw it as one more facet of a world that had already shown him a lot of pain in a short time.

"The lady who came back from that trip wasn't really my mother," he told Jim and Randi. "She tried to be but she wasn't. She was a different person. I'd rather think that my real mother never came back because that's what it feels like. That's the way I'm going to look at it."

Jim understood. He could see Randi, who had resolved never to cry again over the state of the world, pinching her thigh to avoid going back on her word.

Randi, who had never raised a son, took Charlie in. There were several families willing to, including Jim's, but Randi said she felt a special obligation. "That could have been me," she told Jim. "I could have sided with the women on our trip and chosen to come back with them instead of with you and Gary. I could have had her experiences. I could have come home changed like she did."

"You didn't," Jim said. "There are too many close calls in life anymore to keep track of them. Close calls don't mean anything anymore." That was how he saw things. With so much bad shit *really* happening, why worry about the stuff that could have happened but didn't?

"Maybe close calls don't mean anything to you," Randi said. "I'm not sure I'll ever be able to disregard them. Either way, I'm doing it because I would hope Alice might have done the same thing for me."

———

After a few quiet weeks, the folks in the valley had their first frost and the leaves began to change color. While it was a beautiful time of year in the Appalachian Mountains, it also brought the awareness that it could be a long, lean winter. Everyone doubled their efforts to store food and lay in a supply of firewood. Jim imagined this anxiety might have been the way his pioneer ancestors felt going into fall and winter, wondering if they had enough.

The group at the superstore dispersed after Barnes and the other men were killed, many of the families now left without husbands and fathers. Those remaining made the decision to seek other family members to live with. Some tried to remain at the superstore but as word leaked out about their diminished numbers, local citizens began showing up and forcing their way in to look for supplies. Eventually everyone left the superstore and found shelter elsewhere. The store became a ransacked, rodent-infested ruin.

With the sheriff's assistance, Hugh managed to get all of his radio equipment out safely. He found one of the last empty houses in the valley with a fireplace and set up there. He erected several antennas around his new home with the help of the neighbors. As Hugh had expected, the valley was excited to have a radio operator among them. Perhaps now they could hear something of the world outside of their county.

The days got shorter and people began going to bed earlier to conserve their light sources. One cool evening, as everyone was gathered at Jim's for a communal dinner, the lights flickered on for a moment and then went back off.

Everyone sat there in silence, then looked at each other in confusion. They wondered if they'd all imagined it. Had it been a mass hallucination? Then everyone was jabbering frantically amongst themselves, trying to figure out what it meant. They came to no conclusions and the lights didn't come back on.

Two weeks later, it happened again. There was a flicker, then darkness again. Hugh worked his radios and found that there was an effort to get coal-fired power plants back in operation again. There were no details and no prognosis, but the military was involved. Folks tried not to get their hopes up that normality could be around the corner, but it was difficult. They wanted their old lives back. Even Jim, who had seemed to thrive in his new circumstances, wanted his old life back. He was ready to drag himself back into the office and deal with people's mundane problems all day. Life was simpler now but the consequences immeasurably higher.

Then amid the anticipation that recovery may be around the corner, word trickled in through ham radio that what was being referred to as the *die-off* had begun. People around the country were dying at a rapidly accelerating pace. Pantries were depleted, illnesses from untreated water was everywhere, and diarrhea was suddenly a leading cause of death again. Violence was escalating. There was no shortage of ways to die.

As the days got colder and shorter, Pete and Charlie became close friends. They were around the same age and were both adapting easily to this new way of life. They began to pull long hours at Pete's observation post every day. Whatever sense of purpose Pete had found there, Charlie was finding it too. Whatever about this new world had made Pete into a man was doing the same for Charlie.

Watching them walk off to the observation post each morning, Jim had to admit that this was not the world he wanted. As much as he prayed for a *reset* and as much as he idealized off-grid life, it was hard to care for a family here. It was hard to keep people safe. The old world was *his* world and he wanted it back.

This was Charlie and Pete's world though. The way in which it molded them was not something he could undo. The things in them that it fixed, he would not be able to unfix. Even if the lights came back on tomorrow, would those two ever be able to fit back into the space they'd occupied before? Would they be able to put down their guns and just go back to school as if none of this had ever happened?

Somehow Jim doubted it.

Made in the USA
Columbia, SC
03 June 2024

36557051R00135